THE SECOND MAN

EMELLE GAMBLE

SOUL MATE PUBLISHING

New York

THE SECOND MAN

Copyright©2016

EMELLE GAMBLE

Cover Design by Tammy Seidik

This book is a work of fiction. The names, characters, places, and incidents are the products of the author's imagination or are used fictitiously. Any resemblance to actual events, business establishments, locales, or persons, living or dead, is entirely coincidental.

All rights reserved. No part of this publication may be reproduced, stored in a retrieval system, or transmitted in any form or by any means (electronic, mechanical, photocopying, recording, or otherwise) without the prior written permission of both the copyright owner and the publisher. The only exception is brief quotations in printed reviews.

The scanning, uploading, and distribution of this book via the Internet or via any other means without the permission of the publisher is illegal and punishable by law. Please purchase only authorized electronic editions, and do not participate in or encourage electronic piracy of copyrighted materials.

Your support of the author's rights is appreciated.

Published in the United States of America by
Soul Mate Publishing
P.O. Box 24
Macedon, New York, 14502

Print Book ISBN: 978-1-68291-189-1

ebook ISBN: 978-1-68291-185-3

www.SoulMatePublishing.com

The publisher does not have any control over and does not assume any responsibility for author or third-party websites or their content.

Praise for Emelle Gamble's work . . .

"SECRET SISTER is one of those books that leaves you re-thinking everything you once believed . . . Along with having a . . . unique and captivating plot, it offers a shocking turn of the paranormal kind . . . I cannot recommend it strongly enough for those of you that enjoy a book that not only touches your heart but has you tingling in anticipation for whatever comes next." **Fresh Fiction- Fresh Review**

DATING CARY GRANT **. . .** "It really is a love story, not just a break up story, and it was so well written and had unique plot, that I just couldn't put this book down until I had finished it. I loved it . . . and for any of you who are looking for a fun, yet serious . . . romance, this one is for you." ***Long and Short Reviews***

For Kathy Rose,

with love and thanks for all you did for Lorraine

Acknowledgements

Thank you to cover artist Tammy Seidick of Tammy Seidick Design for her fabulous and compelling design.

Thank you to Debby Gilbert, Publisher, Soul Mate Publishing, for her insight and patience during the editing process.

And, as always, thank you to Phil-the-fist for everything else.

Prologue

Last December
Paris, France

Ben Pierce cautiously opened his hotel room door. It was nearly midnight, and he was not expecting anyone.

"Hi, Ben. Sorry to show up without calling, but I misplaced my damn cell." The man standing in the hallway smiled and held out a bottle of Prunier cognac. "I brought a nightcap to apologize for missing our dinner tonight."

"Hey, no *problemo*. Come on in." Ben waved his visitor into the suite, looking impressed by the expensive liquor. "I waited for you at Marigold for an hour. You missed a great French meal."

"I'm sure I did." The man glanced around the room, relieved Ben was alone. "This is nice. You here for the conference by yourself?"

"Two other guys from my office in D.C. are down the hall. They drew the short straw and have to room together." Ben pushed his heavy glasses up the bridge of his nose. "What about you? What are you doing here in Paris?"

"I'm here for work."

"You look like you're doing well." Ben squinted at the man's expensive suit and glossy shoes and then met his visitor's eyes. "I didn't recognize you at the newsstand this morning, until I saw your name on your briefcase. You've changed, buddy."

"You mean you didn't notice this?" His guest swung his right fist near Ben's face.

Ben chuckled and held up his own hand, which sported an identical class ring. "All hail St. John's College! Are we a couple of dorks or what for still wearing these things?"

"I'm sure we're not the only loyal alumni out there." The man's glance swept Ben head-to-toe. "I couldn't place you either when you tapped me on the shoulder. But I should have, you haven't changed much at all from your yearbook picture."

"Liar. I'm losing my hair and I'm growing what my old man would call a paunch." Ben grabbed his belly. "It's the geek career making me soft."

"Fifteen years takes a toll on all of us."

"Some of us more than others." Ben headed for the bar across the room. "Have a seat and I'll get some glasses."

The visitor did not sit down, but continued his reconnaissance of the suite, noting Ben's cell on the table near the window and the laptop on the floor by the sofa. The drapes were drawn. "So you said you're a tech guy? Programmer?"

"I'm an analyst. I don't pound out code, I crunch incoming data streams. Not nearly as sexy."

"You work for the government?"

"Yeah."

"What department?"

Ben grinned. "If I told you I'd have to kill you."

"Yeah? Well then, please do keep that to yourself."

"I'm kidding, man. I work for Treasury."

"Guns or money?"

"I can't get that specific. But you can call me Double O-Ben."

Both men chuckled.

"What are you into?" Ben asked. "Attorney or banker? You got to be some kind of posh dude to wear fancy Italian kicks like that."

"Finance," his guest replied with a glance down at his shoes.

"I wouldn't have guessed you'd be doing something that business oriented." Ben carried two glasses and the bottle of cognac over to the table and sat down. "So how the hell have you been? You bump into anyone else from college since you graduated?"

"No. But it was inevitable to happen someday. We might be ten thousand miles away from St. John's, but our world is getting smaller, don't you think?"

"You mean because of the Internet? I guess. I don't do any of that social media shit. Bosses don't like it." He opened the bottle of cognac. "You want some?"

"Sure." The man walked toward Ben. "You mentioned this morning that my college is having a reunion next year. Do you know where and when is it going to be?"

"April, I think. You didn't get an invite?"

"No."

"The search committee must not have been able to find you. You hiding?"

"In plain sight." The man raised his eyebrows. "Or I'm being blackballed."

Ben frowned as if remembering something unpleasant. "Yeah, maybe. Lucky you. I only heard about it since my sister, Marissa, is the one coordinating the thing. Anyway, it's going to be held in Santa Barbara. You want to go?"

"Maybe. Reunions are reputed to be fun."

"Fun?" Ben snorted, leaning back in his chair. "A bunch of people you hardly remember comparing notes and being snarky about who got fat, and reminiscing about glory days that probably didn't happen the way they recall. I didn't go to mine a couple of years back. Not my idea of a good time."

"Mine either."

Ben took a sip of his drink. "Could be good for you. You look all rich and successful now, and I'll bet a lot of them wondered what the hell became of you. You might even run into Jill Farrell." A moment of silence passed.

"There's a name from the past."

"You had it bad for her, right?"

The man did not smile. "You remember that, huh?"

"I remember the important stuff." Ben smirked and swirled the cognac around in his glass, inhaling the sharp, caramel fumes. "Jill was a hottie. Might still be."

"Do you think she'll be at the reunion?"

"Her family lived in Santa Barbara, I think? So yeah, she'll probably show up if she's around. Girls seem to love those things."

"That could prove interesting."

"Interesting in a good way or a bad way?" Ben asked. "I graduated two years before you guys, but now I seem to remember Marissa chattering about some kind of the drama with Jill a few years ago." He frowned. "Do you know what I'm talking about?"

"Not really." The man flashed a shark smile and grasped the lapel of his topcoat. The blood-red stone in his ring glimmered in the light. "May I take this off and hang it up somewhere?"

"Closet's by the entrance." Ben picked up his cell to check an incoming text. "I can call downstairs and see if they'll bring up a sandwich or something, if you haven't eaten."

"Don't bother."

"Actually, I could go for something too." Ben took a deep hit off his drink, looked up, and then froze, his breath catching in his throat.

The man he had admitted without question into the suite was standing eight feet away, aiming a gun squarely at him.

A Sig Sauer, Ben's trained eye identified. With a silencer. "What the fuck, man?" he rasped, the cognac burning his throat.

"Sorry, Ben. It's not personal."

Ben gripped the heavy crystal tumbler, measuring the distance to the man's head.

"It would be a waste of good booze," the visitor said, as if reading his mind.

Ben set the glass down and crossed his arms. "What the hell is going on?"

"I saw you on your cell phone," the visitor said. "Right after we met this morning. Who did you call?"

Ben blinked. He had made two calls recounting his unexpected encounter with his old classmate, telling both people, ". . . he looks like a freaking movie star now. But there's something off about him."

"Man, this has turned into one bizarre night," Ben said.

"Tell me about it." The man with the gun stood straighter, the gun swaying slightly.

Suddenly Ben lunged at his visitor. The man shot him before Ben could lay a hand on him.

Three times.

The visitor listened for a moment, but no knock sounded at the door.

He stepped over the body and picked up Ben's cell phone to check the call history, and then dropped it on the floor with a sigh.

Despite his aversion to the States, it looked like he was going to have to show up in California, take a temperature or two, and see if old Ben had set off any alarms.

The man who killed Ben Pierce thought of the woman his victim had mentioned. He nodded. She was a hottie. Maybe the reunion would not be all bad.

Unless he had to kill her, too.

Chapter 1

Santa Barbara, California
April

Jill Farrell picked up her ringing cell phone and checked the caller ID. Despite the tough day she was having, a smile pulled at her lips.

"Carly! Hi!"

"Jill? Can you hear me?" The woman's voice sounded far away, but as comforting as a church bell.

"Yes, I can." Jill forced some cheeriness into her voice. "What a great surprise to hear your voice. Where are you?"

"We're in Rome at the airport. Hamilton had business in Milan, and I made him take me along. But I wanted to check in and see how things are going. How's Dorothy doing? Any decision yet on the assisted living plans?"

Jill pursed her lips and glanced across the room where her mother sat on the couch, her eyes half-closed, her face showing no sign that she was aware of her surroundings.

"Mom's no different." Jill swallowed. "I'm moving her to Friend's House today, as a matter of fact. In a couple of hours."

"What? Oh my god, not on Good Friday? I thought you were going to wait until the summer."

"That was the plan." Jill leaned back and hugged her arm to her chest. "But Mom's doctor was adamant we take the first slot that opened-up. She has been roaming around at night, not sleeping. The doctor felt it was time to consider a locked facility because one night, a couple of weeks ago she actually got out of the house and scared me to death.

She could have been hit by a car or worse, so I didn't have much of an argument to postpone it any longer." Emotion tightened her throat. "I can't believe things have worked out like this."

"Oh, Jill, I'm so sorry. But we've talked about this so many times. You are doing the right thing. Assisted living will give Dorothy a level of care you can't provide, and frankly, shouldn't even try to provide on your own. You have to work, and have a life. You know your mom would agree this is the best option for her, don't you?"

Carly was right, Jill knew. Her mother would never have wanted to be a burden. But still . . . "I know that. I do, but it hurts. She's so young, you know, only sixty-three."

Static crackled on the phone and then Carly's voice cut back in. ". . . What time is it in California?"

"Ten-thirty a.m."

"At least I didn't wake you up. Now look, there's another reason I'm calling today. A happier one. The reunion."

"What reunion?"

"St. John's college reunion! It's in two weeks, remember?"

Jill stood and raked her hand through her hair, checking the clock on the fireplace mantle. She already had her mother's things organized, but she felt like there were still a million things to do. "I remember talking about it with you months ago, and agreeing we were not going."

"Well, I've changed my mind. Hamilton and I have been discussing it, and we decided this morning he could work it into his schedule and travel with me. Which means you need to change your mind. Now. Especially because I just heard . . ."

Carly's voice was obliterated by several seconds of static. "Carly, are you still there?"

"Can you hear me?"

"Hi. Yeah, you keep breaking up." Jill sat next to her mom and pulled a throw blanket over her mother's legs. Gently she patted her knee to wake her but Dorothy continued to doze.

"Isn't that exciting?" Carly asked.

"Did you just say you're coming to the reunion?" Jill replied. "You're coming to California?"

"Yes. Next week!"

"That's fabulous news. Are you bringing baby Julia? Your dad will be thrilled!"

"He is. Although I told him we're staying at the Biltmore, not with him. I'm bringing the nanny, too. Anyway, I wanted to ring you first thing so you can call and change your regrets to an RSVP, because I am not going to that thing without you. Especially if Max Kallstrom is going to be there."

Jill put her hand on her chest. "What did you say?"

"Didn't you hear me a minute ago? Max Kallstrom is coming to our reunion! God, after all these years we can find out what the hell happened with him after the car accident. Do you think he can walk? I know all we heard was that his pelvis was broken, or something in the smash-up."

An image loomed in front of Jill's eyes like a ghost.

It was Max Kallstrom, the first day she met him.

She had driven from Santa Barbara to LAX in her dad's old jeep, and had stood for an hour holding a sign with Max's name on it outside the international arrival gate.

Glancing at the guys walking out of the terminal, Jill was expecting a blond, ski-god type, but Max was dark haired with green-flecked eyes. He had a wide-shouldered, lanky frame, and that brilliant smile.

"Are you Max Kallstrom?" Max asked when he stopped in front of her, his accented voice tentative. He had a huge backpack slung over his left shoulder.

She pointed to the sign in her now clammy hands. "No, I'm Jill Farrell. I'm here to pick up Max Kallstrom. Are you Max Kallstrom?"

They had collapsed into laughter and had been inseparable from that day on.

Until . . .

"Jill? Are you there? I just asked if you think he can walk."

There was a long pause, then more static.

"Max is coming back to the States?" Jill asked. "Who told you that?"

"The person running the reunion, Marissa something, told Hamilton a couple of days ago when she called to be sure we weren't attending. Ham couldn't wait to tell me the news, because he remembered about you and Max being a big item, and how Max, poof, disappeared right before we graduated. Anyway, you see my point, right? You have to go to the reunion now."

Jill shook her head, feeling slightly sick. "I honestly don't know if I want to see him, Carly. I mean, he never ever tried to contact me. Maybe he doesn't want to even now. I'm not sure I want to risk being rejected all over again."

"Rejected? Oh, come on. The most he'll be is embarrassed the he acted like such a jerk all those years ago. I bet he's coming just to see you."

"I don't know."

"Well, I know. And if you're worried about running into Andrew Denton, don't be. We can handle that little creep, if he is ballsy enough to show up."

Jill's eyes widened. She hadn't considered the fact that her ex-husband might also be in town due to the reunion. "Ugh. Let's not go there. Surely Andrew wouldn't come, after all that happened?"

"I doubt he would, but if he does, we can handle it. So just get tickets. This is going to be a blast. Okay?"

"I'll call and see if I can still go to the final dinner, at least. Although I'm not sure it's a good idea, Carly. We can talk about it more when you get here."

"Hang on a minute, Ham wants to talk to you," Carly said.

"Jill?" Hamilton's deep, lovely voice came over the airwaves. "Did I hear Carly say you're thinking of missing the reunion? You have to come. You're the biggest reason she wants to fly all the way around the world to California."

"Hamilton, how are you?" Jill smiled. Even though she had only seen him a couple of brief times in the few years since he and Carly married, it was nice to know her best friends' husband was coming, too. "Well, like I told Carly, I'll call and see if I can get tickets to the dinner. But no matter what, I'm so glad to hear you guys will be in town. I can't wait to see you all."

"We're not taking no for an answer about the reunion. Carly needs her best friend by her side."

"I'll try, Hamilton. I will. Have a safe trip back to London."

"Jill?" Carly's voice came back on the phone. "Look, I have to run. Love you and I can't wait to see you!"

"Me too, dear friend. Safe flight."

"Oh, and we'll need to go shopping." Carly suddenly sounded like she did when she organized prom boot camp in high school. "Don't buy anything until I get there. And make us mani-pedi appointments. And hair appointments, okay? Cut and color for me. Nothing starts for a few days after I get in, so we'll have time to get gorgeous."

"Okay." Jill doubted there was enough time in life for her to get gorgeous, but she smiled. "Will do. I'll see you soon!"

Three hours later, Jill pulled into the sunny lot of the Friends Manor House, a long-term care facility on the edge of Santa Barbara, and parked clumsily near the entrance. At the front door stood a six-foot, purple blow-up Easter bunny.

Good Friday.

Jill winced. *Of course it is.* A holiday that seemed to provide the worst of times to her family. The troubles began many years ago on another April 17, when her infant sister Rosie died in her sleep, a victim of SIDS. No one understood that syndrome then, or believed in it, except those victimized.

The very next year, she was stung by a bee and had nearly died of anaphylactic shock.

Then, three years later, her dad fell from the roof on this holiday, dropped headfirst into a thicket of bird of paradise. He walked into the house covered with scratches and debris, his face bruised and bleeding.

That night at dinner, Jill announced the day was cursed for them. Her mother made the sign of the cross and told her to say a rosary and stop being silly, but her father had nodded briefly, his face frozen as if he had seen a monster at the window.

Her dad told her later that they shared the ability to look at life for what it was, while her mother tended to see things as she wanted them to be.

Jill got out of the car and walked around to the passenger's side. She opened the door and leaned in to undo her mother's seatbelt. "Hey, Mama. Are you hungry? Or thirsty? You didn't eat much today."

Her mother stared at her as if she had never seen her before.

"We'll get something soon as we get you settled, okay?"

"What day is this?" Her mother pulled the seatbelt back toward her chest nervously, as if it were a vine she had somehow entangled herself in.

"Friday. It's Good Friday."

"What's good about it?"

From anyone else this would have been a wisecrack, but her mother did not wisecrack anymore. Jill patted her hand. "Lots of things. The sun is shining, and we love one another. A bounty of blessings."

Dorothy blinked, but there was no sign she remembered that bit of family sentiment she had repeated to Jill a hundred times when she was growing up.

Jill parted her mother from the strap of the seatbelt, relieved Dorothy did not physically resist her effort. Her mother was heavier now than she had ever been, and when she did not want to move, it was difficult. Jill took Dorothy's hand and gently tugged so she would know to step out of the car.

Her mother did not budge.

"Who's that man?" Dorothy jerked her arm toward the front entrance of the facility.

Jill turned to look. "No one is there."

Despite this reassurance, Jill saw that her mom seemed frightened. Her mother had added this query about an invisible man to her list of repetitive questions this last week.

Jill feared the paranoia the doctor warned her would get worse was increasing. "Come on, Mom, it's okay. Let's go in."

Dorothy didn't move. "What day is it?"

"Friday. The Friday before Easter."

"I need to go to church," Dorothy whispered.

Faint hope gathered in Jill's heart, even as logic scolded that Dorothy did not understand what she had just said. "Do you want to go to mass? I'll take you this afternoon if you want to go."

Dorothy looked down. After a moment, her eyes started to close.

Jill gripped her by the elbow and the older woman finally leaned forward and stepped out of the car. Her mom blinked in the sunshine as they walked slowly together toward the front door.

"This is going to be a great place to go out walking. It's beautiful here." Jill led her into the building and down the long central hallway. She wanted to show Dorothy around her one hundred and eighty-four square-foot private room before they did the final intake interview with the director.

She had brought most of her mother's things over earlier, thinking the less unpacking, the less upset the move would cause. They stopped at the entrance to her room and Dorothy froze.

"What's wrong?" she asked Jill.

"Nothing. Nothing's wrong." Jill pushed open the door of the apartment. "This is your new home. The place I've been telling you about. Look, you've got two windows that face out on the bird feeder. I'll bring you some suet and we can nail it up there."

Dorothy turned the opposite way and stared into the clothes closet. "Birds?"

"Birds. Yeah, a lot of them." Jill pointed out that her clothes were already hanging in the closet, and her toiletries in the cabinet in the door-less bathroom. She described all the family portraits on the wall, her eyes aching briefly at the one of her dad and baby Rosie.

But her mom was not listening. She was shuffling around in circles in the center of the room. She had not reacted to any of Jill's slow, loud explanation of where everything was, or to her gently spoken reassurance as to why this move was a good thing.

Jill took her arm and guided her back to the doorway. "Now that you've seen the place, let's go get you officially signed in. Then we'll go to the dining room. You hungry?"

"What day is it?"

"Friday, Mom. It's Friday."

"It's awful."

"I know, honey, I know. Change is tough, but you'll settle in. And I'll come every day to see you." She patted her mother's arm, hoping what she was saying would comfort them both.

They walked in silence for several seconds.

"Don't cry," Dorothy whispered at the end of the hallway.

Tears burned hot against her eyes but Jill refused to let them fall and upset her mother even more. "I won't, Mama." She smiled at her mother in what she hoped was a comforting manner.

But Dorothy's expression held only confusion.

With a stab of anguish, Jill realized her mother was talking to herself.

Chapter 2

Jill arrived back at her townhouse to find the place dead quiet, and stuffy, the drapes closed to the views she loved of trees and sky.

The heartache she had been coping with the past months morphed into anger. She trembled as she walked to the bedroom, recalling how Dorothy had always said she was a good child, except when she threw tantrums, which she had done from two years of age to four.

I want to throw a tantrum now.

The reality of what her mother's future held cut like a razor impaled in the beating tissue of her heart. All the facts said she had done the right thing moving her mother to a care facility. But Jill struggled every day, especially today, to accept that her mom was as sick as she was.

"Cancer of the personality," the neurologist had commented. "Alzheimer's erases the personality, which is of course made up of all our memories and habits . . ." he had added, as if that simple explanation might make her feel better.

Jill stood at the dresser. In the mirror's reflection she looked ten years older than her age; her oval face was haggard, her blond hair limp. Her eyes had aged about a century since this morning.

"Yeah, taking this face to a reunion is just what I want to do now." Jill shook her head wearily and took off her watch, then her blouse, then her earrings, feeling stiff and out-of-sync with grief. Her eyes rested on a photograph on the bureau, her mother smiling and content as she held baby Jill in her arms at her christening.

She turned away and forcefully yanked down the shade in her room, and grabbed her purse to get her phone. It was not inside the pocket she usually kept it in and she knew she had left it in the car.

She threw the purse at the wall.

Tears flooded down her face, as the dam of emotions she had kept at bay for weeks finally burst. She kicked off her shoes. One struck the lamp on the night table and over it fell, causing a crash that sent her reading glasses and uncapped water bottle onto the floor.

She picked up the bottle, sopped up the puddle with her shirt, and fell on the bed. She pressed her face into the pillow and sobbed as hard as the night her father told her Rosie had gone to heaven to be with Jesus. Just as exhaustion was about to carry her away, she realized the front doorbell was ringing.

Jill swore, grabbed a handful of tissues, and blew her nose until her head spun, and the moron at the door escalated the noise to include knocking.

Really loud.

She stomped to the foyer to look through the peephole. There was a man out there. She saw shiny black shoes and pressed trousers, an arm covered by a suit coat. But she could not see his face because he was holding a huge vase of flowers in front of it.

Who the hell sent me flowers on Good Friday?

Quickly she combed her fingers through her hair. Feeling anything but presentable, and disoriented from crying, she opened the door wide.

"Happy Easter!"

The voice was vaguely familiar, deep, though not warm or sexy.

The dizzying smell of roses buzzed up Jill's raw sinuses like wasps. "What address are you looking for?" She rubbed the side of her nose.

"This one. This is 16805 Laurel, isn't it?" He still did not move the flowers so she could see him.

Jill considered saying he had the wrong address and shutting the door, but she was standing next to Spanish tiles painted with the numbers 1-6-8-0-5 hanging on the wall.

"Yes, that's the address, but . . ."

The man moved the vase from in front of him. "Hello, Jilly."

Jill gasped. There were only two people who had ever called her Jilly. One was her dad, who had been dead for five years.

The other had no reason to send her flowers, or know her current address. Except he did, because he was standing right in front of her, close enough to punch.

"What are you doing here?" Jill demanded.

"I brought these for you. Here." Andrew Denton, her ex-husband, held the vase out to her.

Jill crossed her arms over her chest. She had called the cops the last time she had been alone with Andrew.

And an ambulance.

"No thanks. What are you doing here?"

"Oh, come on Jilly, lighten up. Can't an old friend pay a person a visit?"

"We're not friends."

Andrew smiled tightly. "I was hoping you would give me a chance at least. I've changed, you know." He scanned her body with one glance, not showing any enthusiasm for what he saw. "And you've certainly changed. I came over to ask if we could bury the hatchet, on what seems like just the right day for that. May I come inside?"

"No."

"Why not?"

Jill stared at her ex. Andrew was much the same, auburn hair and icy blue eyes, but somehow completely changed from the man she last saw over a decade ago. He wore an expensive, dark suit, like an attorney, and any appearance of youth was now gone. He was lean and intense, the man behind the eyes more complicated than she remembered.

When they were together, he had worn his hair short around his neck and ears. It was longer now, combed straight back and gelled. There was a scar at his right temple, small and flat, and perfectly round.

"Because I can't think of a single thing we have to talk about," she finally replied.

"Grudge holding doesn't become you." He set the vase on the ground at his feet. "We should talk some things out."

"No, we shouldn't. I'm leaving the past where it belongs. Dead and buried."

"Okay, so we won't talk about the past. We'll focus on going forward and celebrating all we have in common."

"Which is nothing." Jill swallowed, her mouth dry.

"Not true. We're alumni from the same college. The same class. And our reunion is in two weeks."

The reunion.

Twice in one day she was being forced to travel back and time and think about a man and a broken relationship. Although her short marriage to Andrew, four years after they graduated, was not the same thing as her college romance with Max Kallstrom, two reminders in one day that she wasn't a very good judge of men's characters was distressing.

"I don't have tickets for the reunion," Jill said. "So don't worry about running into me, okay?"

Andrew stuck his hands in his pockets. "What? Why? I'm sure everyone will want to see you."

She pursed her lips. "I need to get going, Andrew. So if there's nothing else . . ."

Andrew took a step closer. "Don't close the door. At least catch me up. I'd like to know about your family. How's Dorothy doing?"

"My mother's great. I'll let her know you asked about her. Goodbye." She moved to shut the door but, quick as a pickpocket, Andrew's hand slapped against the wood.

Though unhappy to see him, Jill wasn't particularly afraid of Andrew, primarily because he no longer seemed to be under the influence of the various illegal drugs he was pumped full of the last time they were alone together. "Please move your hand," she said. "I mean it."

"Not until you agree to sit down and talk to me. How about dinner later this week?"

"No."

His eyes narrowed. "We can go to brunch at Shacks on the Beach. I checked, and it's still in business. See how hard I'm trying? I remember it's your favorite place in Santa Barbara. Doesn't that count for something?"

"Not really." This aggressive bantering, which Andrew obviously thought was flirting, was something she did not remember about him. "I need to go inside. Let me close the door."

He dropped his hand to his side. "Okay, but listen for just one minute. You know, you're not making this easy."

"Neither are you." Jill squinted up at him. "What are you really doing here? You know I'd never willingly spend time with you after what happened between us."

He blinked. "I meant it when I said I want to make amends. What happened between us was stupid, and I have a lot to apologize for, particularly my drug taking. But I'm clean now. Have been for years. And if you don't mind me saying this, you weren't completely innocent, either, were you?"

"I have no idea what you're talking about."

The two of them stared at each other for a long moment. Jill knew Andrew was trying to re-open old wounds, but she was not going to do it. There were memories from the past she cherished, but those of her short marriage to him were not ones she wished to revisit, freaking reunion or no reunion.

He sighed. "Okay. Have it your way." Andrew pulled a business card out of his jacket pocket and stuck it in the flowers. "Max Kallstrom is coming to town. Did you know that?" His voice was strained.

Jill flushed. "What does that have to do with anything?"

"I thought it might be reason enough for you to reconsider coming to the reunion. You'll have the chance to see the man you were still in love with when you married me."

Their glances met. "Andrew, I'm sorry you came all the way over here hoping to get into the blame game, but I am not going to do it. Okay? We're done. Nothing either of us can say can change anything."

"I get you hate me. And that you're still angry about my behavior." Andrew shook his head. "But there's something else I need to discuss with you. It's important. There are some strange things going on I want to tell you about before the reunion. Can't you just give me an hour?"

"No."

"But," he said.

Jill shook her head. "No. Goodbye. Please don't come back," she said and shut the door. Hard.

And locked it. And threw the deadbolt.

And stared out the peephole for five minutes after her ex-husband drove off.

Jill said a few swear words she did not like to hear, much less use, and went into the kitchen where she watched the street for another ten minutes. She wanted to call someone, but the only person who came to mind who would make her feel less freaked-out did not know who she was anymore.

Once she was convinced Andrew was gone, she opened the front door and frowned at the roses, long-stemmed and perfect, swathed in silver tissue with green glass marbles at the bottom of the vase.

Even if the last person she wanted back in her life had given them to her, there was no way she was going to do what crazy people did in the movies and chuck the flowers in the garbage. She carted them inside, relocked the locks, and set the vase on the kitchen counter.

As if it might bite, she carefully plucked out Andrews's business card, tore it in half, and threw it into the trash.

She added water to the buds, which were tightly closed but sweetly fragrant, and carried them into the living room. Her heart raced as she sat down and stared at them on the coffee table.

Cherry vanilla, white roses edged with pink. Her favorite.
Did Andrew remember that?
And how did he know Max Kallstrom was coming to the reunion?

For a moment her mind froze, overloaded by the sensory shock of the past crashing into the present. Particularly two men from the past.

Max had disappeared from her life completely fifteen years ago, the night before college graduation, and never so much as called or wrote one word to her since then. His family had him shipped home after a terrible car accident had nearly killed him, but they had never responded to any of her calls or letters.

So why is Max coming back to town now? After all this time?
And what the hell did Andrew mean that there were strange things going on with the reunion?

"Shit," she swore softly.

Good Friday had delivered another basket of rotten eggs to her door. Taking her mother to the nursing home was horrible enough, but the visit of her biggest error in judgement, one Andrew Denton, and the imminent reappearance in town of her biggest romantic heartbreak, would forever mark this current holiday as one of the worst.

Chapter 3

Jill stared out the kitchen window, which she had done four different times since she had gotten out of bed that morning. A mug of tea cooled in her hand. Yesterday's events felt unreal, and if it was not for the riot of roses in the living room, she would have believed she had dreamed the part about her ex-husband showing up.

Outside the unmistakable sound of a Harley motorcycle reached her. The bike appeared seconds later, the driver's helmet shiny black like his leather jacket. As she watched he made a slow circle around the cul de sac and then disappeared. She had never seen that bike in her secluded neighborhood before, and she wondered who it was.

Jill blew out a nervous breath and stared at her unvarnished nails, unable to remember her last manicure. She poured out the coffee and opened the refrigerator. Her stomach was growling, but she was not sure she could eat. She had slept until ten, thanks to yesterday's dramas and the sleeping pills, and now felt queasy and hungry, all at once.

She closed the fridge, grabbed a box of wheat crackers, and went and sat on the sofa. The whole house smelled like roses. They had started to unfurl, looking as spectacular as their fragrance.

As she crunched, she experienced an odd sensation of watching herself from above, as if she had stepped into someone else's life. She wished Carly was already here. Her friend's pragmatic approach to life always helped ground her, and made Jill feel like she could handle whatever came her way, even when she couldn't.

Jill swallowed. *I better make those appointments.* It would at least distract from the emptiness she felt in the house now that her mom was not living here.

Reminders of Dorothy were everywhere: her favorite afghan on the sofa, her slippers in the closet, her jewelry box in the drawer.

The Delft teapot, a gift from her grandmother, sat on the kitchen table, waiting for her mom to pour.

An image of Max Kallstrom bloomed unbidden in her mind.

He likes tea instead of coffee. With sugar and lemon, sweet and sour.

Her mother had teased him about it when Jill brought him home for dinner, all those years ago.

Jill shook her head. Was it possible Max was coming to the reunion to see her? Would it make a difference, after all these years?

They had become lovers within weeks of him arriving at college her senior year. She had loved him completely, and trusted his declarations that he loved her and that they had a future together.

The car accident had changed his life, and hers too.

Jill stuffed another cracker into her mouth. If she saw him again, Max could certainly provide some long-needed answers to a fifteen-year-old mystery.

But do I want to hear them?

Could anything he said erase the hurt and pain? Could any explanation not end with the simple fact that she had not mattered enough to the only man she had ever truly loved?

Jill got up and brushed the cracker crumbs away. It was time to get some things done. Put something else in her mind except for questions she could not answer.

She started with phone calls. Despite telling Andrew she wasn't going, Jill spoke to a reservation committee member and found out she could still get tickets for the reunion dinner, though it was unclear if there was still room at the other events. She bought the dinner ticket for Carly's sake, still not convinced she would actually attend.

The woman she spoke to said she would have Marissa Pierce, the event chairman, call her back about the other reunion events.

"I see Marissa left a note by your name that if you called, she wanted to talk to you. She must have been expecting you to change your mind."

"Really?" Jill chewed her lip. This was the part she hated, talking to people she had not seen for years. The memory of Marissa Pierce flitted in and out of focus, chubby and blonde braids, with a nervous laugh. Her older brother, Ben, had been a sweetheart, if a bit of a stoner.

Why would she want to talk to her?

"Okay, thanks." Jill called and made a couple of appointments for her and Carly, including one to get her legs waxed, which she had not done for years.

After that, she cleaned house and did some errands, ending the day by driving to Friends House to have dinner with her mother.

Dorothy was not settling into the swing of things easily. She kept getting up in the dining room and trying to get out of the building, and despite Jill sitting with her for two hours, her mother was so anxious and stressed the nurse on duty gave her a mild sedative.

Jill drove into her garage at twenty minutes past eight. She grabbed the mail from the front box and then hurried into the kitchen. Two bills. A letter from the community college where she taught. A thick packet from Friends House addressed to 'Gill Farrel.'

There was also a heavy cream paper envelope, addressed

correctly. The return address said Pandora Security, with a Beverly Hills address.

Jill's stomach tightened and she went back and checked the locks on the front door, then flipped on the kitchen light and turned on the teakettle. She sat and opened the envelope. Inside the single sheet was handwritten.

Jill-

I need to discuss an important matter with you. Please call me at either of my numbers as soon as you can.

Andrew

"Damn." Jill stuck the letter back in the envelope and stared at it. There was no stamp. Which meant someone other than the postman had stuck it in her mailbox today while she was out.

Who?

The teakettle hissed and a chill skittered down her back. A second later, the doorbell rang. Jill nearly jumped out of the chair. She put her hand to her throat.

Get a grip.

If it was Andrew again, she was going to threaten to have him arrested for postal felonies, or whatever the crime was for people messing with other people's mailbox.

Jill blinked and hit the front porchlight and peered through the peephole.

Please don't be Andrew.

But it wasn't her ex.

It was another man. He wore a sports coat and jeans. Relaxed and in profile, he was looking out at the street instead of at the door. His thick, dark hair curled around his collar.

It was a man she had not laid eyes on for fifteen years, but Jill realized with a jolt that she would recognize the curve of his face as long as she lived.

It was Max Kallstrom.

Jill pulled the door open, half-expecting she had imagined the man's identity.

But it was him.

Max turned, his face wreathing into a huge smile.

Several observations flamed simultaneously through Jill's thoughts.

He's older, and even more handsome than I remember.
And taller.
And he looks like he can walk just fine.

"Jill? Jill Farrell?" he said.

"Max. I don't believe it." She leaned against the doorframe, thankful for solid support for her quaking body.

"Yes. It's me, Max Kallstrom." His gaze roamed her face and body, his smile sincere, though his green eyes were cautious. "You remember me? From St. John Vianney? I was your foreign exchange student during your senior year, and we had classes together." He named the year. "Fifteen years ago! It is a long time, *ja?*"

She blinked. *Is he really asking me if I remember him?*

Jill gripped the door tighter. "Yes, yes. Of course I remember you." Suddenly she had the desire to throw herself in his arms, touch his face with her hands, and feel his broad chest against her breasts.

Just as suddenly she wanted to slap his face and scream, "What the hell happened to you? How could you disappear like you did? How could you break my heart?"

The warring impulses overwhelmed her. Jill crossed her arms and stood up straighter. "I'm just surprised to see you, especially after all this time." She heard the sarcasm in her voice.

Max did not appear to.

"Me too! In fact, I think I am more surprised than you that I'm here on your doorstep." He held out his hand to shake hers.

Jill shook quickly and then pulled away and waved toward her house. "Please. Come in. I'll make us some tea, or get you a drink, or whatever you want."

"Thank you. Thank you. I should have called, I know, but I wasn't sure how to reach you by phone, or if you still had the same name." He stepped into the foyer.

"It's the same. My name. Jill Farrell."

Their glances met and held.

"I know. I know that now," Max said. "This was the only online address for J.R. Farrell. I took a chance that it was you. The woman on the reunion committee said she couldn't give me your private information, but to check listings in Orchard Beach."

"So you finally found me."

Max blinked. "Yes." He moved past her, his sleeve brushing her arm. He stopped at the kitchen entrance, resting his hands against his waist.

Jill closed the door and they stood in silence.

Both waiting.

She stared at him. Perfect nose, straight and prominent. Beautiful skin. Silky eyebrows and those wonderful green eyes, clear of worry. The biggest difference was that Max the grown-up carried himself with a certain gravitas, not with the devil-may-care energy of his twenty-one-year-old self.

"I can't believe you're here," she said.

"I very much wanted to see you before the reunion," he said on top of her words.

They both laughed nervously. She gestured toward the living room. "Do you want to come sit down? But can

I get you something first? Tea? Whiskey? I have red wine. California cabernet."

"I'd love a coffee," he said. "Black, please."

She started to say, you drink coffee now, but bit her tongue. "Of course, it'll take just a minute." Jill pulled her fingers through her hair and cringed over her unkempt appearance.

"Why don't I come in the kitchen with you?"

"Oh. Sure. Come on in." She directed Max with another nervous wave, feeling as if she was giving erratic signals to an airplane about to land. She relaxed her arms against her sides and walked into the room, which felt very much smaller with Max Kallstrom in it.

"This is a very nice house. Have you been here long?"

"A few years." Jill turned her back and opened the cupboard. Her mind was a jumble and she was glad for something to do while she fought to clear it. She took out mugs, and sugar, and coffee. *What is he thinking about me right now?*

She took the pot out of the coffee-maker and ran water into it. "So, did you just get into town today?" When she turned he was watching her, his elbows on the table, his hands folded together.

"Yes. I've been in the States for a week. I was in Washington DC for a few days, and I flew into LAX this afternoon."

"Oh. Are you still living in Sweden?"

"No. I live in Paris. For four years now."

"Oh." She flipped on the pot and sat across from him as the water burbled through the filter, the kitchen filling up with the smell of coffee. "What is it you do for a living?"

She remembered he wanted to farm. His family raised sheep, but only for wool, not meat.

"I run my own business. Investments." He cocked his head. "I am not a high roller, like your Wall Street types.

Nothing that glamorous. I administer a fund for a group of investors who aren't interested in making money. They give money away, via grants, to non-profits. Primarily in African countries."

"That must be interesting. And rewarding." Jill squeezed her hands together in her lap.

"What do you do, Jill?"

Her mouth was dry and her tongue dragged against her teeth when she spoke. "I teach English at a community college. I have several foreign students from Africa. The Sudan. A couple from Kenya. They're great."

"I lived in Kenya for a year. Nairobi." He nodded. "Did you always want to teach?"

The confusion of emotions swelled inside her. It was not because she was talking trivia with a man who she had not seen for fifteen years.

It was not because he was a man she had once loved, or that her immediate reaction to him was one part happiness and another part fury.

It was because Max was acting as if she was a complete stranger.

What the hell? Does he think he can just show up and not apologize? Doesn't he realize he needs to explain why he dropped out of my life?

The pain she felt surprised her with its intensity, and she realized she had lied to herself, telling herself she was completely over his abandonment of her. The humiliation and shock felt current, and raw.

"Yes, I've always wanted to teach," she managed. "Since I was a kid, all I wanted to do was teach. I remember telling you that was what I wanted to do when we were in college. Many times." She had tried to say this lightly, as if she was making a joke, but her voice cracked.

"I see." His expression was guarded.

"I did my student teaching when you were here in the States, in fact. At Orchard Beach High School. Right down the road."

"Did you?" Max did not take his eyes off her face.

She leaned toward him. "Don't you remember all those conversations we had about what we'd do after graduation? I'm sorry, I don't mean to sound so, so . . ."

"Disappointed." It was not a question. "And hurt."

"I'm not hurt." Her voice was too loud as she pulled her head back. "I'm just, well, surprised. I mean, I know it was a long time ago, but surely, all that time we spent together . . ."

"Jill," he interrupted. "I don't know of an easy way to tell you this, and I'm sure you are expecting me to say something else, apologize most likely for not getting in touch with you before now. So I would like to tell you something right now. Before we say anything else to each other."

"Go ahead." She swallowed.

"I don't remember anything. I don't remember you. At all," Max said. "I'm sorry."

Chapter 4

Jill tried to swallow, but her throat would not work. "What do you mean? I mean we were . . ." Her voice broke. "Close. My god, you don't remember any of that?"

"No."

"Oh, I see." But she didn't. *Is this some kind of cowardly bull he thinks he can pull to get out of apologizing?* "I don't know what to say."

"I'm sure you don't." Max hung his head for a moment and then extended his hand across the table. "That's why I came here tonight. To explain this to you so you wouldn't be embarrassed if we ran into each other at the reunion." His voice roughened with emotion. "I am so sorry to hurt you like this."

She ignored his hand. "I'm not hurt so much as confused. Please stop saying that."

"I don't believe that. You have to be. You were in love with me." He said it matter-of-factly, his rich baritone filling the room.

"Now wait just a minute." Jill pointed her index finger at Max. "We were just kids fifteen years ago. And while I took our time together seriously, I wouldn't call what we shared love."

"Why not?"

"Why not? What kind of love affair ends like ours did? I'd say we were a couple of kids in heat, and that was it." She stood up and glared at him, aware she was losing control of her emotions.

Max's mouth tightened. "Let me get the coffee. Please, sit down." He motioned toward her chair and she sat.

He got up and poured the cups, setting hers carefully in front of her.

"*Tack.*"

"*Du ar valkommen.*"

Jill flushed. A long-buried reflex had led her to say 'Thank you' in his native language, and he had replied that she was welcome.

She gulped her coffee and felt like an idiot. She was out of her depth here. She couldn't think of a thing to say, she just wanted to scream.

Max returned to his chair. "I'm sure you think I'm a complete jerk. And I think I just made everything worse, blurting out what I said. But it isn't easy for me to explain." He took a sip of coffee. "I have a lot to tell you about what happened to me. It may take a while."

"I've got a few minutes. Shoot." Jill took another mouthful, scalding her lips, and flushed to her waist. The last thing on earth she wanted was to hear Max explain why he did not remember her at all.

"Well, let me begin."

As Max quietly narrated his story, the hurt that had nearly choked her began to fade. Jill realized she should have considered that something like what he was explaining had befallen the young man she had, in fact, been very much in love with.

The car accident, which he could not remember, had left him with a serious concussion, as well as several broken bones and a ruptured spleen, Max explained.

He had nearly died at the scene from blood loss, and then again a few weeks later, back in Sweden, when he developed a clot in his brain. After an operation to alleviate the cranial pressure, his doctors had put him in a medically induced coma for weeks.

After years of physical therapy, his body had returned to nearly what it had been, but his memory had not. He had lost several chunks of his past, the year he was ten, for example, and most of his college years, including his time in California, up to and including the accident. Some of his other lost memories had returned over time, but their year together was wiped-out.

"This is why I decided to come to the reunion." Max's voice was tight from his long narrative. "I thought if I connected with people who knew and remembered me, visited places I'd been, that it might trigger something."

"Why do you want those memories back?" Jill asked. "After all this time, I mean."

"I don't want empty spots in my life. Life is short, and I want all of it. Forgetting the year I lived here, the people I knew, it seems too much of a waste." He looked at her searchingly. "I have a seven-year-old daughter. Olivia. She asks me questions all the time about my past, and what I did as a child and a young man."

"A daughter. So you're married?" Jill gripped her fingers together.

"I'm divorced. Olivia lives with her mother outside of Paris. While I see her often, it's not enough."

"I'm sure that's difficult."

"It is." Max met her eyes. "Do you have children?"

"No."

"When you do, you'll understand why it haunts me that I've lost pieces of my past. Children grow so fast, one gets a sense of how short one's life is, and how important each day is. If I lose that part of my past forever, my life will have been cut short. I don't want that."

Jill thought again of her mother. Healthy in body at sixty-three, but not really alive in the present, helpless against an incendiary illness that had turned vast swathes of her past into ash.

And now more of my own past is going up in smoke as I sit across from another person who doesn't remember me.

With this sobering thought, Jill got to her feet. She wanted to be alone. She wanted blackout sleep.

"Thanks for coming by, Max. And explaining all this. I appreciate it."

"I had to, for me. And for you." He took a step toward her, only two feet separating them. Max reached into his jacket pocket and brought out a worn envelope that he handed to her. "When I closed up my parents' home in Sweden last year after my mother died, I found this."

Jill stared at the envelope. The postmark was fifteen years ago, from the Christmas after Max had disappeared from her life. She knew what the card inside was. And what it said. She had sent it.

Echoes of the words she had written filled her head. "So your mother didn't give it to you when it came?"

"No, but she kept it. I found some photos also. Several of the buildings at St. John's College. I contacted the administration and was directed to a very kind professor there who knew me, and you. Dr. Mary Millard. She told me about our class, and that we were a serious couple. I scanned the photos I found and emailed them to her. She and I exchanged several messages and she told me about the reunion." Max inhaled. "She's the one who suggested I should come and see you."

Jill could not find her voice. The relief she had felt at hearing why Max had not contacted her began to turn to despair. Her memories of their intimacy seemed fragile, and she realized that when they began to fade, there would be no one in the world to help restore them.

She tried to smile. "I'm glad you took Dr. Millard's advice. To come to the reunion. I love Dr. Millard. She was always great. Very insightful."

"She's a wonderful woman. She said to tell you she hopes you'll make some time to talk, that she missed you at the last reunion."

Jill leaned against the counter. "I'm not too big on reunions."

"She mentioned that, but said she hoped you would attend this one. Are you coming?"

"I'm not sure."

Max stuck his hands in his pockets. "I have snapshots of you and me I left at the hotel. And one of you with your hair tied up in a band. I don't know what you call that."

"A ponytail."

"Yes." He grinned, and for a moment the old Max, his eyes warm and teasing, was standing in the room with Jill. "Yes. Ponytail. Olivia wears those. You may have sent the photos in letters, but I didn't find any of those. Only the card."

"You must have been surprised when you read it."

"I was. After I contacted Dr. Millard, I was furious at my mother. Which is very sad because she's gone and can't explain why she acted as she did." He stared at her intently. "The most urgent reason I came here tonight was to ask your forgiveness for abandoning you. You must have hated me."

"I could never hate you." As soon as Jill said the words, she wished she could take them back, for her voice revealed too much of what she had once felt about him.

Still felt, about the old Max.

"I'm relieved to hear you say that." He blew out a breath and smiled a familiar crooked smile. "Thank you."

"Why do you think your mother didn't give you the letters?"

Several moments passed. "I have no good answer for that. She had issues her entire life with depression. Constantly worried about the state of the world and my father's safety. He traveled all over Europe for his career."

She frowned. When they were in college, hadn't Max had told her his father was a farmer, not a man with an international travel schedule? "That doesn't explain why she didn't give her son a letter from a friend."

Max blinked. "Bluntly, I think she blamed you, and America, for my accident. For making her live through the pain of thinking I would die."

"I see." Jill nodded.

"Do you?" He shook his head. "I never did understand her."

"No?"

"No. She was not happy a day of my life that I recall." Max appeared uncomfortable, as if he had said more than he wanted to. "But enough about childhood. Let me just say she was a tough woman to deal with."

Besides sending the letters, Jill had made a telephone call to his mother. In her mind she heard the echo of the dismissive, angry tone in his mother's voice. "Maximilian is not here. Do not call this number ever again." The words followed by the disconnect buzz of the telephone.

It would not help anything if she told Max about that call. "So, both of your parents are gone then?"

He nodded. "Yes. And yours?"

"My father died seven years ago. My mother is alive, but in an assisted living facility. As of yesterday, actually. She has Alzheimer's disease." She swallowed.

"This happened yesterday? And now I show up? Pretty bad timing on my part."

"Things happen when they happen. You had no way of knowing."

"Your mother is young, though, yes? How old is she?"

"Sixty-three."

"Life is filled with tragedy." Max shook his head. "I'm sorry for her, and for you, Jill. I know how frustrating it is, not to know your own past. Not to remember those who love you." He shuddered. "Do you have sisters and brothers?"

"No. I'm an only child."

He crossed his arms over his chest. "I've been very insensitive tonight. I shouldn't have just dumped all this drama from my past on you. And I shouldn't be asking you all these questions about, about people I should remember."

"There's no need to apologize. It's an unusual situation, all around. There aren't any rules to cover this kind of thing, are there?"

"No. No rules for this." Max glanced at his shoes, and then up at her. "Well, that's the whole story then. I hope it's helped in some way, to tell you about it."

She felt raw. "Thank you for thinking of me. What are you going to do to try and remember. Talk to other people, too?"

"I don't know. I think so, although it's awkward." He sighed and stood up. "Thank you again for being so kind, not just slamming the door."

"I'm not that kind of girl," Jill said, trying to keep it light, but she sounded hurt.

"I can see that." He stepped toward her. "I was a lucky man."

She looked down, her face red, and then quickly back at him. "I could help you. Try to help you, I mean. If you want me to."

"What?"

"I could drive you around, share my memories, and help you reconstruct some of the gaps. If you have time, you and I could talk again, meet . . ." Jill cleared her throat. She should have thought more about this before she spoke, she realized. But Max had always done this to her. Made her drop her guard because he was so honest, so open. "Maybe that's a dumb idea."

"No, my gosh, no. It's so generous. You'd do that for me? I'd appreciate hearing anything you could tell me, details about things I said and did." He paused. "We were lovers, *ja?*"

She put her hand to her throat. "I, we. Yes. We were."

"If you don't mind, I want to know about that, too. Our past." His eyes flashed. "My doctors said I might remember something, particularly something as emotionally charged as an intimate relationship."

"It'll be a pretty one-sided story. I'll always be the one in the right." Again she tried to joke and keep her voice light. She failed.

Max blinked, digesting what she had offered. "And your husband? Or boyfriend? They won't mind you doing this to help me?"

"There's no one who would mind."

Suddenly Max pulled her into a hug. "I must say again, old friend, I am sorry. For your pain all those years ago. And I hope now that you know the facts, you'll never worry again what kind of man you were in love with."

Jill relaxed in his arms for a moment, reveling in the strength and solid feel of him, the realness of him, but then pushed away, terrified she might revive a passion only she could recall.

"Like I said, we were just kids when all this happened. You disappearing from my life was a blow, yes, but I recovered. I married another man a few years after you left, as a matter of fact."

"I see." He leaned on the kitchen counter. "And were you happy?"

"No. Not at all. But it wasn't because of you." She cleared her throat, a bubble of happiness growing inside her. "So let's wipe the slate clean. You've apologized. Thank you."

"You're welcome." Max glanced at his watch. "I don't know your schedule, but may I take you to dinner tomorrow? We could fill in the details about what's happened with each other the last decade or so. It can be a very unusual blind date. *Ja?*"

At that moment, Max was exactly the same guy she used to know, full of charm and energy. "Ah, I'm not sure of my schedule then . . ."

"You need time. Of course. I understand." Max held out a business card as they walked to her door. "Here's my cell number. Will you call and let me know about dinner?"

His hand was warm and she saw relief in his face. And something like joy. *Attraction?*

Slow down, she told herself. "Of course. I'll call you tomorrow some time."

"Thank you, Jill." He cocked his head sideways, a twinkle in his gorgeous eyes. "Don't forget."

"That's ironic for you to say."

He looked stricken for a moment, and relieved when she chuckled.

"I won't forget," she said. "Talk to you later."

They exchanged brief kisses on the cheek before Max walked away. Jill watched him, his stride relaxed and easy. Jaunty even. He was relieved. She closed the door and leaned against it.

She did not feel relieved. Her legs were rubbery and, for a moment, she considered slipping down to the floor and taking a nap in the foyer, but one thought gave her enough energy to head for the bedroom.

While she had been dreading tomorrow's Easter lunch with her mother at the nursing home because it would mark a new era of loss, she now had something to look forward to that might be positive. The man she once loved, and lost, was back, seeking a chance to reconnect. *That had to be a good thing, right?*

Jill shook her head, wishing for a moment she could see into the future.

Later that night, the man who killed Ben Pierce stared out his hotel room window and the starless dark sky.

He was not particularly sentimental, but Jill Farrell had

triggered a confrontation with the painful truths he seldom allowed into his thoughts.

He could have taken a different path, despite his father's example, and become a different man. *Am I getting soft? Soft would be deadly.*

He sat for a moment longer and then turned out the lights and lay down in the strange bed. The sheets were cool but his mind remained fevered.

With a groan, the man turned over and squeezed his eyes closed.

It was the reunion.

Perhaps he should abandon his plan, and not expose himself to so many people all at once?

No.

If he wasn't bold now, when so many people who could reveal the truth about him were gathered in one place, he would live in fear for the rest of his life.

And the next time someone discovered the truth about him, he could lose everything.

He thought again of Jill Farrell and sighed.

Chapter 5

Friend's House was bustling with visiting family. Jill parked the car and grabbed the plastic-encased orchid corsage she had brought for her mom. Her mother had always acted surprised when her father presented her with one, even though he had made the gesture every Easter Sunday they were together.

Her mother's surprise today would surely be more real than in old times.

"Jill, wait up!" a man shouted as she reached for the door.

She turned in surprise to find Carly's dad, Dave Hart, dapper as always in a plaid sport coat and dress pants, hurrying up the sidewalk.

"Dave! Hi!" They hugged at the doorway, the bright sunshine making her squint. "What a nice surprise. Happy Easter."

"Happy Easter to you. Carly called last night and told me your mom moved in here ahead of schedule, so I thought I'd come see her." He squeezed her arm. "How are you, honey? You look great. Excited that my girl is hitting town?"

"I can't wait to see Carly. And the baby. I bet you and Leslie are excited too." Jill said this even though Dave's second wife did not get along very well with Carly, probably a big reason why her best friend was staying in a hotel.

"We are." He took her arm and they walked inside, registered, and headed for Dorothy's room. "I hear a lot of your old comrades in arms are coming in for the reunion. That Norwegian kid, too, right?"

"Swedish. Max. Yes, that's true." She kept silent, not ready to share with anyone that she had already talked with Max.

Dave nodded. He was an ex-cop, an old comrade of her dad's days on the police force. Her father had held Dave in high esteem and said he was a great listener, not a lecturer, and was a man he could always trust.

"How's Dorothy doing?" he asked.

"She's only been here two days, but yesterday she seemed anxious. It's going to take time." They stopped so Jill could enter the door code, set at 7777. The residents in the Alzheimer's wing had to be kept locked in. Jill had doubted the wisdom of a code with all digits the same number, as people forgot codes, but might accidentally keep hitting the same button and get out.

Dave held the door for her, but closed it quickly as a resident Jill had been warned about, Mrs. Meeks, dressed in head-to-toe polka dots, rushed toward them.

"Hi there, Mrs. Meeks," Jill said. "Happy Easter."

"Where are my roller skates?" Sandy demanded. "And Frisky. Where's my dog?"

"I haven't seen him."

Mrs. Meeks squinted and then meandered back toward the dining room.

Jill and Dave continued down the hallway. "I've seen her waiting by the door every time I've been here. She knows there's a way out. The Alzheimer's is not quite as advanced with her as it is in my mother case."

"This disease is so harsh. If your father was here, it would kill him to see Dorothy in a place like this."

"It would be tough for him, but I can't help but think that maybe Mom wouldn't have gone downhill so fast if Daddy had still been around."

Dave squeezed her arm. "He wouldn't have done anything more than you have. My wife's sister has Alzheimer's, and her doctor says it's not stress or grief or anything else that makes a person get worse. It's the body making too much of that protein that clogs up all the brain cells, and the fact we don't have any medication to stop it."

"I know, I know. I've read a million articles, but still . . ."

"You've done the right thing by Dorothy, all down the line. She's lucky to have you to make these decisions for her, kiddo."

"Thank you for saying that. I try, but I wish I could do more." Jill knocked lightly on Dorothy's door then opened it and found her mother sitting in the chair by the bed, rocking slowly back and forth.

"Hey, Mama. You've got a couple of visitors."

"Buketa bucketa. Uncle Bill. Bucketa, bucketa," her mother whispered.

Jill touched her shoulder. "It's Jill, Mama. And Dave Hart is here to see you."

Dorothy squinted up at them. "Who's that man?"

"It's me, Dave. How you doing, beautiful?" He kissed her on the forehead. "Nice place you got here. Lots of light."

"Uncle Bill. Uncle Bill. Uncle Bill," Dorothy replied.

She did this often, repeated words and phrases. But until lately she'd only done it late at night, when she was tired.

Jill took a rattling breath. "She's sleeping too much lately. I'm going to talk about the meds with her doctors this week. Don't take it personally that she doesn't seem to know you."

Dave's expression reflected shock. It had only been a month since he had seen Dorothy, but it was clear she was getting worse every day. "Don't worry about me. And it's hard to adjust to new surroundings. It's like that for everyone. She'll settle down."

"I hope so." Jill set the orchid down on the table. Her mother was wearing a lavender print dress and tennis shoes. "Why don't I fix Mom's hair and we'll walk up and see you in the lobby? Would you like to come have a bite with us in the cafeteria before you go?"

"No. No, I wanted to give Dorothy a hug." He made no move to do that, however, as her eyes had closed and she was leaning back in the chair. Instead, he hugged Jill. "I'll see you next week when Carly gets in. All you kids can come over if you get a chance. Even that Swede."

"Okay."

"You take care now."

"I will. Thank you for coming to see her, Dave."

"Sure thing." His eyes glistened. With a last glance at Dorothy, he hurried out of the room.

He had lasted about three minutes, but Jill didn't blame Carly's dad for making a quick retreat. It was disconcerting for anyone who had known her mother to see her as she was now. She thought of Max, who would not remember her mother as she once was, and then pushed all the jumble of emotion that was Max out of her mind.

She glanced at her watch. It was a quarter after twelve and the luncheon started promptly at twelve-thirty. All residents were to be in their chairs then, according to the hot-pink flyer that was pasted on her mother's door.

"Okay, Dorothy. Time to wake up."

She touched her mother and Dorothy opened her eyes.

"What day is this?"

"Easter Sunday. Look what I brought you." She held up the corsage.

Dorothy turned in Jill's direction. Due to the progression of her Alzheimer's, she had difficulty focusing. "Hello."

"It's Jill, Mom. How are you feeling today?"

"Fine." She blinked several times. Her eyes, once a clear bright blue, were faded and infused with an odd, shining spark inside the irises, almost like the red-eye look you see in poorly taken photos. Jill had noticed this glint for several months, but when she asked during check-ups what caused it, none of Dorothy's doctors seemed to see what she described.

"Can I put your corsage on? I thought you might like to wear it today. They're having a special meal in the dining room for Easter."

Dorothy didn't look at Jill as she wrestled the creaking, snapping piece of plastic open and pinned the thing to her mother's dress.

"That looks beautiful."

Dorothy sniffed and made accidental eye contact. "It smells funny."

"Do you want me to take it off?"

She sniffed again. "I have a cold." She sniffed twice more. Dorothy did not have a cold, but she constantly sniffed as if she had hay fever.

Jill wondered if this was a survival instinct. Maybe the pieces of her brain that still worked told her to rely on other senses more now. Maybe she thought her sniffing instincts could lead her out of the forest of confusion that was her daily life.

"The orchid looks nice on your dress, mom. That's the one we got you last summer. At Nordstrom's."

Her mother turned and waved at the window. "Who's that man?"

Jill stared outside. "There's no one there."

A long silence followed and Jill knew that was the end of the conversation.

Dorothy felt around her neck for the antique locket she wore at her throat. It was the only piece of jewelry she decided their mother could keep while living here, as the nurses could work around it when they bathed her.

Dorothy received it from her mother when she was only a child, and had given it to Jill when Jill was sixteen. Dorothy had asked to wear it again last year when they came across it emptying out the family home.

With a shock, Jill remembered that inside was a strand of her mother and father's hair in one side of a locket, the other of which held some of her own, intertwined with a strand of Max Kallstrom's hair.

She had put it in one night after she had cut his hair for him, joking that she would shave him bald if he did not sit still. Jill blinked. "Guess who I saw last night, Mom? Max Kallstrom."

Dorothy rubbed the locket, but said nothing.

"Do you remember my boyfriend when I was in college? Max with the dark hair. He loved tea with sugar and lemon."

Tears trickled down Dorothy's face.

Jill hugged her. "Oh, please don't cry. Do you remember Max? From Sweden?"

"Buketa. Buketa buketa buketa," Dorothy said and moved out of Jill's embrace.

Jill swiped her hand roughly over her eyes. "Okay then. Why don't we go eat? They're having ham and scalloped potatoes. And there's cake for dessert."

Dorothy's eyes met hers in the mirror. "I want to leave," she whispered.

"I know." Jill said. "I know."

When she got home at three P.M., Jill considered calling Max to say she was not up for dinner, or anything more. Half of her brain had argued a hundred times to just leave the past alone, and not invite the new Max into her current life.

The other half of her brain had told her to let go and help the guy. She could have a new relationship with him. They could be friends.

But she couldn't make up her mind what she could handle. She considered calling Carly, but dismissed that. She wasn't sure what she was feeling yet, so she was going to give herself more time.

Time to decide what she could handle. She accepted Max's story about why he hadn't contacted her for all these years, but she wasn't completely ready to forgive him.

Why?

Fear, she realized. For even though he had no relationship memories of her, hers of him were suddenly as hot and merciless as a bed of coals.

Can I be around this new Max and not see the man I loved?

Jill blew out a breath and went and took a long shower, followed by a short nap. When she woke up she felt refreshed. Outside her window a soft breeze sent the aroma of honeysuckle into her room, and she decided it would be foolish to not at least have dinner with Max.

Spending time with him would give her new memories of the man, and help her overcome the past ones, or at least partition them from reality.

The stiffness and anxiety she had felt last night, she realized, was because her feelings were still stuck in the past. She needed to make some in the present, and dilute the power the old ones had over her emotions.

Satisfied she had given the situation enough consideration, Jill called and agreed to meet Max at seven. He was more business-like on the telephone, and she relaxed even more.

Think of him as a new friend, she told herself. *Because that is what he is.*

She chose her clothes more carefully than she remembered doing for years, white slacks and a soft silk blouse that wasn't too clingy, along with her favorite navy jacket. She added hoop earrings and a delicate pearl and gold chain, dabbed a touch of lavender perfume behind her ears, more to relax herself than tempt anyone, and slipped on her sandals.

Max rang the bell promptly on time and she greeted him with a genuine smile.

He leaned across the threshold and kissed her cheek, his mouth warm on her skin, and held her close a moment longer than necessary when they hugged hello.

Jill did not ask him to come in, just pulled the door shut and smiled, listening to him complain mildly about traffic as he walked with her to his rental car. A silver convertible, and the top was down.

"I hope you don't mind. But sunshine at seven in the evening is addicting to a boy raised in a place where it's only around a few hours a day, six months of the year."

She pushed her hair behind her ears. "No, this is great. How is Södertälje?" She said it carefully, as he had once taught her to. "Do you get back much?"

Max held the door for her. "No, not much."

He explained he went to the city where he was born because of a client, and named a huge pharmaceutical company. "And Scandia has a big office there. I have worked with them in the past, so I chat up a finance guy I trust to tell me the truth about European markets. I don't make it out to the hamlet where my folks' house was, but I do go. Last Christmas I took Olivia for a visit. I wanted her to see it in all its snowy glory."

"Did she love it?"

"*Ja.* She did, I think." He grinned and they drove off.

Jill guided Max through her neighborhood and up into the hills toward Ashley, the rustic town where she had grown up, a half hour from Santa Barbara, in the hills near Los Olivos.

"I want to thank you again for agreeing to see me." Max kept his eyes on the road. "This is like a first date for me. Not for you, I guess. Although I am certainly a changed man, *ja?*"

"Not so changed," she said, surprised that this was true. "I thought we could drive by my parents' neighborhood, maybe get out and walk around a bit, and then come back to dinner someplace along the water."

"Great. Seafood? Is that what you like most?"

"I do like seafood, but my favorite is Italian." The best for that was a place called Geno's. She and Max went there many times, but Jill wasn't ready to take on those memories, as it was the place they ate the night they became lovers. "But Shacks on the Beach in Santa Barbara is great on a night like this. Great view of the ocean. I made a reservation for nine."

"I love the beaches along the Pacific. Nowhere is more beautiful."

"And all the girls in bikinis don't hurt the view, right?"

He chuckled. "Is that what I did when I was here before? Ogle girls at the beach?"

"No. You were very gallant." *You only ogled me*, she thought, remembering the admiration in his eyes. "Turn at that first street. My folks place is a few minutes up in the hills."

Max asked many questions about her family. How long they had lived in the area, and what her parents had done professionally. She kept her answers light and informative, watching his face, listening to his inflection to see if he seemed to find anything she said familiar, but he was reacting as someone you sat next to on an airplane would. He nodded, politely, interested.

But that was all.

They pulled up in front of the house and Max put the car in neutral.

She had sold the rambling ranch, her childhood home, early last year when her mother moved in with her, and it seemed already a foreign place. The new owners had painted the stucco a darker tan, and changed the weathered rust-colored trim to a bright blue. They had also cut down all the bougainvillea that covered the front wall of the house, Jill noted, missing that soft, beautiful red flowering vine she had sat under many a summer day.

Max stared at the house. He wore sunglasses so she could not see his eyes, but the intensity of how he set his jaw showed he did not remember being here.

"It's a nice place," he said.

"It is. You want to get out and walk around? I know the neighbors, so we could stroll up the driveway and look into the backyard. You ate a lot of hamburgers out on the patio back there."

"Sure."

Her parents' old neighbors, the Holmes, were not home so they had enough time to leisurely look around at the back yard of Jill's family home. The trees and patio were the same as they had been, but the yard was dug up and a huge pit bull barked his dissatisfaction at seeing them.

Jill pointed over the cement and brick wall, telling him where the BBQ had been, and how they sat under the orange trees, but not in the summer or spring because of the bees. Max smiled and nodded, remembering none of it.

"Is this hard for you? To be here with so many memories?" His voice was rough with emotion.

"Not so much. Not now. I'm kind of numb to it. It seems like someone else lived here, it's so different."

"I felt like that when I closed my parents' house. It was exactly the same as when I grew up, but I felt like I was dreamwalking through it. Because I was such a different person."

Jill nodded. It's the world, and all the people in it, that's changed. Though right now she did not feel different. She felt like the same thirteen-year-old girl she had once been, standing at the fence, looking into the back yard, ready to ambush her friends with a water balloon.

"Shall we head out? There's going to be a lot of our

famous traffic heading down to Santa Barbara this time of night," Jill said.

"Sure. Thanks for bringing me here." Max guided her by the elbow back out to the street.

They drove down the freeway to Santa Barbara, having accomplished none of the memory jarring Max had hoped for. But they continued to chat, and as the miles flew by Jill felt her last remnants of anger melt away, along with much of the tension.

It was not like being with the old Max, but it was lovely getting to know the interesting stranger beside her, as the wind blew her hair and the sun shined down. He was charming and attentive, although his responses seemed more careful than she remembered from the spontaneous younger Max.

At the restaurant, the hostess led them to a table by the windows, which were opened to the night breeze. It was April but felt like summer.

"This is perfect. What a view." Max held the chair for her.

"Like you said, you can't beat the Pacific Ocean for ambiance."

"Ambiance. I like that word. You Americans stole it from the French."

She smiled as Max settled in across from her. They ordered drinks and stared out at the pink and orange horizon, both quiet in the contemplation of the majestic sunset.

"Did we come here together? Before?" Max asked softly.

"Once with my parents, I think. It was pretty expensive for college kids." She folded her hands together on the table. "Is the view familiar?"

He shaded his eyes and stared at the shoreline. "It feels as if I remember sitting here, in this exact spot." He shook his head, "But I don't. I'm sure that sounds confusing. But I'm having that sensation I often had as a child, when I'd heard some family anecdote described so often by others that I felt as if I'd lived through it, even though I wasn't even born yet when it occurred."

"I know you were an only child, like me, but didn't you have lots of older relatives?"

"Yes. On my mother's side only. Five aunts, all with many children." He tented his hands together. "I didn't see them much, but when I did, I always felt an outsider. They were older than I was, and always talking about things as if I did remember. That's how I feel now. Because I've heard how beautiful the beaches of California are so often, in movies, books, and from others, that I feel like I'm remembering visiting this place before, but I'm not."

"And that's not a good enough feeling, right?"

"Good enough?"

"To feel like you remember isn't the same as authentically recalling something. The real memories are what you want. You want those so you can re-live the event?"

"Yes, that's what I want." He leaned toward her. "Is that what you're doing now? Are you re-living what you felt for me, all those years ago?"

Her breath caught. "Well, no. Yes. I mean. A little." She laughed. "I'm feeling grateful that I spent time here with a boy a long time ago. Those were fun and romantic times. Young love is sort of a bonfire of emotions, isn't it? But it was a long time ago."

"It was. And it was unfair of me to put you on the spot." He grinned. "I did it because I'm a bit jealous."

"Of what?"

"Of your remembering. You look like you're happily visiting a place I can't get to. Although thanks to tonight I'm making new memories, and maybe the new ones are good enough."

"Good enough for what? For you to let go of your search for the past?"

"No one lets go of the past willingly. Let's just say, however, that the present is much more interesting to me than it has been for a long time." Max's eyes drifted down her neck and back to her face. "You look lovely tonight, by the way."

A frisson of heat crept up the center of her, and Jill recognized the look she saw in his eyes. When Max was mulling how to shape a request, a plea for something he craved, his eyes sparkled with intensity, as if was marshalling the forces of the world to get his way.

And at this moment, Max wanted something from her. His gaze held hers, as if he was measuring how much he could ask for, how much she would agree to.

Her remembered passion for him rolled through her veins like warm brandy, dragging her back fifteen years. She stared deeper into his eyes, searching for her long lost lover, and saw that he recognized the escalating tension inside of her. "Thank you," she said softly.

He bit his bottom lip. "I have to tell you, sitting here with you, that I feel something I can't explain. Seeing you has filled me with restlessness. An urge to do something more than what I'm doing. It's like having an itch, but not knowing where to scratch."

"Really?"

"Yes. Last night, in bed at my hotel, I couldn't fall to sleep. All I could think of was you. I'd matched a face to the words you'd written, but I still didn't know you at all. All I could think of was spending more time with you. Because I want to . . ."

"Here are your drinks!" The waiter's voice, twice as loud as Max's, cut him off. The young man halted beside their table, noisily delivering napkins, drinks, and a basket of bread and butter.

"Vodka tonic with a twist for the gentleman. A Kir Royale for the beautiful lady." He beamed at Jill, oblivious to the force field he had stepped into. "Have you decided on appetizers? I can highly recommend the crab dip and the seafood chowder."

Max's glance ran over the waiter's nametag. "I think we're good with the drinks for now, Jamison. Give us a few minutes, okay?"

"Of course. Of course. But why don't I tell you about the specials first?"

"Why don't you leave us alone for a few minutes," Max said. "We need some time."

"Certainly sir. Of course." The waiter backed away.

Jill stared out at the ocean. She picked up her Kir and pretty much chugged it. Cold white wine. Crème de cassis. Gulping like a novice, she felt a sudden thirst that she doubted one drink would quench. Everything about her body felt swollen. She was like a kid, all hormones and want, mentally and emotionally out of whack due to her body's attraction to Max.

Jill crossed her legs and took a deep breath. She hated not being in control. Things needed to slow down. Especially these feelings about Max, which despite her caution to herself, seemed to be coming back with a vengeance.

She needed to remember that she was a stranger to him. He was not feeling what she was. She had to be careful.

"Now, where were we before Jamison hijacked our conversation?" Max asked.

Jill downed the last drops of her Kir. "I don't remember. Why don't we discuss some of the people you're going to meet at the reunion? But first could you order me another one of these." She held up her glass.

"I will, but are you feeling okay?" His eyes were still full of heat. "Your face is very flushed."

"I'm a bit hot." Jill set the empty glass down and picked up her water. "But I'm fine. It's been a long and tiring day."

"Yes, of course, I'm sure it has. We should have had an earlier dinner. How did it go with your mother this morning?" Max was still watching her, but the energy that flowed between them moments before dissipated into the ocean breeze like smoke.

She gave him a brief blow-by-blow of the attack of the corsage pins. "I don't think she remembered what happened as soon as I got the pins out, and by the time we got into the dining room, it was forgotten."

"This must be difficult for you."

"Yes. But what hurts most is that I imagine how much more difficult it is for my mother." Jill picked up the menu. "Why don't we order, and then I'll start a run-down on some of your relationships with people you knew in college. It'll give you a head start when you meet them."

"That would be great." Max motioned for the waiter.

Jill sensed he was troubled. She remembered he did not like to avoid talking about things that were on his mind.

But he was sensitive enough now to understand she was pulling back from the flirtation they had shared, and gentleman enough not to press her.

Thank god.

Because she did not feel like she could handle anything more emotional than chitchat. Certainly not a sentence that started with him lying in a hotel bed last night, thinking about her.

Chapter 6

Dinner was a pleasant blur. Jill told Max about Carly and Hamilton, who Max had never actually met, as Hamilton left for Oxford before Max had arrived from Sweden.

She followed with thumbnail descriptions of a dozen more people they had hung out with during the college year they shared. In the car heading back to her place, Max expressed concern at the number of names she had mentioned.

"It's a long list," Max said, turning into Jill's townhouse development. "I'm not terrible with names, but hopefully everyone will have badges so I can have a chance at keeping them straight."

"I'm sure they will. And it will be interesting to see if any of them seem familiar."

"I have expectations, but not much hope."

"Why's that?"

"Talking to you hasn't led to a breakthrough with my recall, and I imagine I was closer to you than to anyone else." Max pulled into her driveway and put the car in park, but did not shut off the ignition.

During the fifteen-minute drive home, Jill felt Max retreating emotionally. While she had been attacked by a second wave of what honestly could be described as lust when he had taken her arm to help her into the car, he had shown no sign of feeling the same.

Now, sitting inches from her, he was even less engaged. "We're here. I bet you're ready for bed."

Jill stretched her neck to the left and breathed deep, clutching her hands together. "Yes, I am tired. But I had a great time tonight. Thank you for dinner."

"You're welcome," he said. "I'm sorry we never got to discuss much of your past. All you did was fill me in on mine."

"Which part of my past are we talking about?"

"I'd like to hear about what happened with your ex-husband, if it's something you want to share."

She took a deep breath. "I don't like to talk about Andrew Denton, if you want to know the truth. I made a huge mistake marrying him, and he and I didn't part on good terms."

"No?" This one word was filled with curiosity. "Sounds like a story."

Might as well get it out in the open, Jill thought. "It was. Andrew and I were casual friends when we were in college, but we got together a couple of years after we graduated. He was very persuasive, said he'd carried a torch for years, which was flattering."

"He fell in love with you in college, when you were with me?"

"I guess, but I never saw any sign of it during college. Anyway, after dating him for a few months, we got married. Pretty quickly after that, I found out he had a very significant drug problem. He lost his job, and ran wildly through what money we had, and I realized I'd made a huge mistake. The night I told him I wanted a divorce, he pulled out a gun."

"What?" Max moved closer, everything about his demeanor surprisingly protective. "He threatened you?"

"No. He wasn't threatening me. He said he was going to shoot himself if I left him. He was not rational, but I didn't think he was serious. Stupidly I grabbed for the gun, and we wrestled for it before it went off."

Max's face hardened. "Were you hurt?"

"No." She took a breath. "Actually, I shot him."

"You shot your ex-husband?"

"Well, I winged him." Jill touched the side of her forehead. "The bullet glanced off his skull about here. I don't think he even had to get stitches."

"Holy Mother."

"I know, right? Aren't you glad you asked? I bet you are asking yourself about your choice in women back then."

Max shook his head. "No, I'm not doing that. But I'm glad to be warned you're not a girl to mess around with."

Something about the way Max said 'mess around with' in his soft Swedish accent struck her as hilarious.

Jill put her hand over her mouth but could not stifle her laughter, which rumbled out of her for several seconds. "Oh my god, Max, now you're going to think I'm a nut case, laughing over shooting someone. It's not funny, I know. It wasn't funny at all at the time. It feels unreal telling you about it."

"I don't think you're crazy at all. I'm sorry I brought up something so painful. I seem to excel at that."

She squeezed his hand. "It's good you did. Imagine if someone else at the reunion mentioned that sordid tale. You'd think I was a psycho." She shook her head and the three Kirs she had at dinner sloshed around in her stomach. "I don't feel very well. I think I'm drunk."

"Poor girl." He patted her knee. "Come on, we'll get you inside."

She held up her hand. "Give me a minute, okay?"

"Sure." He sat back. "Did you say your ex-husband, this Andrew, went to jail?"

"Yes. That night he was charged with a couple of felonies, but his family had money for a big-time lawyer, and I think after a short time in prison he got sent to rehab. I divorced him, and that was that."

"And you never married again?"

"No." She blinked, uncomfortable that she felt she had to make it clear she wasn't a desperate spinster, or something.

"I don't talk much about this, but I'm glad you heard it from me. I'm sure you'll probably hear other references to it at the parties."

"Why would anyone bring that up?"

"Because Andrew is going to be there."

"You ex-husband is coming to the reunion?"

Jill pictured him standing on her front porch two days ago. "That's what I hear."

Max sat mulling this information in the darkness. A car drove slowly down the street and circled, the headlights illuminating him in profile. "You mentioned I never met Hamilton. But did I know Andrew? Were he and I friends?"

"Yes, you knew him. No, you weren't friends."

"Why?"

"You thought he was a *skit huvud*, which you told me means asshole, if I remember correctly. That's a direct quote."

"It appears I was a good judge of character."

They shared a chuckle. Several moments passed. "Are you feeling well enough to go inside now?" he asked.

"Yes." She wanted suddenly to tell him about Andrew's warning about the reunion, but bit her tongue. She was a mess of opposing impulses, she thought, and it would be best if she called it a night.

"When would you like to get together again, Max? I'm going to be busy Tuesday, taking my mom to the doctor, and Carly and Ham are coming in Thursday."

"Can I take you to lunch tomorrow?" Max asked. "I thought maybe we could drive over to St. John's and see Dr. Millard."

"Sure. Going to the college is a great idea. What time?"

"Let's shoot for noon." He grinned. "No pun intended."

She smacked his arm. "That was a cheap shot. But okay, I'll see you then." She stepped out of this car unsteadily.

Max came around the side of the car and shut the door.

She put her hand on his arm. "You don't have to walk me to the front door." She pointed to the entry, twenty feet away. "I left a light on. Always leave the porch and the foyer lights on. My dad was a cop, and he reminded us of that every single time we went out. I'll be fine."

"I know you will." Max wrapped an arm around her shoulders. "But I'm walking you to the door. I know how to behave on a first date if I want a second one."

"Ahhh, smooth operator."

He threw his head back and laughed, the sexiest sound she had ever heard.

"You don't think you're smooth?"

"No," Max said. "I'm about as far from that as a man can be. But thank you for the compliment."

They stopped at the front porch. "What happened to your dad? His name was Patrick, right? You said he died several years ago, *ja?* Very young, too."

"Yes, he was. Only sixty-four. He'd never been sick a day in his life, but seven years ago, on Holy Wednesday, he got up at his usual 5:30 and said to my mother, "Did I pay the paper?" and then he fell dead of a heart attack."

"I'm so sorry. But what is Holy Wednesday?"

"The Wednesday before Easter."

"Why is it holy?"

"To commemorate the day Judas was paid thirty pieces of silver to betray Jesus."

"I don't see why that would make it a holy day," Max said.

She opened her purse and began pawing through it. "Me either. We Catholics aren't known for logic. It's more about magic and faith."

"What did your dad mean, do you think?"

"No idea. Although I've wondered if he didn't actually ask, 'Did I pay the piper?' He was an ironic kind of guy."

Max shook his head. "But your mother was sure he said paper."

"I never asked her."

"Ask her now."

"It's too late for that, I'm afraid." Jill grabbed her house keys, her eyes hot with sudden tears.

Max took the key ring from her and opened the front door. He made no move to follow her inside. "I'm so sorry to hear this about your parents, Jill. I know how it feels to be . . ."

"Alone?" she said.

"You get some rest, okay?" Before she could move away, Max put his hand on her chin and kissed her on the lips. It was gentle, but nearly melted her earrings.

She drew away and saw that look again in his eyes, that look she had not seen for fifteen years, until tonight at the restaurant.

Max wanted to come in the house. He wanted her. The new her he had just met.

But nowhere nearly as bad as she wanted him. The old him. The new him. All of him.

Good god.

Jill froze. If she kissed him again, if she pressed her mouth on any part of his face, or felt his chest or thigh against hers, or his strong arms around her, she would be lost.

"Good night." Her voice was cool.

Max gave her an intense look when she stuck out her hand, but he took her hand in both of his and squeezed it gently. "Good night, old friend. See you tomorrow."

Without a backward glance, he walked to his car.

She stepped inside and closed the door. It took her a full minute to get control of her breathing.

These feelings can't be trusted. I don't even know him. Not this him. And he doesn't know anything about me, this me, or any me I ever was.

Jill locked the front door, dropped her purse on the

kitchen counter, flipped off the entry light, and walked down the shadowy hallway to her bedroom.

She undressed in the moonlight, feeling as if she was sleepwalking. She pulled her underwear off and dropped it in a heap and kicked off her sandals. Leaning down, she turned on the lamp on her dressing table and frowned.

Where is my jewelry box?

She grabbed her robe out of the closet and for the first time noticed the room around her.

Jill gasped, blinking several times as her heartbeat increased. The contents of her chest of drawers on the wall opposite were dumped onto her bed. Her closet was open, and boxes and shoes and clothes lay in heaps outside of it.

"What is going on?" The realization that someone had broken in to her home filled her with panic. She held her breath, listening.

Is whoever did this still here?

Goosebumps rose on her naked skin and she soundlessly slipped on her robe.

Where's my phone? She looked around wildly, remembering she had laid her purse on the counter in the kitchen. She took a step and the doorbell rang.

Without another thought, she ran for the front door.

Max. He must have decided to come back.

Her heart pounded so hard that she could not hear herself think. She grabbed the doorknob, threw the lock, and pulled it open.

"Max! Thank god." Jill stopped, clamping her teeth together abruptly.

Andrew Denton stood in her doorway, a quizzical look on his face.

Jill sucked in her breath. Frantically, she looked past him, but the driveway was empty. Max was long gone. "What are you doing here?" she said.

"I sent a note saying I needed to talk to you. I know it's Easter Sunday, but I thought this might be the best time to catch you, so I risked coming by. I left you a phone message, too, about an hour ago. Didn't you get it?"

"No." *Not that it would have mattered,* Jill thought. "Look, I don't have time right now. I need to call 911."

"Why? What's happened? Are you all right?"

Jill pulled the belt on her robe tight. "I got home ten minutes ago and discovered the house has been broken into, so I need to call the police."

Andrew whipped out his phone. "Sit down on that bench. You look like you might faint. Do you know if whoever broke in is gone?"

Jill stared at her house. "I didn't see or hear anyone, but I haven't searched the place." She turned. "Wait, no, don't call the police from your cell, I'll do it from inside."

Too late.

Andrew held up a finger to silence her. "Yes, Operator. My name is Andrew Denton. I need officers at the scene of a residential break-in at . . ."

Jill listened numbly as Andrew gave the police the address, her name, and described her as uninjured. Her arms and legs began to shake and she sat down on the stone bench beside her front entry. Surreal was the only word that came to mind to describe her life at that moment.

She stared at the car at the curb.

"What rooms did you go into when you got home?" he asked.

"I stopped first in the kitchen, and then went to my bedroom. It's been ransacked."

"But you got undressed?"

"I got undressed in the dark. I didn't notice the mess until I turned on the light."

"It must have been a fun night out."

"It was," she said, not liking the tone in his voice.

"Have you been drinking?"

Jill squared her shoulders. "What the hell, Andrew, why are you questioning me like this? You sound like a freaking cop." She pointed to the curb. "You better leave now, before the real ones get here."

True to form, Andrew walked closer. "I'm asking what the police are going to ask. And I should stay until they get here, because I called in the report. You don't want to explain you sent me away because you can't stand the sight of me. They might treat your story of a break-in differently if you begin the interview by recounting a story that ends with you shooting me in the head."

The sound of sirens echoed around Jill, louder with every second that passed. "I just winged you."

"Dick Cheney would be proud."

Jill scowled at his attempt at a joke. She got up. "I'm going to go in and put my clothes back on. Stay here. I'll be right back."

"Don't touch anything else," Andrew said. "And put some shoes on. People feel much more vulnerable to questioning when they are barefoot."

Jill had the urge to flip him off, but instead she stomped into the house and grabbed her clothes off the floor and dressed, and then slipped on her shoes. She fretted about why Andrew was back again, and what the hell Pandora Security was.

Is he armed? With that sobering thought, Jill stepped out of the bathroom two minutes later and found him in the living room with three Santa Barbara cops.

Shit.

"Officers, this is Jill Farrell, the victim. This is her home."

"I'm not a victim," Jill said. "This is my house, but I wasn't here when this happened, officers. I'll answer your questions. Not Mr. Denton. He's leaving now."

"No, I'm not."

"Yes, you are."

The cops exchanged glances.

Andrew narrowed his eyes. "I'll wait in the other room, Jill. We still have something to discuss."

"Is everything okay here, Miss Farrell?" the taller of the two cops asked.

"Yes," she said, sending Andrew a look that should have killed him. "Okay, wait in the kitchen."

The cops stayed for less than thirty minutes and did not dust for prints, or take pictures, or seem all that interested once they saw the damage. They said it was most likely neighborhood kids who had broken in looking for cash or jewelry.

When they checked they found the sliding glass door to her patio ajar, and the lock showed signs of being jimmied. Jill explained that she always kept a piece of doweling in the track to keep that from happening. The officers found it leaning against the inside of the window, as if she had forgotten to put it in place.

Which was probably the case, she realized. With all her mother's recent doctor appoints, she could not honestly remember the last time she had secured the door.

The cops toured the rest of the house with her and found both of her bedrooms were ransacked, and about ten storage boxes in the garage had been ripped open and emptied onto the floor, but as far as she could tell nothing was taken.

She agreed to call if she found anything else missing, and accepted their scolding about leaving her place locked up securely.

She closed the door, and immediately panicked over not thinking about something that might have been stolen.

Dad's gun!

It was stowed in the very back of the closet, unloaded, and not worth much to a pawnshop, but certainly would have been of interest to the punks who broke in.

Jill flung open the closet door and felt around behind the jackets and coats for the peg the revolver and holster hung from. Her hand found the smooth, worn leather of the holster, and the comforting weight of the gun.

With a sigh of relief, she left it where it was and headed for the kitchen. Her unwanted guest was sitting at the table, the smell of coffee in the air.

She sat across from Andrew, who had helped himself to a box of cookies from her pantry. There were crumbs on the table in front of him.

"Okay. What the hell is it you want from me?" Jill said.

"Are you okay?"

She folded her arms over her chest, realizing her blouse was unevenly buttoned. "My house was burgled, half the clothes I own are on the bedroom floor, and despite my asking you to stay away, you're camped out in my kitchen. Why?"

"I think you might be a touch more grateful I was here to help," Andrew said. "Anyway, we do have something to talk about."

"I'm made it clear a couple of days ago that we have nothing to discuss."

"Oh, trust me, we do." Andrew tented his hands together, his blue eyes bright.

Jill stood. "If this is about the past, for god's sake, we were over with a decade ago. I don't have anything more to say about it. So if you want to rehash the arrest, or our domestic violence, I don't care to participate."

"I'm not here about that," Andrew said.

"Then what do you want?"

He blinked. "I'm sorry to hear about your mother. I understand she's in a long term care facility."

"And how do you know that? Jesus, are you stalking me?"

"No, of course not." Andrew sat more upright. "You've decided to go to the reunion, I understand."

Jill blinked. "Who told you that?"

"It doesn't matter. I made inquiries."

"Then why did you ask?"

"Fair enough. Look, I know you don't want to spend any time with me, but I'm going to tell you something now that you might not believe, but you must. It's very serious. So please listen for a couple of minutes before you say anything."

"First, you tell me what Pandora Security is?" she asked. "I want to know what it is you do before I say anything else."

"It's my company. I'm an investigator."

She leaned forward. "You were in jail for attempted murder. How did you get a license to be an investigator?"

He flinched. "My criminal record was expunged because I went to rehab for two years. I have worked very hard to put my mistakes behind me. Especially the ones I made the night you left me."

She softened, but only a little. "Good. Good for you."

"Thank you. Now look, it's unfortunate you have to deal with so much tonight, and that my showing up makes you feel awkward, but what I have to say can't wait until it's more convenient. It's too important."

"To whom?" Jill said.

"To people in our government, and out of it. Quite possibly to you and your family."

"This is crazy." Jill sat and crossed her arms. "You've got two minutes to explain this."

"I work primarily with government clients, both here and in Europe, and South America. I was contacted a few weeks ago by the state department on behalf of another agency. They requested I informally look into the murder of an alumnus of St. John Vianney College."

Jill gasped. "Murder? Who was murdered?"

"Ben Pierce." Andrew's voice was steely. "He was two years ahead of us. His sister, Marissa, was in our class. Do you remember either of them?"

Jill's heart fluttered with shock. She pictured Ben, heavy black glasses and smiling face, at the desk next to her in English. He had put off his required liberal arts classes until senior year, and always kidded her that he was copying off her exams.

"I did know Ben. And I remember Marissa. She's handling the reunion, right?"

"Yes. Have you talked to her?" Andrew stared at her.

"No. Not personally. What happened to Ben?"

"He was an ATF agent. Last December, while attending a technology conference in Paris, he was murdered in his hotel room."

"That's horrible. But why are you telling me about this?"

"Because I need your help. I'm assisting in the investigation."

As she had with Max a couple of hours ago in his car, Jill was unable to control her nervous emotions. A full-out chortle rolled out of her. Because what Andrew said was so preposterous, she could not give it the credence his unsmiling face said it deserved.

"Are you joking? I'm a community college English teacher, for heaven's sake. What could I possibly do to help in an investigation?"

Andrew leaned closer. "It's believed the man who killed Ben also has a connection to St. John's. Possibly a fellow student."

"What?"

"Yes. Ben left a rather cryptic message the day he was murdered. He said he had run into an old classmate, and that there was something off about the guy."

"That's rather ambiguous. This sounds like a movie," Jill said. "And you still haven't explained why you're telling me this."

"If Ben's killer was a fellow student, there is a very real possibility he might attend the reunion. So I need someone to act as another set of eyes and ears inside the parties, and watch for suspicious behavior."

Jill was slightly nauseous. "If you're talking about me being some kind of what, spy for you, that's ridiculous. I have no idea what you mean by suspicious behavior. What exactly would I be watching for? I mean, aside from someone pulling a gun on someone at the reunion."

"There's no need for sarcasm." Andrew colored. "I would like you to go to the events, all of them, and observe. See if you notice anything odd or unusual. Watch if anyone seems nervous, or asks a lot of questions about Ben."

Andrew reached into his coat pocket and took out an envelope. He pushed it across the table at Jill. "I'm prepared to pay for your help. Sign the non-disclosure form inside. Once I get it back from you, I'll give you a check for $10,000. For your findings. And your time and trouble."

"$10,000?" Jill's eyes opened wide. "For my *findings*? I don't even know what a finding is. I've got no experiences with something like this."

"Your dad was a cop," Andrew said.

"And my mother could quote a hundred bible verses and make pie crust from scratch, neither of which I could do on a bet. What's your point?"

"I need your help, Jilly," Andrew said softly. "Can your country count on your help?"

Jill's legs felt unsteady. "I can't imagine a single good reason to get involved in this."

"Don't say no," her ex-husband replied. "Sleep on it. And please don't mention what I've confided to you tonight to anyone else." He stood.

Jill stared at him. She felt there was something more to this story, something that Andrew had not said. "Do you know anything else? Why does ATF, or whoever it is you're working for, think this person is one of our classmates?"

"There was some evidence found at the scene that I can't share." Andrew's expression was serious.

"Well, do they suspect someone in particular though?"

"For your information, yes, from what I understand the feds are looking hard at five or six people. Classmates who live or travel often to Europe, and who are in the technology or finance fields. Someone who may have been at the conference that Ben was attending." Andrew held Jill's glance. "I don't know the names on that list, but I wouldn't be surprised if Max Kallstrom was one of them."

Jill gasped. "What? Why?"

"He's in investments, from what I've found out. Lives in Paris. And that whole disappearing act of his fifteen years ago? Fits perfectly with someone who might seem a bit off to Ben Pierce, if you ask me."

Jill stared at her ex-husband. She moved her mouth but no words came out.

"I knew this would shock you, but I thought you should know the man you're hot to hook up with again could be dangerous."

She blinked and a few things became clearer. "Are you targeting Max because of your misconceptions about what ruined our marriage, Andrew? Is this some jealous thing?"

"No. Of course not."

"No? Then why single out Max? From what you said, several men in our class will be under suspicion. You included, since you travel all over the world. There's no other evidence Max is involved, is there?" Her heart pounded in her ears.

"No, no, there isn't. Yet." Andrew's eyes were steady. "And for your information, I'm not jealous of him. But considering Kallstrom is the reason you never gave our marriage a fair chance, I think you owe it to me to help in this investigation."

The room seemed to spin around her and Jill felt hot and cold. She grabbed the tabletop as the taste of Kir crept up her throat.

Chapter 7

Jill stared at her bedside clock. Ten minutes after eight in the morning and she felt like she had been hit by a truck.

Either the restaurant had poisoned her Kir, or she had been struck down with a bug intent on doing what Andrew had failed to do: beat her into submission.

She had thrown up twice last night before Andrew had knocked politely on the powder room door and told her he was leaving, but would be in touch soon.

After that, all she remembered was the good old dry heaves, which basically made her wish for death, or an exorcist. She had had bone-rattling chills, and been in and out of bed until 3 a.m. The last time she must have passed out because when she woke up an hour later she was stretched out in the hallway in front of the bathroom, her hair glued to the side of her face.

She swallowed. It was not the best idea. With one hand on her forehead and the other on her stomach, she got out of bed and walked directly into the shower. She turned on the cold water and for ten minutes let the torrent both wash and sober her up.

A few minutes later, she once again stood staring out the kitchen window at the street, a mug of coffee in her hands. It had taken her about eight minutes to make a pot.

She replayed the events of last night in her head. The break-in by unknown juveniles was aggravating. The news about Ben was heartbreaking.

Jill took a gulp of coffee. And Andrew's request was beyond ridiculous, as were his suspicions about Max.

Max.

Jill blinked and remembered her body's reaction to him last night. After all these years it was the same as it had been when she was a kid. She had her share of other lovers since Max, including Andrew, but none had ever flipped on all her switches as he had.

"I think you have an unhealthy obsession with the unobtainable past," a psychologist she had gone to suggested to her years ago, after her divorce from Andrew. He opined she had chosen Andrew because she knew he would never measure up to Max, and that she was in limbo, waiting for the Swede's return.

She had dismissed that opinion, and had managed one or two other serious relationships since Max, but she had never felt the same depth of attraction for any man.

Until last night.

I need to get a grip on my libido. While her instincts said Andrew's speculation about Max was jealousy inspired and had no basis in reality, it made her focus on one fact she could not ignore.

She did not know this Max. Certainly not well enough to let sexual instincts direct her interactions with him.

I'll call and put him off for a couple of days, tell him to go see Dr. Millard by himself. Get my head together.

Jill felt an immediate pang of regret at the thought of not spending the day with him. She shook her head and it felt as if her skull was full of sand. Catching a whiff of the too-ripe bananas on the counter, she breathed deep to stave off another bout of retching.

The wall phone rang. Jill winced at the sound and picked up the receiver. "Hello?"

"Ms. Ferrell?"

"Speaking." She wished again the ancient thing had caller ID.

"Are you okay, Ms. Ferrell?"

"Fine," she rasped. "Who is this, please?

"This is Megan Jenkins from Friend's House. Everything is okay here, so don't ever worry if you see my number on your caller ID. If it's an emergency, we'll say so right away. Anyway, I was checking to see if you received our notice in the mail?"

Jill's mind flashed on the misspelled envelope she'd received a couple of days ago. "Ah, yes. But I haven't had a chance to go through it yet. Is it something important?"

"Yes, ma'am, it is. It explains about the new rates. I was calling to see if you had any questions about them."

"New rates?" Friday they had given Friend's House a check to cover the first two months of Dorothy's care, $8,475 a month for living in the Alzheimer's wing. That included meals, laundry, and medication supervision. When she told Carly about it, she said for that price, it should have included a weekly massage from Ryan Gosling.

"What are you talking about?" Jill asked.

"Would you like to go find our letter? Then I can answer any specific questions you might have."

"I will in a minute. But why don't you tell me the new rates now."

"Well, okay. Your mother's new monthly fees will be $9,090 as of July 1st. HEVCO, our parent company, has done their best to hold down costs and is pleased to announce that they don't expect another increase until January of next year."

"What? You're going to raise the rates again that soon?" She thought HEVCO should change their name to GOUGECO, but didn't share that. "Tell the director I'd like to discuss this with her tomorrow when I pick my mother up for her appointments, okay?"

"Certainly. But I'll be glad to give you a breakdown."

"I don't need a breakdown." *I'm going to have a breakdown*. She had worked out that the money from the sale of her mother's house, along with Dorothy's Social Security and her father's pension benefits, would cover her mother's care for about five years.

They would then get her qualified for Medicaid, who would not help with expenses until an Alzheimer's' victim was down to her last two thousand dollars. Which is going to happen a lot quicker now, thanks so much, HEVCO.

The image of Andrew offering her $10,000 darted through her brain. That money would help, she thought. *No way.*

Jill said goodbye and grabbed the mail and fished out her phone from her purse. She glanced around the wreckage of her room that she had not picked up last night.

She punched in Max's number. Her call went to voicemail. She hung up and glanced at the clock. It was eight forty.

Two hours later, she had read through the stack of mail, paid bills, vacuumed, and restored order to her bedroom and the guest room. The garage boxes were repacked and taped. They were all things from her mother's house, crockery and photo albums and Christmas decorations, and Jill could not imagine what teen delinquents had hoped they would find in them.

I better try Max again.

She sat down on her sofa, her attention caught by the roses. They were fully opened, their fragrance rich and sweet. She remembered other times flowers had filled the house, happier times. Max had given her flowers once, wildflowers he had picked along the shore.

She inhaled, smelling salt water and summer. *It was a trick of the mind,* she thought. She had to be careful and not get too sentimental. With a frown, Jill hit redial.

Max answered on the second ring. "Hi! I was about to call you. Is everything all right? I saw you tried to get me a couple of hours ago when I was in a meeting."

"Hi, yes, everything's fine." *Except since I saw you I was burgled, poisoned, and propositioned for undercover work by my nutty ex-husband*, she thought. "I was calling about today, and . . ."

"Good news there!" Max interrupted. "I talked with Dr. Millard early this morning and she's going to meet us at the Canyon Inn for lunch about twelve-thirty. She's thrilled we're coming to see her, and told me again it's been way too long since she's talked to you. Is noon still a good time to pick you up?"

She did not want to stay in this house today, brooding about her mother's finances or the past. Or Andrew's half-baked paranoia. After all, she had agreed to help Max. "I think it would be better if I meet you there." Jill cleared her throat. "I have some errands to run afterwards, and I don't want to intrude on your business calls."

Silence. "Oh. Okay, and then later maybe we can have dinner?"

"I'll let you know about that. I'm not sure how late I'll be, and I need to swing by and see my mother." She winced. She had not thought of doing that until now, and she should have. "Okay? So I'll meet you at the Canyon Inn by twelve-thirty?"

"Sure thing."

Jill hung up and stared at the roses.

She grabbed them and carried them out to the patio so she would not have to see or smell them, stuck the dowel in the sliding door, and locked it, and went to take another shower.

The Canyon Inn, built on the edge of a cliff high in the mountains above Santa Barbara, offered a breath-taking view of the Pacific Ocean and Channel Islands.

Due to traffic caused by an earlier accident, and an anxiety attack over clothing choice, Jill was fifteen minutes late. She trailed behind the waiter and found Dr. Millard and Max chatting at a table on the outside patio.

"Jill, darling, how great to see you! What's it been, ten years?"

"Surely it's not that long ago?"

Millard frowned. "I think it has been at least that long, you were newly married." She darted a glance at Max. "Or should I not bring that up?"

"My past is public knowledge." Jill remembered the many calls she fielded in the aftermath of the shooting scandal, thanks to coverage in the local papers. "And I already filled Max in on the seamy details."

"You mean how you shot the bastard?"

"She just winged him." Max raised his eyebrows. "Or so she says."

"What a pity," Millard retorted.

Jill gave Dr. Millard a hug. "It is wonderful to see you."

Max pulled out a chair for Jill. "Everything okay? I was going to call to see if you'd been held up."

A wisecrack about the burglary last night flitted through her brain, but she swallowed it. "Traffic? What can I say, I should know better on a Monday. Everyone is back to work except we educators. Thank god for Spring break."

They ordered drinks. Dr. Millard a bourbon and soda, she and Max stuck with iced tea. Her professor looked eighty but was probably mid-sixties, Jill thought. She had been a chain smoker for decades, and die-hard beachgoer who bucked the healthy lifestyle trends ascribed to Californians out of independence and addiction.

"I do wear sunscreen," Millard said in response to Max's comment on her tan. "But I'll bet all that chemical goo is going to kill me before the sun does."

"I wear it every day too," Jill said. "I freckle more and more. Climate change is eating the ozone, right?"

"That's true." Max smiled at her appraisingly. "But your

skin is lovely."

"It is," Millard chimed in. "Your family is Irish? Your kind looks gorgeous until they hit sixty. Then the men all look like drunks, and the women look exhausted."

Jill smiled at Max's expression. It was clear he did not remember Professor Millard was famous for her cutting, but true, comments. "Sounds like you've seen my aunties and uncles." She picked up the menu. "So what sounds good for lunch?"

They placed their order, chatted for a few moments about the spectacular views and the ever-present sunshine.

"How does it feel to see this guy after all these years?" Dr. Millard asked, watching Jill with interest.

"Nice but a weird. It's like fast-forwarding your own life when you see a person for the first time in such a long time."

"Neither of you look different to me," Millard offered. "Except you're both more beautiful. Max was too skinny as I remember, kind of gangly. And you were always ducking your head down, as if you didn't want anyone to look at your lovely face. I like these current versions of you."

"Thank you," Jill said. "You look great yourself, Dr. Millard. I always admired your jewelry, and I think of you when I see anyone wearing great Navaho pieces."

The music teacher touched the heavy squash blossom necklace hanging from her neck. "I've got more than I can wear now, and I give it away every chance I get to people who appreciate it. Except for a few pieces that were my mother's. She got them in the 1930s and 40s. They're worth quite a bit now, but priceless to me." She put her hand on Jill's. "Max told me about your mother and the Alzheimer's. So sorry, dear girl."

"Thank you."

"It seems you're surrounded by people with memory issues." Millard turned to Max. "Has Jill been able to stir up anything familiar inside your head?"

"She has." Max's eyes flashed. "Nothing clear enough to qualify as a recollection, but something's happening."

"It's been intriguing," Jill said quickly. "Last night at dinner I filled Max in on several of our classmates and things we'd done. I hadn't thought of some of the events for a long time, like the time our bus broke down in Tijuana and we were escorted to jail for a couple of hours. Talking to him is bringing it all back for me."

"I'm looking forward to the reunion events," Max said. "I'm going to be honest with everyone, and tell them up front I don't remember them. Should get the party off to an interesting start."

"You'll only have to tell a couple," Millard said. "They'll tell everyone else. Start with Jill's best friend, Carly Hart. She was our own personal Internet when they were in school."

"Carly does like to talk." Jill said. "She and Hamilton are coming in on Thursday night."

"Carly married Hamilton Stewart?" Millard asked. "I'd forgotten that. He didn't graduate from St. John's, did he?"

"No. He finished his undergraduate course work at Oxford senior year. And he never came back. Fell in love with London."

"How did Carly get together with him?"

"She ran into him by chance in Greenwich when she was on a trip for the Metropolitan Museum." Jill smiled as she remembered Carly's excited call during her European excursion. "She said she hadn't liked him much when he was at St. John's, but once they rediscovered each other, she fell in love and the rest is history."

"Hamilton was a bit of an odd duck," Millard said. "Orphan, if I remember. Only relative was a cousin or something in Great Britain, or somewhere. But a brilliant and accomplished musician. Does he still play piano?"

"I don't know. I have only actually seen him a couple of

times since they were married. He's busy with his banking career. Carly said he flies all over the world."

"Does he work for Lloyds Bank?" Max asked. "I feel like I may have run into someone by that name at a conference."

"I don't remember who he works for," Jill said. "That would have been a wild coincidence, you running into him. Ham's about the only one of our friends who wouldn't know you from college if you met on the street."

"Good. I won't have to worry about explaining to him at least why I didn't recall our time together." Max sighed. "It's very awkward, this situation I find myself in."

"Don't feel embarrassed by it. Leave that to this one's ex-husband." Millard pointed to Jill. "I was astonished to hear Andrew Denton is going to show his face in town. The man never did have any shame."

"No?" Max said gently.

"No. I knew he was trouble for the moment I met him," Millard said. "He's dishonest to the bone. Cut every corner there was while he was at school."

"Perhaps he's changed." Jill took a deep breath. "I mean, everyone changes, right?"

"I seem to remember some cliché about a tiger not changing his stripes," Millard said.

"Jill gives everyone the benefit of the doubt," Max said. "Was she always like that?"

"Yes," Millard said. "I'm not sure it's a positive thing."

"No?" Max asked.

"Don't be too trusting," Millard said, wagging her finger. "The world is not always as it seems."

"I'm not too trusting. I suspect everyone. I'm a teacher, remember. Always on the lookout for fake 'my dog ate my homework' stories." Jill smiled nervously at the approaching waiter. She considered asking Millard if she had heard about Ben Pierce's death, but that question would take the conversation in a direction she was not ready for. "Oh good, here's the food."

The trio dug into their lunch, chatting about the people Jill had covered with Max last evening, and a few more Millard knew some interesting things about.

After they were done, Millard suggested they meet up at the college as they walked to the parking lot. All agreed a tour of the classrooms and dorms where Max had spent a year of his life was in order.

"Do you want to ride with me?" Max asked Jill as they crunched through the parking lot.

"No, let's drive separately. I have to run some errands afterwards."

"Right, you have errands. Anything that might jog my memory involved?"

"No. I've got to go see my mom and a few other things."

"You don't want company?"

"I thought you had business things to do during the day?"

"I did. Wrapped it up this morning with a two-hour call to New York." Max put his arm on her shoulder. "I cleared the day for you."

Her heart rate jumped. "Well, why don't we firm up a plan for dinner tonight? I should be back home by six or so. We could grill burgers at my place." Jill gulped after she said those words, second-guessing if she should have made the offer.

Max and me. Alone. Is this a good idea?

"Home-grilled hamburgers? I would love some of those." He stepped closer. "When I'm not with you, a hundred questions come to mind to ask, and I'm afraid I'll forget some. So a whole evening together sounds terrific."

They stopped next to her car and he put his other hand on her waist and pulled her closer. "I think I might be remembering how it felt to be with you, before. Some kind of knowledge in my blood, if not my brain. You are very kind, and caring. I was a very lucky man."

Parts of her body began to respond with the yearning she felt last night. "I think we need to go slow here, Max."

Max dropped his arms. "You're right. Forgive me, but I'm finding myself a bit out of control around you."

"I'm not thinking all that clearly myself," she said. "But we'll talk more about, about everything, later. At dinner." She raked her hand through her hair. Dr. Millard, behind the wheel of the same ancient Mercedes she drove fifteen years ago, honked as she headed up the hill to St. John's campus.

"Let's head up to the campus. Follow me, okay?"

"I will." Max grasped her arm. His eyes darkened with that look she was becoming very familiar with. "Don't lose me."

"See you there." Jill slipped into the car. Her hand was sweating as she put the key in the ignition. She glanced in the mirror as Max's convertible pulled up behind her, waiting for her to move.

He wants to make love to me. A burst of liquid heat spread through her. "Sweet Jesus," she murmured, and put the car into gear.

Chapter 8

Jill and Max toured a couple of the classrooms in the Liberal Arts building where Dr. Millard had her offices, and then went on to the gym. But they could not get into the dorm rooms, as they were locked because the students were away for the holidays.

"Let's go down to the theatre, then we'll stop in my office," Millard directed. "We'll take Max to the scene of the Senior Talent Show. If that doesn't prompt his brain, nothing will."

Jill nodded. A month before they graduated, the seniors produced a charity show for the college and community to raise money for scholarships. Favorites from the Forties, was the name of the event that year. She could see the program in her mind, a black and white photograph of Bing Crosby wearing a tux on the cover.

"I performed in a talent show?" Max frowned. "What was my talent?"

"We sang a duet," Jill said.

"But I can't sing," he protested.

"That's correct," Millard said. "Jill sang and you more or less sat there through one of my favorite Jules Styne, Sammy Cahn classics."

"I sang?" He put his head back and laughed. "Wow, that must have been scary."

"No, you're not listening. What Dr. Millard said is right. I sang," Jill teased. "You kind of mumbled the lyrics in your Swedish accent. 'Kiss Me Twice' never sounded so international."

"'Kiss Me Twice?' I don't know that song." Max's expression tightened. "How does it go?"

Jill grinned and cleared her throat. She was not a great singer, but since all Irish Catholics grew up in church choirs, she could carry a tune. She launched into the charming old love song about a second chance at romance after a long, long time.

Millard and Max clapped.

Jill grinned self-consciously and made a tiny bow.

Max shook his head. "You sound moody and sexy. Like Norah Jones."

"Wow, I'm sure Norah Jones would be alarmed to hear that you think I sound like her, but thanks."

"Is anything coming back to you after hearing that great rendition?" Millard asked.

"No." Max seemed far away. "Memory of music is stored in a different part of your brain than daily events. So I was hoping." He shrugged. "But nothing."

"Give it time," Millard said. "Alright, come on you two, let's go see where the magic happened." They walked around the building to the back steps and went inside.

The 300-seat theatre was dim and musty. Dust motes danced in the light pouring in from the high windows at the back. Millard narrated the current year's program highlights and Max walked around, sat in one of the creaking wooden seats, and then they all headed backstage.

Millard took them through the green room and dressing areas, pointing out the new light controller and automated curtain apparatus, before they trooped across the performance area.

They stopped center stage. The professor pointed down at the orchestra pit. "We still use live music for the Christmas Chorale. The board of directors tried to replace our vintage Bennett upright piano, but I raised a fuss so they left it alone." She shook her head. "Newer isn't always superior."

"I agree," Max said. "I have a 1976 Mustang. It's my prized possession and I love it, even if it stays in a garage next door to where my daughter lives in Paris eleven months of the year."

Jill lowered her head. *Max keeps his car near his ex-wife.* She did not know what to make of that, and with a pang she didn't want to label, wondered if he was really over her.

Fifteen minutes later, the three of them were ensconced in Dr. Millard's office. With a rush, the years dissolved and Jill felt like the intimidated student she had been years before.

A huge poster of conductor Andre Previn hung on the wall facing Dr. Millard's desk, as it always had, while busts of Beethoven, Mozart, and Handel teetered on the top shelf of her bookcase. Leather boxes stuffed full of vinyl records were everywhere, and an ancient turntable system held the place of honor on the credenza beside her desk.

Jill and Max took the cracked leather desk chairs opposite her. "Thanks for the tour, Dr. Millard," Max said. "I appreciate your taking the time to revisit all my haunts."

"I enjoyed it. And thank you for lunch." The professor picked up a manila envelope lying on her desk and handed it to him. "I put a package of memorabilia together for you to look at, Max." She turned to Jill. "Do you have the Senior Yearbook from your class? Someone has taken the school copy out of the library without filling out a slip. If you have one, I thought Max might benefit by having a look at some of the faces."

"I should have thought of that," Jill said. "Yes, I'm sure I have mine somewhere."

It might actually be in one of the boxes I repacked yesterday. She had not stopped to look at each of the books scattered around the floor of the garage, but the box marked 'Jill college stuff' was one the burglar had dumped out. "I'll check. Good idea."

"Do you want to open that packet and ask us questions about anything?"

"No," Max said quickly. "No. I'd rather look at it by myself."

Jill heard strain in Max's voice. The visit to the past was proving difficult for him in a way he might not have anticipated, she realized. Like looking at photographs of relatives you never knew.

Jill turned down Dr. Millard's offer to stay awhile and listen to Shaw's Chorale recording of "Handel's Messiah," which Millard deemed the best she had ever heard, hugging the professor at the door.

"I'll see you soon."

"At the cocktail party, the real fun begins," Millard said. "Don't worry about it, Max. Your classmates were drinkers. They'll move past your odd tale quickly and hit the bar."

"That's good to know," he said.

Millard waved them off, and they headed to the parking lot.

Jill stopped beside her car. "Okay, well I'll see you tonight at my place."

"Are you sure you want to get together tonight?" Max's fingers clutched the envelope Professor Millard had given him. "I realize I'm expecting a lot from you. I'm worried I might be taking up too much of your time."

"I wouldn't have offered if I didn't want you to come over. But don't feel obligated."

His eyes flashed. "No, don't misunderstand me. I want to. Very much." His eyes were intense. "It's just that I realized when we were walking around with Professor Millard that this must be awkward in many ways. I don't want you to feel uncomfortable with me."

"I don't. Actually, the more obvious it is that you don't remember me, the less stressful it is." Her face reddened. "But you need to remember that I *do* remember you. The old you, anyway. In many ways it feels like I'm catching up with an old friend."

"One with a very bad memory?"

Jill smiled. "Well, there's that."

Max visibly relaxed. "You are a very forgiving person. Not many people would make such an effort."

It wasn't difficult to be kind to him, she realized, although she didn't trust herself to say that. "See you at seven?"

"Yes. And I will bring wine, and dessert, okay? You like chocolate, don't you?"

"See, you do remember things about me."

"I'm a good guesser." Max opened her car and Jill slipped inside.

"Thanks. See you later." She buckled her seatbelt.

"Drive safe."

"You too." Jill backed out and then braked to adjust her mirror. She caught the image of Max sitting in the rented convertible, his cell phone pressed to his ear. His expression was serious, and quite suddenly, he looked like a complete stranger.

Goosebumps raised along Jill's neck. "Don't be too trusting", Dr. Millard had warned. She would remind herself of that, Jill told herself. She put the car into gear, and drove quickly out of the lot.

Ben Pierce's killer stepped out of the shower and dried off quickly. He had a lot to do before his date tonight.

He stood in front of the mirror and wiped the steam off the foggy hotel mirror. He combed his wet hair straight back and then slathered shaving foam on his face, his eyes taking stock, considering if she would find him much changed.

Too much changed.

It's been fifteen years, he thought. But he was intent on getting her into bed. He needed to know if she would question how things were different now, if she would press him about anything he could not explain away.

He pressed the razor against his cheek too hard, nicking himself. A trickle of blood dyed the white cream on his left cheekbone. He dabbed it with a septic stick, angry with himself for the slip, and continued shaving.

He dried his face and stared at the image, turning from side to side. Satisfied, he threw the towel on the floor and hurried to dress.

At 7 p.m., the doorbell rang. Jill found Max, arms full of bags and a huge bouquet of tulips, waiting with a smile on his face. "Delivery for Miss Farrell."

"Hey, come on in."

Max followed her into the kitchen.

Earlier she had pounded a package of ground sirloin into patties, and had sliced tomatoes and onions and cheese. These makings for dinner now sat covered on a platter on the counter.

"Set your bag on the table. Can I get you something to drink? Beer, wine, soda?" Jill took the flowers and grabbed for a vase to put them in.

"Why don't I pour you a glass of wine?" Max pulled out a good Chablis, as well as a bottle of black currant liquor, crème de cassis. "Or I can make you a Kir? You enjoyed those at the restaurant."

She put her hand on her midsection. "No. I think I'll stick with sparkling soda for right now. But we'll make Kirs one night when Carly is here. She loves them, too."

"I'm looking forward to meeting her. Again. And I'll have to quiz Hamilton to see if he remembers meeting me."

Hamilton works in the financial market, Jill thought, the random fact making her frown. *And he lives in Europe. Is he on Andrew's suspects list, too?*

Jill settled the tulips in the vase and wished her brain would stop reminding her of her conversation with Andrew. But his words echoed like background music in her thoughts, along with a melancholy mourning for Ben Pierce that she could not share with anyone.

She set the vase in front of the kitchen window and took the chair opposite, where Max sat watching her.

"How was your afternoon? You went back to your hotel?" Jill added seasoning to the bowl in front of her, full of chopped potatoes, onions, pickles, and mayonnaise.

"Yes. I made some calls. Took a swim in the hotel pool. I think I scared some kids with how pale I am."

"You don't look so pale."

"I would say I am at least ten shades paler than the average Californian." He leaned toward her. "Potato salad, *ja?* Our Swedish version, *Farskpotatissalad,* uses sour cream instead of mayonnaise. And fresh dill."

"I think you made some of that for us, when you were at the house for a barbeque once." Jill put the lid on the bowl. "Would you stick this in the refrigerator for a few minutes? And I'm sorry I keep mentioning things you don't remember. You've had a rough day already."

Max put the bowl in the fridge. "It was disappointing that nothing came back to me up at St. John's today. But I'm still trying to remember. I appreciate you helping me." He came back to the table. "I hope you know that."

"I do." A smile tugged at her mouth. Jill got up and pulled some utensils from the drawer. "Shall we eat dinner outside? It's warm, but I think it'll be nice."

"Whatever you want to do." Max took the table settings from her. "I was thinking about your mother today. How are you coping with all of that?"

"Pretty well. I feel helpless, pessimistic, even. But I also accept the reality that she isn't going to ever get better. It's frustrating, as it is for you not being able to remember, I'm sure."

"That is the word. Frustrating. Powerless. I hate it. Just waiting to see what happens next. It's like watching a horror movie."

Jill rubbed her suddenly chilled arms. "For me, the worst pain comes from not understanding why it happened to her." Her voice dropped. "Even my faith can't help me accept that, nothing can. The randomness makes me so angry."

"I understand how you feel. Being at the mercy of an injustice fills me with rage, too." Max squeezed her shoulder with his left hand. "And I don't mean the accident that robbed me of my recall. I was never unfaithful to my wife, but Claudine cheated on me. For years. She's married to the man now. He's my daughter's stepfather. It kills me to accept it some days."

"Wow, I'm sorry to hear that. That must be very difficult."

"It is. But it won't help anything if I let my anger control my life, or direct my dealings with Olivia's mother and her new husband. Anger is the most corrosive emotion of all. I hope you don't have any left for me, because of my disappearing." Max's eyes locked on to her face, searching.

"I don't. I don't blame you at all anymore."

Max put his hand gently on her face. She thought he would kiss her again, as he had done last night. She wanted him to, but instead he moved away from her, leaving her to worry about what he had seen in her face.

"Sure you don't want a glass of Chablis while I discuss being a loser in love?" His voice was husky.

"You weren't the loser in that relationship, your wife was."

"That's generous of you to say."

"Just speaking the truth as I see it." Jill cleared her throat. "Why didn't you kiss me?"

He froze and then slowly turned. "You wanted me to."

There was a hint of a question. "I don't know what I want."

He nodded. "I know. That's why I didn't kiss you. Yet."

"Yet?"

"Yet." He crossed his arms over his wide chest and took her in with one hot glance. "I have no right to say this, but the next time I kiss you, I am not going to hold back like I did last night."

"That sounds like a warning."

"It is."

Her lips hurt, she wanted so badly to kiss him. Instead, she turned and reached into the cabinet. "I think I will have some of that wine." She took two flutes out and placed them on the counter.

Max poured two glasses. *"Skol!"* He handed her one.

Jill raised her glass. "And let me toast you, old friend." The wine went down crisp and cool. "So what do you say? Shall we light the grill?"

"Yes." His eyes warmed. "I'm very, very hungry."

"Well then, follow me." She balanced her glass on the platter of food and headed outside, feeling as if something had been decided between them.

He tilted his chin up and pointed to the food. "You're sure you have enough to fill me up?"

"Oh, I have enough." She turned and smiled at him. "Don't worry. I won't send you back to the hotel hungry."

Chapter 9

One thing hasn't changed a bit about Max, Jill thought. *He can still eat his weight in hamburgers.*

She had made four for the two of them. He ate three. And potato salad. And fruit salad. And now they were tucking into the cream cheese frosted brownies he had bought at Helen's Sweets, her favorite bakery in Santa Barbara.

"Shall I open another bottle of wine?" he asked.

"Why not?" So far her stomach was handling the bombardment, and she was content to sit in the April dusk forever.

Max went out to his car for more wine and came back to the table with the second bottle, as well as the envelope Dr. Millard had left with him.

He pushed the package toward her. "I spent an hour looking through that stuff after I left you. There's a program from the senior class musical inside, and some photos. Also a couple of newspaper articles about the car accident."

"Wow." Jill emptied them out in front of her. The first, from the Santa Barbara Beacon, had a headline on the front page. "Vigil for Swedish Exchange Student." A photo of the twisted wreckage killed her appetite.

As she scanned the story, images from the night Max was nearly killed unspooled inside her brain.

It was the middle of May. She had bought a new dress that afternoon, a short flowery sundress, and new shoes. High heels with straps that went around her ankles. Telling her folks she was not going to eat with them, she sat quietly through dinner and the clean-up, getting more aggravated with each passing minute that Max was so late.

Then the phone rang. "Oh my god, Jill! Something's happened," Carly had screamed through tears.

The cops had come to the Hart's door and told Dave his vehicle was involved in a one-car accident, and that the driver was not expected to survive.

Jill, her father, and the Harts, along with many of their St. John's classmates, had rushed to the hospital, only to be told by the doctors no one could see Max.

Jill stared at the photo of the car.

Dave's compact sedan lay on its side, split open like a cat-food can by the emergency responders so they could pry Max's body from the twisted steel.

"I don't remember seeing this photo before." It was from the local Sunday paper, and the colors were still strong. Green trees, black road, blue sky above twisted white car parts.

"It's gruesome. I'm surprised they published it. Looks like blood spatters all over the ground, doesn't it?"

Jill peered closer. Splotches of dark brown blotted the ground and stuck to the metal wreckage. She turned it over and slid it back inside the envelope. The second article, written a month after the accident, noted Max had been flown home to Sweden for further treatment. Underneath was a group shot of St. John's students at a vigil on graduation night.

Jill's eyes widened. She was standing in the center of the group, dressed in cap and gown. Tears ran down her face as she stared at a lit candle clutched in her hand.

"This was taken graduation night. I don't remember much of it," she said softly.

"It was humbling for me to see how your classmates remembered me on their special night. And disconcerting, as if I was looking at photos of my own funeral."

A shiver went down Jill's back. "It was unreal. I mean,

I saw you the morning of the accident. We made plans to go out, and then ten hours later, everything was over."

"I'm very sorry." Max sighed as he stared up at the stars winking to life in the purple-orange sky. "I caused you and your family so much sadness, and I ruined your graduation."

You ruined my life, Jill thought. *But not forever.*

She stared down at the photo. Carly stood beside her, her arm around her shoulders. Jill squinted, recognizing several faces in the crowd. Including one young woman in blond cornrows. Marissa Pierce, standing behind Carly. Andrew was there, too. At the far side of the crowd, his expression feverish and excited.

He was probably high. Jill slipped the clipping in with the other and picked up her wine. "You didn't get anything back after looking at these morbid mementoes, huh?"

"Nothing." Max brushed a stray lock of hair behind his ear. "I realize I may have to soon accept that a year of my life is gone for good. It's disappeared into a void and may never come back." He tapped her on the nose. "Which means I can't get us back."

"I've still got us." She tapped her head. "Up here." She tapped her heart. "And in here."

Max leaned closer. "How are you feeling about us right now?" His eyes moved up to her forehead. "In there?" He placed his hand on her heart, gently, the swell of her breast beneath his palm. "And in here?"

"Confused, more than anything," she whispered.

"Confused?" He moved his mouth an inch from hers, cupping her breast, he rubbed his thumb against the light fabric. "I'm not feeling at all confused about you."

"No?"

"No. I don't remember you as a college girl, but in these past three days I've come to know you as the woman you are now. Kind. Caring. Gentle, but strong. I like you, Jill. A lot."

"Humm. A lot, huh?"

"Yes. How are you feeling about me?"

She cleared her throat, aware of her increased pulse. "Pretty good."

"Well then." He met her eyes and the years separating them from who they were then and who they were tonight melted away.

Jill had only one thought, and that was to kiss Max. So she did, burying both hands in his hair, she pulled them together. His lips were taut and smooth and warm and she felt a rush of heat and want and relief. She opened her mouth to him and he claimed her completely.

He stood and pulled her into a full body embrace that lit-up the rest of her willing flesh like a Christmas tree. Moving his hands down her back, Max dug his fingers into her bottom as she grasped his shirt.

She wanted to lick him and undress him and touch every plane and muscle and bone. Max slid his hands under her shirt onto her shoulder blades, massaging them as he ground his pelvis against her.

"Let's go inside." She broke free of his mouth, her lips swollen with his taste.

"You're sure that's a wise idea?"

"No." She blinked. "But I want you."

Max picked her up in his arms and carried her inside, down the cool hallway to the bedroom. He put her on the bed and pulled his shirt off in a single motion.

Jill lay looking up at him, admiring his muscular arms, and the thick hair across his broad chest. Her breathing was shallow and excited. She pulled down her jeans and panties and kicked them onto the floor, and then wrestled her tee shirt and bra off her heated body.

Max watched her from the end of the bed, gasping when she got up on her knees, facing him. She opened her arms wide. "Come here," she said. "Let's make some new memories."

He unzipped his pants and slid them off, but stood where

he was. He was fully aroused under the snug briefs, but he seemed to be waiting for her to look at him, all of him, before he made another move.

He stuck his thumbs in the waistband and pulled his briefs off. The light in her bedroom was dim, but the reason he was waiting for her to look at him was suddenly obvious.

Jill caught her breath and sat back on her haunches, her arms falling to her sides. She stared at Max's left thigh and groin area, where a swarm of angry, arcing scars marred his once-perfect body. The disfigurement was the worst on his hipbone, where the damage was centered in a smooth, sculpted hollow, below which stretched a five-inch scar line glimmering like a river against his skin.

Surely the remnants of a post-accident operation which had repaired, but forever marred, his beautiful body. "The accident?"

"Yes. I took the steering wheel to the gut. Crushed my hipbone. It's been replaced, but I was lucky to not be, ah, mangled any worse than I am." He grinned and touched his hip. "I set off alarms whenever I go through airport security. And my leg is pretty horrible to look at, isn't it? I'm sure I'm not the man you remember."

Jill heard vulnerability, and a kind of plea, in Max's voice, as if he feared she might be unwilling to accept him, all of him.

"No one's the same as they were before." She ran her hands over her breasts and belly. "I'm fatter, and I think I have some stretch marks on my ass." She smiled. "But I'm betting you can look past that."

His eyes narrowed and his voice lost the joking hesitancy of the moment before. "You're a vision. And more desirable than I imagined, which I did all night the last two nights, by the way."

Jill crawled across the mattress, well aware of the effect her breasts were having on him. She sat on the edge of the bed and pressed her hand against his body, thrilled by the tension she felt in his body. She put her mouth on the scar field and kissed it, licked it as Max trembled and placed his hands on the back of her head. She moved her lips in a line across his abdomen and then put her mouth on him.

Max groaned and Jill trembled as her brain tumbled back to the last time they had made love. She remembered the length, the thickness, the taste of this man she had never forgotten. She had her first orgasm with Max, her first true coupling of flesh and emotion with another person.

And now he was back in her life.

Max grabbed her shoulders and slid her up the length of his body. He plunged his tongue into her mouth as his hands guided her onto him, him into her. He lowered them both to the bed and began to move; sure, urgent, his body demanding her to arch her back more, open her legs wider, move faster with his thrusts.

Jill gave him everything willingly, more than willingly, desperately. When she came, she screamed his name and wrapped her arms and legs around him, leaving the past behind as every nerve in her body reveled in the delicious, astounding present.

At 3 a.m., Jill and Max untangled themselves from her bed sheets to sit in the kitchen and finish the brownies. Max made tea in Dorothy's favorite teapot, and poured Jill a cup.

"I'm too tired to pick it up." She stirred in a cube of sugar.

"I'll hold it for you." Max lifted the cup to her mouth. "Drink."

She took a sip and smiled.

Max sat across from her, naked save for his briefs, and bit into a brownie the size of his hand.

"My mother wouldn't approve of you sitting at the table without your shirt," she said.

He swallowed, a smile tipping his mouth. He gestured with his left hand. "Okay, give it back to me."

She lay her hand on the pale yellow polo she was wearing. It was turned inside out, the green alligator logo sat over the rosy flesh of her left breast. "Nope. I'm keeping this forever. You'll have to drive back to your hotel naked."

"I'll catch up on my tan."

"I'll rub suntan lotion on your back."

He put his fork down. "I'll return the favor." He reached across the table and touched her face. "After I make love to you three or four more times."

Her breathing quickened. She was sore and sated but more than willing to go back to bed with him. Although she doubted her trembling legs would carry her.

"My house was burglarized the other night," she announced.

"What? When?" Max slowly put down the last brownie.

"Easter Sunday. After you dropped me off, I found the house had been broken into." Jill touched his arm. "Sorry, I didn't mean to upset you. They didn't take anything that I can tell. The cops said it was probably kids looking for drugs or cash lying around."

"How did they get in?"

Jill recounted the details, leaving out the complicated sideshow of Andrew's visit. "I only brought this up so you'd go out and lock the rental car before we go back to bed. If the little bastards are breaking into houses, cars could be next."

"I think you should have a security alarm installed. You're here by yourself now."

"It's a safe neighborhood. Don't blow this out of proportion."

"I'm not." Max folded his arms, his expression serious. "Has this happened before?"

"No. And I doubt it will again. I'll be better about locking up."

"Do you have a gun?"

A beat of silence passed as her smile faded. "Why do you ask?"

"Don't all Americans have guns?"

"Well, actually I do. My dad's old service revolver is in the back of my coat closet."

"Do you know how to use it?"

"Yes, I do. Have you forgotten I shot my ex in the head?" She smiled.

He didn't. "Is it loaded?"

"Duh. No, I'm the daughter of an ex-cop. No loaded guns in the house."

"But you know where the bullets are?"

She did not know. Had no idea. But she was not going to tell Mr. Dead Serious that fact. "Yes, of course."

She took another bite of brownie and eyed his nude torso, wishing she had not blurted out the burglary story. "I'll let you have your shirt back if you want to go outside and lock the car. And then you can get a box for me in the garage. I think the St. John's yearbook is in the one marked 'Jill college.' The punks who broke in didn't find anything of interest in it, but we can at least look at photos."

"They searched through your garage, too?"

"Yes. Boxes of my mother's things." She shrugged. "Come on." She stood and held out her hand. "Put your pants on, let's go. We've got things to do."

Max's mouth was set stubbornly. "I think you should call about an alarm system."

"I hear you. But first things first. Let's get the yearbook. And then come back to bed."

Max finally smiled. "Okay."

A few minutes later, he slipped once again out of his jeans and they collapsed on the mattress. Jill lay on her stomach, his shirt cozy around her shoulders in the cool hours of the morning.

Max draped his arm protectively over her and watched as she chattered about the young faces on the pages of the yearbook.

"Who is that?" He squinted in concentration at one student's photograph.

Of all people, she thought. "It's Marissa Pierce. From the reunion committee."

"This is Marissa?" Max frowned. "She looks like someone I know, from when I was growing up."

"Really?"

He nodded. "Ingrid. Ingrid Keppleman. Her grandparents lived next to my parents." He squinted at Jill. "I never said anything like that fifteen years ago, I take it. That this woman resembled Ingrid?"

"No. But then, I didn't hang out with Marissa myself when we were in college, so I doubt we three were ever together."

"Oh." He touched the page. "She's so familiar. But that's not strange is it? Don't some people say everyone in the world has a double somewhere?"

"I've heard that but I never believed it." Jill wrinkled her nose. "We're all different in some tiny way at least."

"Even twins?"

"Yes, I think so. I've known two identical sets, and there were big differences, in personality, but also in looks." She stared at the yearbook photo. "Are you sure you don't remember her?" Jill swallowed, thinking maybe this was a breakthrough of some kind. "Take your time and think about it."

He stared at the black and white head shot and finally shook his head. "No, she looks familiar because of Ingrid. I don't know her." He closed the book and put his hand behind Jill's head. "I told you, it's probably time to accept that the past is gone."

"Only a couple of years of it, here and there, right?"

He nodded and pulled her tight against his nearly naked body. "Ja, but still. I hate to lose the one we spent together."

"It might still come back." Jill lay on her side, face-to-face with Max. She felt his body harden into full arousal against hers. "We'll have to keep working on recreating the good parts."

"Ja." That look of hunger was back in his eyes. "I want you."

"Again?" She slid the palm of her hand down his chest and abdomen, and inside his briefs. "But it's so late. Maybe we should just get some sleep." She rubbed her fingers against his skin.

Max groaned and sat up. He kicked off his underwear and then crawled across the bed and turned her on her stomach. He straddled her and pulled the shirt off over her head.

"You have a beautiful ass." He rubbed her buttocks, squeezing the soft flesh, and then leaned forward and licked the middle of her back, slowly moving his mouth lower down her spine. "I'll let you sleep in a while," he murmured.

Max pulled her slowly closer, the sheet rubbing against her hard nipples, enflaming her body even more. "Is our lovemaking the same, Jill?" he asked. "The same as it was when we were first lovers?"

Her mind swam back through the years to their younger selves, two eager lovers, all arms and legs and intense coupling, bodies covered in sweet sweat. They had been eager to try out anything they could think of with one another during those hot summer nights. "No. We're not the same, so of course it is different now."

He was still. "What do you mean?"

She arched her back and turned to look at him. "It feels like more," she said.

"More?"

"More expert. More knowing. More delicious."

Max smiled wickedly and pulled her body hard against his. "I want you to forget the past. It won't hold a candle to the now."

Chapter 10

Jill struggled to read the clock beside her bed. Eight twenty-two. Max had his right arm and leg wrapped around her, his breathing even in the quiet morning air. She closed her eyes for what felt like three minutes, and then opened them wide.

The clock then read nine fifty-three.

Max was no longer beside her, but she heard the shower running. Jill rolled on her back and stretched, contented as a cat who had spent the night with a vat of cream. Soft light filtered through the shutters, and outside she heard a lawnmower.

What a perfect Tuesday morning, she thought. *I'll make pancakes. I have blueberries. And then we can take a ride to the beach. The Pacific is too cold for a swim, but we can sit and watch the surfers in their wetsuits.*

Magically, it seemed that while she had slept, time had gone out with the tide, and she once again was a twenty-one-year-old college girl mapping out a lazy, perfect day with her boyfriend.

She pulled Max's shirt over her head, reveling in the way her body felt after being so thoroughly made love to. She went to the powder room and spent a minute, amazed that, to her eyes, her face was that of her college self. Happy. Youthful. Full of hope.

In the kitchen, she started a pot of coffee, pulled out the fruit and milk and eggs for pancakes. The clock on the stove read two minutes after ten.

"Shit!" Jill said, whacking her forehead. *Mother! Her appointment with the doctor is at ten-thirty.*

She turned on her heel and ran to her bedroom, nearly knocking Max over in the doorway.

"Whoa! What's wrong? The kitchen on fire?"

"No, damn it. I totally forgot mother has an appointment with the doctor this morning." She grabbed underwear and a clean blouse and then stripped and began to dress.

"Can I help?" Max leaned against the doorframe, wearing only his jeans and a look of appreciation.

"If you could pour me some coffee, I'll owe you." She grinned. "There's a travel mug on the counter. I need to get on the road five minutes ago."

"Why don't I drive? I want to meet Dorothy, again, if you think it wouldn't be too upsetting for her. I'll come along to help."

Jill pulled her jeans up. "It would be great for you to come spend some time with her, but probably not today. I'm going to have to rush her out of there, and she's got two medical appointments and one for an eye exam." She stopped and put her arms around him. His hair was still wet, and his skin was firm and cool.

Max kissed her gently. Then not so gently. Desire coiled in her lower belly and she pushed against him. "Stop that or I'll never get out of here. Coffee, please. I'm going to comb my hair and then I have to run. There's stuff to put breakfast together, if you're hungry."

"Oh, I'm hungry all right." He nestled his face into her neck and gave her a tiny bite. "I'll make the bed and lock up. You go get yourself together, and I'll get you some coffee."

Jill smiled as Max hurried one way down the hallway, and she the other. *I could get used to having him around.* For a moment, she let her mind wander into the future. When he went back to France.

What will I do then? How is this, whatever it is, going to work?

No answers came to her, but the peace she had felt a few minutes ago had fled.

It was about the worst four hours she ever spent with her mother, Jill thought, vowing never again to schedule more than one appointment a day. It was stressful for Dorothy to get in and out of the car, and even worse to try and explain to her mother why they were in the doctor's offices.

Jill pulled her car into the parking lot and sighed. Her mother dozed in the seat next to her, her face drawn, a half-inch of grey bordering the auburn hair Dorothy had colored Jill's entire life. She was going to have to re-think taking her mother to the salon next week as she had planned.

Friend's House has a small on-site facility. *That might be easier, and less upsetting. For both of us.*

She walked around the car and opened the door. Dorothy woke with a start but allowed herself to be helped out of the seat belt. They walked back to her room slowly. She did not look at Jill but walked quicker than usual, as anxious as I am, Jill thought, to get back to her room.

Inside, Jill sat her Mother down at the café table by the window and gave her the sandwich she had bought at the drive through. Dorothy had missed lunch because of her appointments. Her mother eyed it, but made no move to pick it up.

"Not hungry?" Jill handed her an apple slice. "How about this?"

Dorothy took it and nodded, biting into it hungrily.

Jill took the turkey sandwich apart and handed her mother pieces of the meat and cheese and bread separately, which Dorothy seemed more comfortable with.

A few minutes later Jill helped her Mom to her bed for a nap. Dorothy fell asleep instantly. Quietly, Jill covered her with the blue and red afghan Dorothy had knit for her father twenty years ago, and headed out. She checked her phone, which she realized she had not taken off silent for the last three days.

Max had called twice and Carly once. There were also two calls from a caller marked Private.

"Miss Farrell," a woman said as Jill leaned down to sign-out on the visitor's log.

She turned to find Karen Rose, the director of Friend's House, standing behind her.

"Hi, Karen." Jill slipped the cell into her purse. "I checked my mother back in. It was a long day for her. She'll probably sleep until supper."

"Good. She's been unsettled at night, so I'm sure she needs the rest." The red-haired woman handed her an envelope. "I thought I'd give you this instead of mailing it."

"Thanks. What is it?"

"The receipt for the check for the next two months of your mother's stay."

"You mean the first two months. The check I dropped by on Friday?" Jill frowned.

"No, I put that in the mail to you as soon as I got it. This is for June and July, and the balance to August." Karen raised her eyebrows. "From the funds your husband dropped by yesterday. What a good-looking man he is."

Shock like a blow to her forehead stopped Jill dead. She held up her right hand. "Wait a minute. Who and what are you talking about?"

"Your husband. He was lovely to the staff when he came to visit with your mother yesterday evening. Had a huge box of candy with him, which he left in the dining room when he took Dorothy back to her room."

Confusion, panic, and anger exploded simultaneously. "Karen, I'm not married. And no one paid anything on my mother's account but me." *Have I left my mother in the care of idiots?* Briskly she handed the envelope back.

"What? Andrew Denton isn't your husband?" The director's hand jerked toward her face in alarm.

"Andrew Denton? He came here? You let him in to visit my mother?"

Karen took a step backward. "Well, yes. I mean, I wasn't aware of the fact you were married, but he explained when he introduced himself to all of us how you kept your own name for professional reasons."

"Shit, Karen. I was married to Andrew Denton, but we've been divorced for a decade. You tell your staff he is never, ever to be allowed to visit my mother again."

"I certainly will. But Miss Farrell, you should understand Friends House personnel aren't a police force. We're an assisted living facility, and anyone can drop in on the residents. We go out of our way to make guests from the community welcome."

"You're not following me here," Jill interrupted. "Andrew Denton is not a guy you want to welcome and let mingle with the residents."

"Why?"

"Because he's nuts. Dangerous."

"Dangerous?" she replied. "What, you mean like a criminal or something?"

Jill had said more than she should have, but she was furious. "No, he's not a criminal that I know of, but he's very troubled and has shown up out of the blue wanting to get back into my life. Which he is not going to do. So I don't want him coming around here. My mom is confused enough. Seeing him, and trying to remember if she knows him, can't help her."

"Do you have a restraining order?" Karen asked as if she hoped Jill did.

"No. But I'll get one if that's what it takes to keep Andrew from visiting again. If he shows up, tell your staff to call me and I'll handle it. I'll start the paperwork with the police to make sure he gets the message, but until then, I need your assurance this won't happen again."

Karen nodded. "I'll tell staff how you feel about Mr. Denton. But as I said, I can't promise anything. We'll do our best."

"Great," Jill said. "Now what else was it that you said? Something about a check?"

"Ah, yes. Mr. Denton gave me a check to cover some of your mother's care." She blinked. "I've already deposited it. Do you think that's going to be a problem?"

"Oh, there's going to be a problem, all right. I have to go now. Just please, please tell everyone here if Andrew Denton shows up they are to call me, and not to allow him to go to my mother's room."

Jill hurried out, her stomach a knot, and got into the car. She started it, but left it in park as she dug out the phone and pressed voicemail. There were no messages from Max, or the private caller.

Could it be Andrew?

She tried to focus, running over several things she could do. She should not have trashed Andrew's business card. With a sigh, Jill finally pressed one of the numbers and put the cell to her ear.

"Dave, hi, it's Jill. Can you possibly come over to my house this afternoon? I have something I need your help with."

"You okay, honey?" her best friend's dad asked. "Dorothy okay?"

"Yes. We're fine. But I need some advice. I don't want to go into everything now, but is your old partner still working at the FBI?"

"Yes." Dave paused a moment. "It's almost three now. How about four?"

"That'd be great. I'll see you then." Jill drove the short distance home, trying to order her mind as to what, exactly, she should tell Dave, and what she wanted him to try and find out.

She pulled into the driveway and her phone rang. It was Max.

"Hey, pretty woman, how did it go? Your mom okay?"

"Well, it was a long and confusing day for her, but all the doctors said she's fine, although she has a cataract that has to be taken care of by the end of the year. Sorry I had to run out like I did earlier."

"Don't worry, please. I understand. When can I see you again?" His voice was low and intimate. "You want to come to the hotel tonight? We can swim in the heated pool and get room service."

"That sounds perfect. How about seven?"

"No, come now." He paused. "I thought you might like a massage first."

A sigh escaped her. "Sounds lovely, but I need a couple of hours. I have some things to take care of."

"Okay. I'll see you at seven. Bring a bathing suit." He gave her the room number and rang off.

Jill paused. She was unsettled, suddenly, at how quickly she had jumped back into an affair with Max, but her brain didn't seem to be able to combat her hormones. She sighed and stuck the phone in her purse, her head full of a hundred conflicting impulses.

I should tell Max about Andrew. But first I need to get Dave's opinion about what Andrew said about Ben Pierce. She slammed the car door and hurried into her house.

Jill related the events of the last few days as Dave quietly listened. She ran through Good Friday's surprise reappearance of her ex-husband, Max's arrival the next day, and the burglary on Sunday. With a deep breath, she recounted Andrew's offer of money if she helped with some cockamamie investigation into the murder of Ben Pierce.

She ended with the discovery a few hours ago that Andrew had visited Dorothy and posed as her husband.

She did not go into what had transpired between her and Max last night, but her nervous voice when she said his name probably told the retired cop everything he needed to know about that.

Dave's expression was apprehensive when Jill repeated what Andrew said about working as a security consultant, and that there was a possibility the murderer of Ben Pierce could attend the reunion festivities. But he kept his questions short and offered no opinions.

Her father had always said Dave Hart was a great detective because he knew how to keep his mouth shut and listen.

Jill was apprehensive telling Dave all these convoluted facts, but was relieved to be able to share the burden of the last few days' happenings with someone she trusted.

"I tried to look up Andrew's company on the Internet, but there's no listing online, so I don't have any way to contact him about his visit to Friends House," she said, wringing her hands together. "And he gave them a check for $20,000, not the $10,000 he first offered me! What is he up to?"

"Sounds like he's trying to bribe you into helping him. Or he feels guilty about what happened, and he's taking a roundabout way to make amends."

"Amends? Like money could erase his behavior. I'm going to give him a check tomorrow to pay him back. I need to find out where to mail it."

"He doesn't know you very well, that's for sure." Dave smiled, but his eyes were serious. "I'll make some calls. My old partner on the force is now with the FBI. Supervisor in the LA FBI field office. I'll ask if he can go across to the ATF folks and make some inquiries about Ben. I would like to hear the circumstances of his murder from law enforcement."

"Andrew told me not to tell anyone about that." Jill folded her arms. "I'm sure he won't be pleased if it gets back to him that I sicced you and the feds on him."

"My guy is a pro, and very discreet. As for your ex, do you want me to go with you to the Santa Barbara police and get a restraining order against him?"

Jill's eyes widened. "I've thought of it, but really don't know. What do you think?"

"I'd hold off. Andrew didn't hurt your mother. He'll say he was being a generous ex-spouse by paying her bill. I doubt he'll go back there. And I doubt the police would consider what he did serious enough for a restraining order."

"Should I tell Max that Andrew suggested he might be on the list of suspects?"

Dave met Jill's eyes. "You haven't said anything to Max yet?"

"No. I told Max about the burglary and the, you know . . ." She made a gesture with her thumb and index finger like a gun. "About how I shot Andrew by accident and why we divorced, but I didn't tell Max he showed up a couple of days ago. Or about all this stuff with Ben Pierce."

"I think you should keep all this to yourself for a little longer, then," Dave said. "If you do tell Max, he'll probably get angry and confront Andrew, as anyone would. Which could make figuring out what's going on that much harder. Let me see what I can find out first."

"Okay." Jill sipped her coffee. "What do you think about the burglary?"

"What do you mean?"

"Is it connected somehow, to this thing Andrew was talking about?"

Dave blinked. "I'd trust the local cops take that it was

kids, honey, but keep your doors locked. I doubt it had anything to do with anything else."

"Okay, but I thought . . ."

"Don't borrow trouble," Dave interrupted. "It's surely just an unfortunate coincidence."

"My father always said cops don't believe in coincidence."

"They don't. But that doesn't mean they don't exist." He finished his coffee and set the mug down on the kitchen table. "So how was it, seeing Max after all that time? Is he the same guy?"

A blush crept over Jill's face and melted into her hairline. "Good. Really good." Briefly she filled Dave in on why Max had not contacted her all those years ago. "After hearing what happened, I don't feel quite so humiliated."

"Good. I like that he made the effort to seek you out, face-to-face, before the reunion. It would have been tough to run into him and find out then that he didn't remember you."

"I'll say. Or if he'd seen Carly first. She's been wanting to give him a kick in the shins for fifteen years. She might have beat him up."

"My daughter is loyal to a fault. Hurt someone she loves, you hurt her. And face the consequences." Dave stood. "I'm going to take off. Thanks for the coffee."

"You're welcome. Thanks so much for your help." Jill followed him to the door. "I can't believe all this drama. I'm starting to dread answering the door for fear someone else from my past will be waiting there. One more reason to avoid this reunion."

Dave hugged her and they stepped outside. "Don't avoid the past. Especially as it is bringing Carly and her baby girl home for a while." He hesitated for a moment. "Have you talked to her lately?"

"No, not for a month or so before she called the other

night." Jill crossed her arms over her chest. "Why? Is there something wrong?"

"I hope not. Just a dad's instincts. She seems, I don't know, unusually stressed over how much Hamilton is having to travel for business. I told her to get him to move back to the States, that we've got plenty of airports here he can fly out of. She said that it wasn't an option."

Jill put her hand on Dave's arm. "You know Carly. She's moody, and now with the baby, I'm sure she misses you more than ever. We'll have a good girl's chat night and I'll make sure everything is okay with her."

"Good. I know she misses you as much as she does me. Probably more." He hugged her again and then hurried down the walk, waving to her from the car.

Jill locked the door and headed for the bedroom. Max had left the house in fine order, the kitchen cleaned-up, fresh sheets on the bed, everything tidy. Her college yearbook was on her dresser. She saw it had a piece of paper bookmarking a page, and opened it.

Max had left her a note on the page with her senior photo. *I look about twelve in that picture*, she thought. Eyes straight ahead, hair blown out and severe as a helmet, her mother's locket at her throat. *Class beauty then and now. XXX Max*, he had written in bold black ink at the bottom of the photo.

Jill blinked. *He forgot he already signed this yearbook.*

She turned to the back pages where there was a photograph of her and him, sitting side by side in St. John's theatre green room. *My girl, once and forever . . . Love Maximilian,* he had scrawled in his beautiful penmanship.

She turned back to her class photo. The new inscription was carefully printed in block letters. She frowned. The handwriting did not look anything like the printing.

No one writes in cursive anymore with computers.

Max had changed a lot, so it should not be alarming that his handwriting was different, except everything was spooking her since Andrew came along with his conspiracy theories.

Jill closed the book.

She showered and shaved her legs. She thought back to last nights' lovemaking, her insides warming in anticipation of another round tonight. Max was a much different lover now, much more skilled. She considered the ways she was different from her 21-year-old self, who Max did not remember.

Sometimes a faulty memory is good. She smiled.

Thirty minutes later, Jill was dressed and her hair was blown dry. She piled a stack of clothes on the bed, underwear and a bathing suit and shorts for tomorrow, as she was sure she would spend the night at the hotel with Max. She added her cosmetic travel bag and grabbed a robe, then glanced around for a duffle.

It's in the hall closet.

Jill went to the foyer and pulled open the door and flicked on the light. The space was jam packed due to the additional coats and boots from her mother's house, but she remembered putting her canvas overnight bag inside the suitcase at the back.

She moved several things out of the way, finally spying the suitcase. She gripped it and tugged, pulling it along the left side of the closet near the peg where her dad's gun hung in the leather shoulder holster.

She froze.

The holster was there, but it was empty.

The gun was gone.

Chapter 11

Max answered on her first knock. "There you are," he said, sweeping her into an embrace.

Jill met his lips, touching his face with her hand, but returned his kiss with less enthusiasm than he was obviously expecting. She stepped out of his arms and walked into the middle of his hotel suite.

He shut the door. "What's wrong? Where's your bathing suit?" He smiled. "If it's in that tiny purse of yours, I say we stay in and I'll let you wear it in the Jacuzzi."

Jill put her purse down and tried to keep her voice neutral. "Do you have my gun?"

Max blinked. "Whoa. That's a strange way to say hello."

"Do you have it? Did you take it without asking me?"

"Yes, I have it. And yes, I took it without asking you." Max exhaled and nodded toward the bedroom. "Your father's Beretta is in the safe in my closet. I bought bullets for it, and a locking case to store it in so you could keep it in your bedroom, not hang it in the closet where you wouldn't be able to get it quickly if you needed it."

His words chilled her. "So when I wasn't there, you searched my house to find it, and then took it?"

"I didn't search, Jill. You told me the gun was in your hall closet." He crossed his arms over his chest. "I would have asked you first, but I only thought of it after you left to take your mother to the doctor. You said it was an old gun, and that concerned me, so I dug it out of the closet and stopped at a shop downtown. It needs a good cleaning, by the way, according to the man at the hunting store."

"You had no right to take it without asking me."

Max's expression tightened. "I'm sorry if I upset you. I didn't imagine you'd be looking for it before I could give it back. But I was worried about what happened, about the break-in at your home."

Jill could not smooth the upset from her voice. "I told you not to worry about that. The cops said it was kids."

"I know what the cops said." His green eyes darkened. "But I am worried. I wanted you to feel safe at night, even if I wasn't there."

"Thanks, but I am very used to be alone at night and I can take care of myself." She turned and walked to the window, her lip trembling.

"Jill." He put his arms around her waist. "*Karaste karlek*. We've started down a new path, but I hope you know I have every intention of seeing you after the reunion is over. I hope you feel the same way."

Karaste karlek meant dearest love. Max had called her that a million years ago.

Jill walked to the wall of windows, fighting for composure. There was a stunning view of the ocean from his room. The water stretched forever, glimmering and opaque as the future.

"I'm feeling foolish for being so impetuous," she said. "I'm not twenty-one anymore. It's not like me to let a relationship develop so fast."

"Don't fight what you feel." Max crossed the space and stood near her. "I'm not. I may not remember the past, but every minute since I saw you last Friday, you've been on my mind. I feel the attraction between us. Something more than memories. I know you feel it too."

She turned. "I do feel something. But I'm afraid I might be confusing the past with the present. I don't really know you at all anymore. And I'm not used to having you in my life, worrying about me. Doing things for me. I'm not used to anything that's going on right now."

"I understand." Gently he slipped his arms around her waist. "You have a lot of upset to cope with, aside from me showing up."

She tried to smile. "Yes, I do. And I appreciate your concern about my safety. But it was shocking to find the gun missing."

"Did you think I stole it? For some nefarious reason?" He tightened his grip on her.

"I just didn't know what to think, Max."

"I see." He dropped his hands to his side.

Jill tensed. *He doesn't see. He doesn't know about the ridiculous things Andrew said. Or Dave's words of caution.*

She cleared her throat. "I'm going to go. I'll call you tomorrow." She grabbed her purse from the table and faced him. "Would you please get my gun?"

"Of course. But don't leave like this." He put his hands back on her. "Stay and talk. This, whatever it is that happens to me when I'm in the same room with you, means something real is between us. Don't be afraid of it just because it's unexpected."

For a moment, Jill struggled to keep her emotions in check, but the sincerity in his voice undid her. She laid her face against his chest, gasping as a rush of varying emotions tore through her body.

Rubbing her back as if she was a child, Max held her so tight she felt his heart beat against her own. After a couple of moments, the storm of emotion passed and Jill moved out of his arms.

She ran her hands through her tangled hair. "I'm a mess."

"You might feel like one." His voice was gentle. "But you are not a mess. You're stunning. I was overwhelmed with how beautiful you are, the minute you answered your door. More beautiful than those pictures of you as a girl."

She lay her hand on his cheek. "This is so strange. I knew you as a boy, and now again as the confident man you are. But you only see me as a thirty-five-year-old woman with a lot of issues and a propensity to weep."

He kissed the side of her wrist. "Tears are an expression of the truest emotions. Come lay down and rest. Sleep. Then I'll order dinner and we'll have a quiet evening, and share everything we can think of to share. Let me take care of you tonight, Jill. Don't worry about anything for a few hours."

"But I didn't bring my things . . ."

Max smiled. "You can use my things. My yellow shirt was a good fit, *ja?*"

At last she relaxed. "*Ja.* It did."

Two minutes later, she lay down on Max's bed. He sat and massaged her back and shoulders until she felt boneless. They laughed about his inherent aptitude as a Swedish masseuse.

Max lay beside her and she slept for hours.

When she woke, Max ordered room service. Waffles, eggs, and bacon at midnight.

She took a bubble bath and then they made love. The passion she had for him the night before amplified into a deeper, more urgent need as she learned more of his most intimate likes and wants.

Hours later, she swam out of a black sleep. The room was dark and the heavy drapes were closed. Jill fumbled for her bag on the bedside table and dug out her phone, shocked it read ten twenty a.m. on Wednesday. It felt as if a week had surely passed since she had last checked.

There were calls. Two from private number. And one from Dave Hart a few minutes ago. She hit voicemail.

"I'd like to come over this afternoon," Dave said. "There are some things I need to discuss with you. Call me back."

"Round two of room service? Shall I order more waffles?" Max asked from the doorway.

Jill hurriedly put the phone down, feeling a stab of guilt. She stretched her arms in the air and allowed a very contented yawn to roll out of her mouth. "No. Just coffee please. I'll jump in the shower."

Max came to the bedside and dropped the newspaper beside her. "I've already had a pot brought up. And croissants. Come sit with me by the window. It's sunny and warm outside and you can see all the way to the Channel Islands."

"Sunny and warm, in other words a standard-issue California day. Let me shower first. I won't be long."

She joined Max a few minutes later, her wet hair tied in a knot on top of her head. He had a toothbrush and toiletries sent to the room, but she had only lipstick and a compact with her.

He's going to see exactly what I look like in the morning she thought, sitting down next to him and pouring a cup of coffee. "What a great suite. Your business must be doing well."

"It is. And I need a bit of space, and a nice view." He grinned at her. "Will you come with me on a trip soon?"

"School is over mid-June. I'd like that, but I'll have to see how my mother settles in. Do you travel a lot?"

"I do." He leaned over and kissed her cheek. "You look like a teenager this morning. *Vacker flicka.*"

Beautiful something, she remembered. "Don't stare too closely." She tore a piece of the croissant off and ate it. Her lips were bruised, and she smiled when she touched them, remembering.

"What shall we do today?" Max asked. "Do you want to go to the ocean? I can rent surfboards."

"It's too cold this time of year for that. And I need to head home for a few hours. I have to go to the bank and . . ." Jill stopped before she said, *and get Andrew a check for $20,000.* "But I should be free by dinner. We can grill again, or we can go out."

"I'll handle dinner arrangements. We'll drive up the coast a ways."

"That sounds great." She sipped her coffee. "What will you do today?"

Max glanced at his watch, an elegant Patek Philippe with a well-worn leather band. "I need to make some calls. And I am going to meet with a potential client at four this afternoon. He lives in Solvang."

"Oh, Solvang. You'll love it there. Is Danish food very different from Swedish? You can get some on every corner."

"I do like it. The Danes feel they are superior to us Swedes, who they say eat rotten herring too often, and the reverse is true, of course. Lots of competition between Copenhagen and Stockholm."

"You both have beautiful queens."

"*Ja.* But ours is prettiest." He touched his dark, silky head of hair. "She's dark like me. No one is suspicious of my being not blonde anymore."

They both laughed.

"Why don't you come with me? If you're done with your errands by three, we can drive up together and you can eat *wienerbrod* and coffee while I meet with my client."

"*Wienerbrod?*"

"It's what you Americans call Danish. Apples, pastry. Frosting. Yummy."

They chatted and Max tried to tempt her with an invitation for one more trip to bed, but Jill demurred and was on the road back to her house by eleven. She stopped to visit with her mother, who was listless and non-responsive, despite the change in medications.

It took her an hour to finish the banking and grocery chores, and she arrived back at her townhouse at a little after one.

She took the gun out of the trunk and put it away carefully, and then stashed the cashier's check under her mattress. She poured a glass of wine and went to the living room to call Dave Hart.

He did not pick up, so she left him a message that she would be home until about seven. "I know Carly and Ham are coming in tonight, too," she added. "So whatever works. I can make myself available tomorrow, if that's better. Thanks again, Dave."

She walked through the entry and out the side entrance into the garage, determined to find Andrew's business card. Since the universe had obviously decided this was the day to bury old, broken relationships, the sooner she gave him back his bribe money, the sooner she could blot out his reappearance in her life.

Jill emptied the trash barrel contents onto newspapers on the garage floor and used the broom handle to sift through it. She found both pieces, but they were soaked with coffee grounds, the phone number illegible.

Cursing under her breath, Jill bundled the trash back up, and went inside to shower and dress. She missed the call from Dave Hart, but he left a message he would be over at three unless he heard from her.

At 3 p.m. on the nose, he rang the bell.

"Come in, Dave."

He seemed anxious.

"Can I get you some coffee or something?" she asked.

"No, nothing for me." He gave her a kiss on the cheek and stepped inside. "Let's sit down. I have a lot to tell you."

She followed the ex-cop down the hallway into the sunny living room, sensing the tension in him. She sat on the sofa and he took the chair opposite.

"So what's up?" Jill folded her hands together tightly.

"As far as I can find out, part of what Andrew Denton told you is true." Dave leaned his elbows on the knees of his khakis.

"Yeah? What part?"

"Ben Pierce did work for the ATF. And he was found murdered in December at a hotel in Paris. The story was never released to the public. There is an active investigation into his death, and the authorities are particularly interested in members of your graduating class."

"Why?"

"Evidently Ben called his supervisor the day he died, shared that he had run into a college classmate, and commented that there was something off about the guy." Dave clenched his hands together. "My buddy at the FBI said Pierce was killed that same night."

"Did Ben's boss ask the guy's name?"

"Yes. But Pierce wouldn't tell him."

"Why?" Jill felt uneasy at the look on Dave's face.

Dave leaned across the desk. "We don't know. The best guess ATF has is Ben wanted to check the guy out more before he said anything else officially. In his line of work, if this unknown friend worked in the security or financial markets, any formal inquiry could ruin the guy, even if he wasn't involved in anything shady, which is what the boss thought Ben meant."

Jill put her hand on her head. "It sounds like the Ben I remember. He was always kind, and careful. I don't remember him every gossiping about anyone." She looked at Dave. "How was he killed?"

"Shot. And the hotel room was set on fire."

"Oh my god, how horrible." Jill covered her mouth. "His sister, Marissa, is in charge of the reunion. It's strange she hasn't sent an email or anything out about Ben's death." She shook her head. "It's amazing she's holding it together enough to be running an event like this."

"I doubt she knows the real story about her brother. They may have simple told her Ben died in an accident."

Jill's face felt tight. "Andrew didn't say anything about that part of the story."

Dave raised his eyebrows. "What part?"

"He didn't mention Ben met with someone from college the day he was killed. All he told me was that a classmate was implicated because of some kind of evidence pointing to St. John's alumni."

"Denton wouldn't tell you everything he knows. By the way, my FBI friend confirmed Andrew is a security professional. He was very interested to hear your ex was involved with this case."

"Why?"

"Rumor has it the CIA has used Andrew in the past when they needed field work done outside of channels."

"What does that mean, outside of channels?"

"It usually means they hire a contractor who knows how to get information without a warrant." Dave blinked. "Like if someone wants to search government records, or a location, but they don't have probable cause, they might ask someone like him to do it for them."

"I don't get it," Jill said. "You mean he breaks in places?"

Dave nodded. "Maybe."

"Do you think he broke in to my house? But that's not possible. He didn't show up until afterwards." Jill pushed the hair off her face.

"Did he? Or was he already here?"

"I, I don't know."

"Did you see him drive up?"

"No. He rang the bell after I was inside for a few minutes. But he wasn't there when I got home a few minutes before that."

"He could have been on another street."

"But this all happened in broad daylight, for heaven's sake!" Jill stood, rubbing her hands up and down the chilled skin of her arms. "And if he did do that, why wouldn't he leave before the cops got here?"

"He might be trying to control things, or get a feel how the police were going to pursue it. I don't know. I'm not saying Andrew did it, but your instincts might have been right last night. The burglary could be connected to whatever the hell the government is looking into."

"But what would he be looking for inside my house?"

"I have no idea. Do you have a lot of mementoes and things from college? Something that might show a relationship between Ben and someone who might be involved?"

Jill laced her fingers together tightly. "No. I don't have anything like that. Only a couple of yearbooks. Some personal pictures. A couple of video tapes and stuff of the talent shows."

"I don't think there's a connection." Dave stood up. "My advice for now is to stay away from Denton. I'm going to talk with another intelligence source in LA, and then I have to pick up Carly and Ham at the airport tonight. I'll call you first thing tomorrow, okay?"

"Sure. Are you going to tell Carly about all of this?"

"No. Let's continue to keep it between us. You two girls will have plenty to talk about besides an unsolved murder that may or may not involve people you know."

"Okay." Jill walked Dave outside. "Tell her to call me tonight, no matter how late, okay?"

"Will you be home by midnight? That's how late it will be by the time I get them to their hotel."

"Yes." She smiled. "You sound like my dad."

"Sometimes I feel like your dad." He pointed at the house. "Keep this place locked up."

"Right." Jill closed the door and leaned against it.

So Andrew has a reputation for breaking and entering. And one of my classmates might actually be involved in Ben Pierce's murder.

She pressed her hand against her chest.

One thing was for sure. She was glad she got her gun back from Max. And that he had bought her a box of bullets.

Ben's killer sped down the Pacific Coast Highway in the fading sunshine, thrilled as the rented car fishtailed along the narrow road.

He loved fast cars and narrow roads, and wished his life allowed more time for both.

Inhaling deeply, the man settled back into the leather seat, relaxing his foot on the gas. Meeting the woman face to face over dinner had gone off as he had hoped, and screwing her senseless had gone even better. She had voiced no complaints, expressed no doubts, and so far was a willing and satisfied partner.

He had enjoyed more than a few moments of it, letting himself go in a way he wouldn't have guessed possible, considering all that was at stake. He also had not expected her breasts to be so lush, or her ass so tight.

It was impossible to tell everything from an old yearbook photo.

But now came the difficult part. He would bed her again, commiserate with her as much as he had to in order to keep her distracted.

It was the others he now had to worry about now.

The man glanced at his wristwatch and pressed down hard on the pedal.

Chapter 12

Max brought along a new, hi-tech case for her gun when he picked her up for dinner. He told her she should keep the gun in it, and lock the case in her bedside table.

Under his watchful eye, Jill did as he asked, but she was nervous having it next to the bed. She decided she would move it back to the closet tonight. It would not be all that handy, but she would feel safer having it in another room.

Her dad always said more gun owners shot themselves by accident than got shot by intruders, and to always keep the ammunition separate.

Jill told Max she wanted to stop and see Dorothy before they went to dinner, and he agreed to come in with her. It was late for her mother to have a visitor, particularly someone she had not laid eyes on for years, but in the evening Dorothy was calmer than in the morning.

They navigated the lock on the door, and nearly let Sandy Jeeks, the resident she and Dave had met last week, sneak out the door.

"Don't hold the door open," Jill said to Max when Sandy approached. "She isn't allowed out without an escort."

"Oh." Max blocked the door with his body and smiled at Mrs. Jeeks. "Sorry, ma'am. Why don't I walk you back to your room?"

"Aren't you a handsome devil?" Mrs. Jeeks held out her arm and let Max walk her toward the lounge. She rushed off back toward the door when it opened, winking at Max.

"She's a handful," Max said.

"I don't blame her for trying to break out of here," Jill said.

They found her mother in the brightly lit TV room, seated in a recliner, her head back, a few wheelchair-bound residents clustered like dozing pigeons around her. A DVD of an old Glenn Campbell special was playing loudly.

"Appropriate," Jill commented. "Campbell fought Alzheimer's for a long time before he retired, but he still remembered his songs."

"The brain is such a mysterious organ." Max touched his head. "I sit and concentrate and try to control mine, but it does not follow my directions."

"That's true for all of us sometimes." Jill put her hand on Dorothy's shoulder. "Hey, Mom."

Her mother's eyes opened and she stared right at Jill. She blinked to clear her sleepy vision. "Hi, honey."

"Hi, Mom. How are you?"

Dorothy squinted and fumbled around with her hand at her neck, feeling for her locket. "What day is it?"

"Wednesday." Jill leaned closer. "It's Jill."

"Jill." Dorothy said her name as if it were a word in a foreign language.

"I brought an old friend to say hello. It's Max. Max Kallstrom. My boyfriend from college. Do you remember how he made Swedish potato salad for you a long time ago?"

"Hello, Mrs. Farrell." Max sat next to Dorothy, at eye level to the recliner. "How are you?"

Dorothy stared at Max and, after a long moment, her mouth began to twitch. Slowly she reached her hand out as if she would touch him, but it hovered, trembling in the air. "Is it really you?" she whispered.

Jill's eyes stung and she bit her lip.

Max took Dorothy's hand in his and kissed the top of it. "It is me. Do you think I look different now? Maybe I need a haircut? You look the same as the photographs Jill has at her house, though," he said. "Your blue eyes are as lovely as the sky."

Dorothy smiled then, a real smile, the smile of a woman who had been flattered by a handsome young man.

But then she shuddered and pulled her hand away, holding her arms close to her side, as if she was cold. "Buketa, buketa, buketa. Go away. Scat." She made a hissing sound and turned to Jill. "I don't like this."

Max and Jill drove in silence down the Pacific Coast highway toward Gaviota, to a restaurant recommended by the concierge at his hotel. He reached for her hand and she squeezed his, but withdrew it from his grasp.

"It's never going to get any better for her." She crossed her arms over her chest to keep herself warm.

"There aren't any drugs to help stall the progression of her memory loss?"

"No. The drugs they give her cause strokes and fatigue and hallucinations. They are worse than useless."

"I'm so sorry. It's grim," Max said softly. "Are you okay financially? I mean, I could look over your books if you like. Give you some free advice about investments."

Jill swallowed, as Andrew's warning that she should worry if someone was interested in her finances skittered along the edge of her brain. "I think we're good. Dad's lawyer's had everything buttoned up pretty tight. But thanks."

The drove for several minutes in silence, the classical music station playing softly in the background. Outside the car, the ocean was grey and choppy at water's edge, and clouds blocked the setting sun. Pale purple and orange glimmers flickered at the edge of the horizon, looking more like fire than fire.

Jill shivered. "I'm getting hungry. Is it much farther?"

"No. It's right up ahead. The food is supposed to be great. Simple but great."

"Sounds like what I need tonight." She turned and stared at his strong, sculpted profile. "Thank you for coming to visit Mom. I think, somewhere inside her mind, she did remember you."

Max pursed his lips. "You don't need to thank me. I wanted to see her. I'm sorry I don't remember her, from before. But I'm glad to have gone tonight. For you as much as anything."

"Well, it's comforting to have company, but harder, too. I feel like I need to protect her. It's hard letting people see her like this. I think she'd hate it."

"It is what it is. I admire you for taking care of her, Jill. She's lucky to have you."

"She was a great mom." Jill clenched her teeth. *Was.*

Ahead a neon sign, 'Sandals,' burned blue in the dusk. Max made the turn into the narrow entrance, the car wheels crunching slowly across the shell-covered parking lot.

It was a tiny seafood restaurant with dining al fresco and locally famous brick-oven bread. They ordered wine and drinks and the smell of hot rolls and the taste of her cool wine began to relax Jill.

"So how did the Solvang meeting go?" she asked. It was time to talk of other things besides things that could not be changed.

"It went well. The man I met with is vice-chair of a foundation." He named a tech company giant and raised his dark eyebrows. "They have a considerable amount of money they want to invest in the securities I am most versed in, although I'm not familiar with the foundation they are hoping to support. I'm going to do a bit more research, but it looks promising. How was your afternoon?"

Her conversation with Dave gripped her mind. "My day was fine." Jill tugged at her hair. "I've lined up a bunch of appointments for Carly and I for a trip to the salon and some shopping."

"You will amaze our classmates with how much you still look like your younger self. I'm sure of that."

"I hope my hair looks better than it did in college. You saw those photos." She frowned. "Are you dreading seeing all those people? And explaining what happened to you a hundred times?"

"I'm curious more than anything, I guess. But now, it's not as important as I thought it would be. It'll be a fun party, where I'll have the prettiest girl from the class on my arm." He winked. "You are going to attend all the events with me, aren't you?"

"If you want me to."

"Of course I do. It will be great for my ego."

"Our female classmates' appreciation over how fabulous you look all grown-up will be what's great for your ego." She thought for a moment of the shock, surprise, and interest people would feel seeing them together again. "It won't be boring, that's for sure."

"Good. I hate boring," Max said.

After dinner, they wandered around the grounds of the restaurant, which bordered a national park. A sign for the hiking trail leading up to Gaviota Peak was nearby, so they decided to walk a bit in the starlight evening. He told her about his daughter, Olivia, and how she was a happy, shy child who had taken the divorce very hard.

"I make it a point to spend at least one weekend a month with her," Max said. "I can't wait for you to meet her."

Jill smiled but said nothing. They headed back due to darkness, mosquitoes, and the fact that Jill's flats were not cutting it on the trail. As they reached the edge of the parking lot, a few more cars had pulled in.

A man in a helmet and leather jacket was sitting on a Harley, as if he was waiting for someone. As they made their way toward Max's rental, the powerful motorcycle engine started up, and the driver made a wide pass around their car and headed out into the breezy night.

He was familiar somehow and she squinted at his retreating form. *Where did I see that bike?* It had an unusual blue flame pattern on the engine cover that she was sure she had seen before.

"We should do this another time in the daylight," Max said, coughing as the dust kicked up. "We'll get you some proper hiking boots and bring a picnic."

"We should." She pushed aside the mystery of the guy on the bike. "When are you going back to France, by the way?"

"My ticket is for next Wednesday."

A week. He's leaving in a week. "You fly to New York, then direct to Paris?"

"All the flights stop at Heathrow, but I'm going to Marseilles this trip. It's Olivia's birthday on the 24th, so I'm going to spend a week there. Then home to Paris."

"It seems a million miles away," she murmured.

"No. It is 6,061."

She chuckled as they reached the dusty parking lot at the restaurant. "You know the exact miles?"

"Yes. I get bonus miles, remember?"

"Not bonus kilometers?"

"No. But that would be," Max paused. "9,754." He grinned. "I was always good in math."

"I'll say. I remember that from college, by the way. You took calculus. For fun, you said. I had no idea what the questions on those tests were even asking."

"You were an English major, *ja?* Good with words but not math?"

"A cliché, but true."

Max put his arm around her shoulders. "There isn't anything clichéd about you."

"Well, as I've said before, you don't know me all that well."

"Yet," he whispered.

"Yet. And next week you'll be six thousand miles away. So this will be it for us for a while." *Maybe forever.* She felt pathetic for the sad tone in her voice.

"Not so long. I booked a ticket this afternoon to come back to the States in mid-June, and I left the return open," he said. "I wanted to ask you what you thought about spending a couple of weeks together when you're out for summer break. And plan a trip so you can come to Europe with me. When do you need to return for the new semester?"

"September."

"Excellent. Maybe you can come for August?"

"I don't know." She shook her head. "I wouldn't feel right about leaving my mother for an extended period of time. She needs me to come by and see her, I think. And that's a lot of time, a lot of money."

"Don't do that," Max said. "Don't look for problems before we actually have some."

"We? Before there is a 'we', both of us need to figure out a lot more things. I mean, where's this we thing going? Realistically?"

"Wherever we want it to go," he said quietly.

Jill pulled away. "I'm not asking you for any kind of commitment. I mean, jeez, I'm not willing to make any myself. It's been less than a week. We've talked, got reacquainted, and become lovers, but we live in separate worlds, on different continents. You have a daughter who lives in France."

Max put his hands on his hips and his voice rose. "What are you doing? Pushing me away? Trying to keep me from telling you I'm falling for you?"

A smile bloomed over what felt like her entire body. Somewhere in her heart, Jill knew she had been waiting for fifteen years to hear this from Max, even now, when a relationship was so impractical. "You're being impetuous. I remember this about you. You got an idea in your head, and that was it. Common sense be damned."

"I am being honest about how I feel. Are you?"

She put her hand on his mouth. "Don't press. You need to learn, to remember, that I'm not like that. I'm like a tortoise. Slow and deliberate. I need to understand what's happening, and think through how to handle it."

"Think? Can't you feel what's happening?" He pulled her back into his arms.

"I do. All I'm saying is the smart thing to do is to slow down, not make any plans for now, okay?"

"No." The look in Max's eyes was intense. "I've lost too much time already with you. I'm not going to lose you again."

"Well, that's good news."

"You're good news," he said.

Jill relaxed against him, abandoning practicality for the moment. She kissed him as the ocean breeze wound around them, unable to cool the heat from their embrace.

After a while, Max broke away and opened the car door. "You'll come back to the hotel with me for the night, *ja?*"

"No, I should go home. Carly's going to call, but more importantly, I'm sure she'll come to the house early tomorrow. So no, but you could come in for a while. I still have brownies, if you'd like dessert." She ran her hand down his pant leg and squeezed his thigh.

He grinned. "You'd have to use those bullets I bought you to keep me away tonight. And since I've heard you're not a very accurate shot, I'd take the chance."

"That's not funny."

"Yes it is." He nudged her with his elbow. "You need to chill. And get into practice for what your friends are going to be talking about at the reunion."

She sighed. "Isn't that the truth? Okay, funny man, let's get going." She winked at him and slid into the car. When she pulled the seatbelt across her lap, she caught movement in the shadows outside to the right of where they were parked.

She peered closely, and made out a man in a leather jacket, arms crossed over his chest, watching them. "Who is that man?" she asked Max.

"Where?" he said, his voice steely cold.

She raised her hand and pointed, but there was no one there. She blinked and shook her head. "I'm seeing things. And I sound like my mother."

"I'll get out and look," he said, his hand on the door handle.

"No. Let's go. Sorry, it was nothing," Jill said.

"Okay." Slowly Max backed the car out and turned toward the highway. Jill glanced in the side mirror nervously but saw only the moonlight in the trees.

Carly Hart Stewart showed up at Jill's door the following morning at eight a.m. with bagels, presents, and enough enthusiasm to launch an Internet start-up.

"Carly! But where's Hamilton, and the nanny, and dear baby Julia?" Jill hugged her, bags and all, and took some of the things from her.

"Ham hasn't made it to California yet, he had to make a detour to Toronto. Nanny and Julia are both sleeping at the hotel. I told them we'd be back there for lunch." She ran a critical eye down Jill's body, from her hair to her bare feet. "Girlfriend, what have you done to yourself? You are glowing, absolutely radiant!"

"I, ah, I've been resting." Max had left at dawn. She had considered going back to sleep for an hour, but she was glad now that she had made herself get up and shower and straighten the house. Although what she did last night besides sleep was obviously written all over her face. "It's spring break, remember? I've been sleeping in."

"Umm, and who have you been sleeping in with these days?"

They settled at the kitchen table, bags piled beside them. Carly unwrapped the bagels as Jill poured steaming water into her mother's teapot. "Well, since we last talked I have a lot to tell you."

"So talk. I'm so screwed up as to time zones, I was going to bring In-N-Out hamburgers, but they're not opened yet." She spread a healthy scoop of cream cheese over her bagel and chomped down on it. "Start with your love life. What's going on there?"

"Okay. But I think it's better if you listen for a minute, and then ask questions at the end," Jill said in her teacher voice.

"Okay," Carly said around chewing. "Shoot."

Jill grimaced, thinking how Max would make that into a joke. "As to my personal life, you know I haven't seen anyone seriously the last couple of years. . ."

"Wait, is that a love bite on your neck?"

Jill slapped her hand over her neck. "Carly, pay attention." She took a breath. "Andrew showed up a second time a couple of nights ago, right after I discovered that my house was burglarized, and . . ." She eyed Carly, whose face was frozen, her mouth full, her eyes huge.

"And Max Kallstrom came to see me after we talked on the phone last week. He explained everything about what happened to him when he disappeared fifteen years ago." Jill cleared her throat. "And we've been out together. A few times."

Carly blinked and swallowed. She pushed her plate away. "Holy Mother. What has your life turned into, a reality show?" She grabbed Jill's hand. "Okay, well, as long as it's Max who gave you that hickey, I'm in for this story any way you want to tell it. Just don't leave out a single thing."

An hour and two pots of tea later, Jill was hoarse from

talking. "Why don't we take a break and go out on the patio. I need to water the plants."

Carly followed, still shaking her head at the dramatic past week Jill had endured. She pointed at the dead vase of roses sitting on the corner of the patio. "What's with those?"

"Andrew brought those. They were gorgeous. But I couldn't stand to look at them after a day or two."

Carly nodded. "I can't believe all this."

"Which? The Andrew brought me roses part? That my house was burglarized? Or the shock of shocks that Max has walked back into my life?"

"All of it!" She squinted and settled into one of the loungers, turning her alabaster skin to the sun. "I still don't understand why Andrew came to see you, though."

"He said he wanted to apologize." Jill was uneasy keeping the news of Ben Pierce's murder, or a possible classmate being a murder suspect, from Carly, but she was determined to follow Dave Hart's advice. "And I think he sincerely wants to preempt the drama of running into each other at the reunion."

"Did he forget that he almost killed you?"

"That's a tiny bit unfair, Carly. He tried to kill himself, remember?"

"He had a gun and was cracked-out on drugs. You could have been dead." Carly crossed her arms over her chest. "But let's move on. How are you feeling about Max? You're smiling and sparkling, but how's your gut sense about this? Do you believe him, about the amnesia thing? That that's the reason he didn't contact you?"

"Yes. I do." She met Carly's blue eyes. "Do you think what he said is plausible?"

"It sounds pretty lame. I mean, amnesia? Really?"

"It's not uncommon with traumatic injuries, from what I've read on the Internet," Jill replied quickly. "I poked around and did some research after Max told me his story.

People often lose their memory after blood loss or a head injury. And he was almost killed in that accident."

"But why did he wait fifteen years to contact anyone from here? He knew he was in California when it happened. It seems to me once he was over the worst of it, which was before you married Andrew, by the way, he would have hopped on a plane and tried to re-connect. Is he saying he didn't consider there were people here who cared about him and wanted to know how he was?"

Carly's doubt deflated Jill's mood a degree. "Why don't you wait and ask him that. He said he didn't know about me, so I'm not sure he thought there was much point to coming back to California. And his parents never gave him my letters. It took him two or three years to be able to walk okay, and after that, I think he moved on. Went to school and got his masters, and got married. He has a daughter. She's seven."

"What? You're sleeping with a married man?"

"No, Max is divorced. I don't sleep with married men."

"Good. I'm a married lady and I hate women who do that kind of crap. So where's the ex?"

"She and Max's daughter, Olivia, live somewhere outside of Paris. She's remarried."

"Does he see the daughter much?"

"He says he does. I think that's why he's living in France." Jill turned off the hose. The bed of flowers was a wreck, but at least the ice plant and the palm trees on the slope were hanging in there. "Max thinks he met Hamilton, by the way." She recounted the story. "Isn't that wild? We would have known more about Max a couple of years ago, except Ham's the only one from school who wouldn't have recognized him."

Carly stared off into the distance. "Ham never mentioned Max's name to me. And I'm sure he would have. I told him all about what happened with you two, although maybe he doesn't remember that. He seems to blank out a lot when I talk to him about college." Carly leaned back and closed her eyes. "God, this sunshine is heaven. It goes right to my bones, which I worry will be permanently frozen by cold and damp ten months a year."

"How is England? Are you still loving it, aside from the temperature?" Jill sat beside her.

"London's an impressive, big 'little' city, if you know what I mean. Easy to get around in. Full of stuff to do, and architecture to marvel at, and the flowers! Flowers are everywhere in the parks, hanging in front of shops, on even the poorest stoops." She opened her eyes and frowned at Jill's garden. "You wouldn't make it in England. They require flowers to actually have blooms in the UK."

"Don't pick on me. You know how summers are here. How's Ham doing with his work?"

Carly closed her eyes again. "He's spending a lot of time in Asia, Japan in particular. When he's home he sleeps and locks himself in his study."

"What's going on, Carly? Are you two having trouble?"

"No."

"Are you lying to me?" Jill asked.

After a long pause, Carly sat up. "Yes. Actually, I think Ham is having an affair. And I think he wants a divorce."

"Oh no!" Jill reached out and put her hand on Carly's arm. "Has he said that? Why would he want a divorce?"

"I don't think he's in love with me anymore." Her voice shattered.

"Carly! Why? You have to tell me more than that. What's happened? Do you fight all the time?"

Her friend, always so strong and confident, hung her head. "No. But he's very distant. Uninterested, even in Julia. I was hoping he and I could get some intimate time together on this trip. Get out to the beach, go for a drive. Be together and catch up. But now, he's not even here." Her face was a picture of misery. "I'm going to be one of those statistics. Married at twenty-five. Divorced and a single mother a decade later."

Jill hugged her friend. "Don't jump to conclusions. You need to talk to him. Maybe get some counseling. Surely he's feeling stressed if you are. You need to confront him."

"I know. But I'm not as good at that as you are. You know he has no family at all. He only had one Uncle when he came to London, but that guy died. So it's just me and our baby. I'm not sure Hamilton knows how to be a member of a family. He lives to work, I think."

"Why did you say you think he's cheating on you?"

"A couple of months ago I found a cell phone I didn't recognize stuck in a zip compartment in his luggage. I asked him about it, and he blew me off, said it was one he used for work, but I think he might have it so he can call another woman on it."

Jill rolled her eyes. "Did you check the activity?"

"It was password protected."

"Lots of people have more than one phone, Carly. That's not much evidence for you to jump to that conclusion he's having an affair."

"I know. We need to go to counseling, but when I brought it up he said our problems were because I expected too much from him." Carly wiped at her eyes and then plastered a huge, fake smile on her face. "But enough about me. Tell me more about Max. Is he still gorgeous, with those big-gun arms to die for? Does he still kill in bed?"

"He's a pretty amazing in all ways." Jill's face grew warm, but she her heart was aching over Carly's revelations. "I can't wait for you to see him. Let's have dinner tonight, okay? When is Hamilton expected in? Tomorrow?"

"That's what he said. We'll see if he shows up." Carly pulled out her cell and scanned the email. "Nothing from him, but there's a message from Marissa Pierce. She's sent out the final agenda for the reunion."

"Cocktails Friday, dinner dance and films of various class functions on Saturday," Jill rattled off. "Which should be a riot, Dr. Millard was in charge of compiling them. And Sunday, presentation of the class gift, a mass of remembrance, and a picnic."

Carly grinned. "For someone who didn't want to go to the reunion, you've certainly memorized the agenda."

"I am. It's because I've been obsessing that I don't have any clothes for any of those things. Except maybe the picnic."

Both women looked down at Jill's jeans.

"You're not wearing those," Carly said.

"No?"

"No. Come on, let's go open that package I brought you. It's a dress from Paris. Your color, baby pink."

Jill walked to the screen door and pulled it open. She heard her phone vibrate on the coffee table. "I'll try it on right now. And then let's go shopping. I made hair and nail appointments for tomorrow morning at 10 a.m. But I need to grab my phone, first." She pointed at Carly's face. "And you need some sunscreen or you're going to get burned, Miss English Rose."

"I know. I'm done here." Carly got up from the lounger and followed Jill inside, but took a detour to the bathroom.

Jill grabbed her cell. The caller ID said private.

Maybe it's Andrew. I can get that money back to him today if it is. "Hello?" Jill said.

"It's Dave. Is Carly there with you?"

"Yes. Is everything alright?"

"I've found out some new information I need you to have. Can I come by now?"

"Sure. But, what about Carly?"

"It's time to share things with her. Carly knows how to keep her mouth shut."

"Oh. Okay, great. Can I call Max and ask him to come over too?" Her heart felt as if it was located in her throat. She put her hand on her neck and swallowed hard.

"No, don't do that. I'll be there in fifteen minutes."

He disconnected.

Jill stared numbly at the phone for a moment, registering that she had missed a call from Professor Millard last night, and two from Max this morning. She put the cell on the table and took a deep breath.

She tried not to worry about why Dave Hart did not want her to tell Max what was going on. But as she sat on the edge of the sofa, doubt filled her heart.

Chapter 13

"I found out why the feds are focusing their hunt for Ben Pierce's killer on your college class. A ring was found at a crime scene in France. It was badly damaged in the fire set to cover Ben's murder. They were able to establish it was from St. John Vianney College, and your graduating class."

Dave and Jill had told Carly the whole story about Ben Pierce's murder, about Andrew and his proposition to her to spy for him, as well as the details Dave had found out surrounding Ben's death.

Carly sat next to Jill on the sofa, and both women stared at Carly's dad.

"But you left out the most important thing," Carly said. "Who did Ben Pierce meet with? Surely someone knows."

Dave blinked. "Both of my sources say no one knows the man's name. And Ben's ring was on his body, so they think the one they found must belong to the murderer."

"And the murder happened in Paris, right?" Jill asked. *Where Max lives.* A coincidence that was feeling more and more sinister to her worried brain.

"Yes." Dave clasped his hands together. "Ben was part of a team investigating a multi-national investment fraud case, and the conference was a cover for him to meet with representatives for several governments."

"One thing I don't understand is, why does Andrew think this classmate, whoever he is, would show up to the reunion?" Carly asked.

"He said he would be checking to see if anyone has been asking questions about Ben Pierce's death," Jill replied.

"That sounds farfetched," Carly said.

"I agree," Dave said. "What the ATF can't nail down is why anyone would kill Ben. Unless the classmate Ben made contact with was somehow linked to the fraud investigation, they don't see a motive for the guy to murder him."

"The cops are sure it wasn't random? Like a burglary or something?" Jill cleared her throat. "That happens sometimes, doesn't it?"

"Yes, but the class ring is a big deal. Personal effects were missing from the hotel, too, although Ben's wallet was found in the room, so it wasn't an addict looking for cash." Dave checked his wristwatch. "Look, I have to head out. You two know a whole lot more than any other civilians, so you need to be very careful with what you say, okay? I understand Ben's family was only told he died in a fire."

"So Marissa doesn't know her brother was murdered." Jill asked.

"No."

"This class ring that was found," Carly asked. "Couldn't anyone just buy one?"

"The FBI checked with the class ring company, and they won't sell a ring to anyone who can't prove they are entitled to it."

"Wow. I never knew that," Carly said.

"Schools don't like it when people fake a connection to their institution, and historically the ring manufacturers have been very strict." Dave sat back and sighed. "At the risk of sounding like a broken record, let me also say I don't want either of you telling Max, or anyone else, about Ben's murder."

"Dad, that's ridiculous," Carly argued. "How can Jill not share this with Max? Andrew implied Max might be involved. I think she should tell him that."

"Are you comfortable trusting Max with that information?" Dave stared intently at Jill.

For a moment the room was silent.

"Are you asking me if I suspect him?"

Dave nodded.

"No, I don't." Jill inhaled. "I can't vouch for his behavior the last fifteen years, but I've found him to be the same admirable guy I knew years ago. I mean he's different in some ways than the boy I once knew, but I am, too. Everyone is. People change in many ways, but still have the same core morals of the person you first meet, right?"

"He's not wearing a St. John's ring, by any chance, is he?" Dave asked.

"No. And I don't remember that he even bought one. But that doesn't prove anything. I'm not wearing mine either, in fact I don't even know where it is." She cocked her head at Carly. "Do you know where yours is?"

"Ham wears his all the time, but I didn't get one. I spent the money Dad gave me on shoes, as I remember." Carly glanced at her father. "But you always have yours on. Right?"

Dave held up his right hand. "Notre Dame. Class of 1973." The stone twinkled in the silver setting, an homage to the virgin mother's holy blue robes. "Same setting as they've always had. Like St. John's. Mine doesn't have the graduating year, though. But yours do. Which is how they zeroed in on your class."

"This is so gruesome to even be talking about." Jill shivered. "To think someone we once knew might have turned out to be not only a crook, but a murderer."

"In this big old world, some people take the wrong path." Dave stood. "Okay, I need to head out. I'll be in touch." He kissed Carly and the two women walked with him to the front door.

Carly's face showed the strain of the conversation. "I'll be over with the baby on Saturday, Dad. We've got a lot going on with the reunion, but I'm staying on another week, so don't worry about not getting your baby fix."

"I won't." He hugged Jill.

"Thanks again, Dave, for all your help."

"Sure thing. You ladies have fun shopping. And remember, keep this conversation between the three of us for now."

"We will." Jill shut the door and turned to Carly. "Wow."

"Wow is right. What a drama!"

"You're not mad I didn't tell you about all this earlier?"

"No, of course not. Dad made it clear he told you not to say anything, so I'm glad you listened to him." Carly hugged her. "How creepy is it that poor Ben Pierce was murdered! I never imagined anything like that would happen to someone we knew."

"It's horrible. And it's also so weird that Andrew is involved in trying to solve the crime. He's the only guy I know who was in prison, and now he's an investigator." Jill shook her head. "He has tried pretty hard to get me to doubt Max. He was always jealous of him. We didn't talk about Max more than once or twice when we were married, but Andrew seemed to resent that I was involved with Max in college."

"That doesn't surprise me. Andrew had the hots for you back then."

"What? I never noticed that. He kept his distance until well after we graduated."

"I'm not surprised you didn't pick up on Andrew's infatuation. Max had your full attention, and he has always been a winner, and Andrew's always been a loser. It's no wonder Andrew was jealous. He hung around and waited for his chance."

"You make him sound like a stalker."

"Well?" Carly narrowed her eyes. "Were you telling my dad the whole truth about Max? You really do trust him completely?"

"Yes." Jill touched her chest. "People can change their appearance and goals, even their basic outlook on life. But that thing that happens when an old friend comes back into your life, that recognition in your heart, that can't be wrong, can it?"

"Sometimes we want something so badly we convince ourselves a lie is the truth." Carly sighed.

Was Carly was talking about herself? "I trust my instincts about Max."

"And I trust you, so that's settled." Carly smiled. "Okay, now for the hard part. Even though there might be a psycho in our midst, we still need fabulous new clothes to show the girls we were in school with how awesome we are fifteen years later. It's time to shop."

"I'm ready." Jill ran her hands through her hair. "I don't know what to do with this mop. Do you think I should go shorter?"

"Maybe. And some highlights." Carly smiled. "But you look so pretty. Like a woman in love. God, has it gone that far already with Max?"

The question brought color to Jill's face. "We're not kids any more. No one falls in love in a week, especially with someone who lives on another continent. I'm attracted to the guy, but I don't think love is what's going on there."

"Love can overcome time and geography when it's real." Carly eyes filled with tears. "Come on, let's go shopping."

"Oh, Carly." Jill touched her friend's hand. "Is there more to tell about Hamilton?"

"No. I was thinking about you."

"Come on, Carly. Spill."

"I've got nothing more to say about that man of mine, other than the fact he's still the man I love." Carly grinned and wiped her eyes. "He's so sweet with Julia, and with me when he is around. I should be content with that I guess."

Jill knew her friend was done talking about her marriage for now. Pushing Carly never worked. "Good. He's probably enjoying this visit to his past. I wonder if he'll be shocked about what we all look like now." She laughed and handed Carly her purse. "Do you think anyone will be unrecognizable?"

"We'll figure out who people are." She hugged Jill. "Though all anyone will be talking about is you and Max! Everyone loves a second chance at love story."

"Is that what it is?" Jill grinned. "We'll see. But for now we need some party clothes."

"This is shocking." Carly followed her out into the garage. "I don't think I've ever seen you eager to go shopping."

"See?" Jill opened the car door. "People do change, like I told your dad."

"They don't change that much," Carly said. "We both need to remember that."

"My god, you are twice as handsome as you were fifteen years ago." Carly reached her arms around Max and gave him a warm hug.

"Thank you." Max winked at Jill, who was standing behind Carly at the bar in the hotel lobby where the Stewarts were staying.

"You're both gorgeous." He released Carly and embraced Jill, kissing her softly on the mouth. When he drew back, he squinted. "Is your hair different?"

Both women laughed and Jill's right hand nervously flew to her hair.

"Yes." Carly answered. "Bravo for noticing, Max. She spent half a week's salary on getting a new look while staying exactly the same. I think she was afraid people wouldn't know who she was."

"I would know her no matter how she altered her appearance." Max smiled wider.

Jill blushed. "So what did you do with yourself today? Were your ears burning? Carly asked me a hundred questions about you."

"I was on the phone most of the time, but I did have a couple of moments where I worried about what was being said about Jill's prodigal lover returning to town." He pulled her closer to him, his arm draped around her shoulders. "Did you tell your best friend I'm better than ever?"

"At what?" Carly demanded. "Jill was very light on details."

"At everything. Especially my English. I bet you can't even hear my Swedish accent now, *ja*?"

They all laughed and Jill relaxed a bit. She had been nervous about Carly's reaction to Max, but so far it was what she had hoped. A few minutes later, they followed the hostess to a booth in the corner of the restaurant.

"Will Hamilton be joining us soon?" Max asked.

"That's the plan." Carly's voice lost a degree of warmth. "He sent his apologies to you both, by the way, for his late arrival. He should be here shortly."

Jill thought of the look on Carly's face when her cell phone rang a couple of hours ago. They had been playing with baby Julia upstairs in Carly's suite when Hamilton rang to say he had landed at LAX.

Carly's mood had changed after she took the call from her husband, and the tension in her best friend's face spoke volumes.

"Where is he flying in from?" Max asked. "London?"

"No, he was in Hong Kong," Carly replied. "At least that's where he said he was." She narrowed her eyes at Max. "How are we girls ever supposed to know where our men really are now, though? With cell phones it's hard to be sure, isn't it?"

Max's expression remained neutral, but Jill's cheeks

pinked. Carly was trying to drag them into the skirmish she was in the midst of with her husband.

"What looks good to everyone?" Jill picked up the menu. "I'm famished. Carly and I didn't have lunch thanks to her 'shop till you faint from hunger' strategy, so let's order appetizers while we're waiting for Hamilton."

"Excellent." Max gestured for the waitress and they ordered food and more drinks.

Jill was enjoying her wine as Max regaled Carly with a story about driving in downtown Los Angeles when someone tapped her on the back.

"Hi, Jill!"

Jill turned toward the female voice and came face-to-face with a woman she did not recognize, holding hands with a man she did.

The redhead smiled broadly. "It's me, Marissa Pierce," she said, throwing an arm around Jill's neck. "And I think you know this guy," she said, pointing with her thumb at her date.

Jill and Andrew locked glances, neither one bit happy to discover the other in such close proximity. Anger flared in her as she thought of his visit to her mother's, but she did not want to broach that subject in front of the group.

"Hello, Andrew," she said coolly.

"Jill."

He seemed slightly off-balance, but not worried enough to indicate he knew she had found out about the check.

"I bet you didn't recognize me, Jill," Marissa said with a giggle. "Most people haven't."

"Well, no, actually, I didn't. But you look great." Jill kissed her old classmate on the cheek, the awkward girl Marissa once was completely obliterated by the stunning woman standing by the table. She bore scant similarity to her old self, except for her unfortunately screechy voice. "I'm sorry I haven't caught up with you on the phone before this, so it's great to see you."

"Oh, that's okay." Marissa smiled brightly. "I've been hard to get a hold of. Between running the reunion and getting reacquainted with Andrew, I've been busy, busy, busy!"

Reacquainted with Andrew. Jill's eyes widened. *Oh my god, I forgot Marissa and Andrew dated in college.*

"Well," Jill said brightly, raising her eyebrows. "I think you both probably remember Carly Stewart and Max Kallstrom from college. Max, this is Marissa Pierce and, uh, Andrew Denton."

Max gave Marissa, whose emerald-green dress was cut to her navel, a brief hug. "Please." He gestured to the chair next to Marissa. "Won't you both join us?"

Carly kicked Jill under the table. Jill kicked her back.

Marissa plopped into the chair. Her huge breasts were dangerously close to spilling out of her dress

"I can't believe it," Marissa gushed. "You all look so amazing. You haven't changed at all, Carly, except maybe for your hair. I idolized you in college, did you know that?"

"Well, no, I didn't," Carly said, an edge of snark in her voice. "You've certainly blossomed, Marissa. I wouldn't have recognized you, except for that voice. Once a cheerleader, always a cheerleader."

Jill frowned at Carly, but her friend ignored her.

"I know, right?" Marissa prattled. "I mean, I've lost a ton of weight, and changed my hair. I could be a totally different person for all you know. I feel like one," she added giddily. "But Max, look at you! I never, ever thought we'd see you again after the car accident. Why the heck did you disappear like that? I thought you were dead."

"Yes, do tell us, Max. We're all eager to hear how you've returned from the dead." Andrew's voice dripped sarcasm.

"Well, I'm back from Europe, not the dead." Max shot a look at Jill as if to say *here goes*, and gave a brief explanation of what happened to him in the aftermath of the car crash. "And when I found out from Professor Millard that there was going to be a reunion, it seemed like the perfect time to reconnect with old friends."

"Seems to have worked out great for you." Andrew cut his eyes to Jill. "Did it hurt your feelings that your old boyfriend didn't remember your pretty face?"

"I don't get my feelings hurt easily," Jill replied smoothly. "When Max told me the truth about what happened, I understood."

"The truth will set you free," Carly said. "This is a well-known fact." She drained her glass.

Jill watched her friend nervously.

"I'm very lucky Jill is such a warm and understanding woman," Max said. "I went to her first to explain when I got into town, and because of her reaction, I decided I could take you all on. But I'm sure Jill's ability to be kind and forgiving isn't news to any of her friends."

"Oh, it might be news to Andrew here," Carly said sharply.

Marissa's eyes widened and Andrew glowered.

Jill realized then that Carly was drunk. Between the wine in her hotel suite and what they had at the bar, she had quite a bit.

"Well, as good as it is to see you all, I'm afraid I have to give you some sad news," Marissa said. "I don't know if you all remember my brother, Ben. He was two years ahead of us at St. John's." Her eyes glistened. "Ben died in a hotel fire in France a few months ago, I'm sorry to say. It's been very tough for me and my family, but I wanted to get the word out as many of you were friends with him."

Jill blinked. Across from her, Max froze and Carly stared straight ahead. Andrew shifted in his seat as a look Jill could not decipher flashed over his face.

"I'm so sorry to hear this." Jill covered Marissa's hand

with her own. "During his senior year, Ben and I had a couple of classes together. He was always so fun to be around."

Marissa nodded. "He was, wasn't he? Always the life of the party. I would have notified his friends about the funeral, but my folks wanted to keep it private. This has gutted my parents. And I still can't believe it."

"Ben would be proud of you for pulling the reunion off, Marissa," Jill said. "It can't have been an easy task."

"Actually, it helped keep my mind occupied. But as for the reunion, boy could I tell you some stories about how hard it is to track some people down. Andrew was a big help when I reached out to him," the redhead said. "He was the one who found Max's address. But speaking of old classmates, did you all see Eddie Fitzhugh's wife? She's a famous model! They live in Switzerland, I think. I had to call three different times before she would speak English to me and put Eddie on the phone." Marissa chaptered on, listing another dozen people and providing vivid physical descriptions, along with a narrative of what careers they were involved with.

Jill filed away the information that Andrew had tracked Max down, as the names Marissa dropped ping-ponged around inside her head. She met Max's glance and saw he was staring intently at Marissa.

Andrew stood up abruptly. "Come on, let's let these folks eat their dinner, Marissa. Good to see you, Carly. Max."

Marissa stood at the same time Max did and grabbed him for another hug. "I'll see you all tomorrow night at the cocktail party!"

Andrew took her by the right elbow and hustled her toward the exit.

Max sat down and sighed. "Well, so that's Marissa." He raised his eyebrows at Jill. "And Andrew. He's a good-looking guy. Not much of a scar."

"He's a dick," Carly said.

"Carly, please."

"He's a dick and Marissa is a bimbo," Carly said. "I mean, I feel bad about her brother, but how clueless can you be to dress like that for an event like this? She looks like a hooker. If I were Andrew I'd be worried she's looking to trade up before the evening is over." She squinted at Max. "Do you think her boobs are fake?"

"I have no comment," Max said with a chuckle.

"Carly, don't be unkind," Jill said softly. "Fake boobs or not, she's just dressing like that to get attention. Actually, I think she's sweet. And I can't imagine what she's gone through losing her brother."

"Yes," Max said, his voice hard. "What a terrible loss."

"Especially under those circumstances," Carly agreed.

"What circumstances?" Max narrowed his eyes, as if sensing he had missed something.

"I'm sure Carly means the fire. Didn't you hear Marissa say Ben died in a hotel fire in Paris?"

"I heard her say in France. Was it in Paris?"

Jill froze and bit her lip. "I think so. I think that's what she said."

Max stared at her. "Wherever it happened, its terrible news."

"Let's talk about something more uplifting." Jill moved Carly's wineglass to the center of the table. "And why don't you eat something? The shrimp cocktail is delicious."

Carly grabbed her glass and waved it at Max. "The Chardonnay is filling me up nicely. Would you pour me another, please?"

Max picked up the wine bottle.

Jill sighed and turned her attention to the restaurant entrance, her brain reeling with the encounter with Andrew. *I need to be careful what I say,* she scolded herself, noticing that Marissa had stopped and wrapped herself around a new arrival. The man she was latched on to was tall and fair, his white shirt and superbly tailored suit proclaiming another man of the world had arrived.

Andrew stood off to the side watching, arms crossed over his chest. His body language shouted that he wished the evening was over.

It was a feeling Jill shared, particularly as she recognized the man Marissa was mauling. "Hamilton's here, Carly."

"Oh, goody," her friend replied, and drained her glass of wine in a gulp.

Chapter 14

Jill studied Hamilton Stewart's profile.

While Max was handsome in a guy next door kind of way, Hamilton had refined and classic features, a firm chin, high cheekbones, and a strong forehead.

His blond hair was lighter than Jill remembered from school, but then, as she sat watching and listening to his back and forth comments with Max about the world financial conditions and markets, she had not known him well before he left college to go to Oxford.

And she had seen him only twice since then.

What she did remember from her college days was that Hamilton was a quiet kind of guy who kept to himself and rarely socialized. She frowned. He had been orphaned very young, and had a rich relative somewhere in the UK who paid for his schooling, if she remembered right.

The most vivid recollection she had was of him playing piano in the student talent show their junior year. He was a near virtuoso, energetic and commanding when immersed in his music, leaving the crowd and Professor Millard in awe over his expertise.

Jill stared at his hands. He wore no rings and had long, graceful fingers, feminine almost. She glanced at Carly, who was also watching him, a rapt look on her face.

Her friend had not touched her meal, but seemed more relaxed than she had been before Hamilton showed up, though nothing about her was the animated and confident woman Jill was used to seeing in a social setting.

Carly had listened without comment when Max repeated the accident and loss of memory details to Hamilton, who seemed completely absorbed in Max's story. She had however, stopped drinking once Hamilton hugged and warmly kissed her hello.

Jill pushed her plate away and tipped the last of the wine into her mouth. The look in Max's eyes said he was ready to leave.

"Are you two ready to take off?" Hamilton asked. "I've been monopolizing the conversation, I fear."

"I have enjoyed myself completely," Max said.

"As have I." Hamilton turned to Carly. "You look ravishing tonight, wife of mine. Did you and Jill spend all day in the salons to get ready for the festivities?"

"We did some shopping and pampering," Carly replied. "Doesn't she look fabulous? While the haircut is great, I think its Max that's put that smile in her eyes."

"I take no credit for anything." Max said. "Except agreeing with you. Jill Farrell is stunning."

"Stop it, you guys. It'll make me break out in zits or something," Jill said.

Hamilton studied her. "They're right. You look like you did when you were in college. Your yearbook photo shows the quintessential California girl. A smile for everyone, and always tanned, blonde, and beautiful."

"Did Hamilton ever tell you he had a secret crush on you back then?" Carly blurted out.

"Carly, don't be silly," Jill said, her face warming.

"My wife imagines I'm in love with everyone all the time," Hamilton said. "But I was, as most of the fellows were, an admirer. And still am."

"Well, if you did have a crush, you had good taste, then and now," Max said. "Your wife is one of the most gorgeous women I've ever seen."

"Thank you, Max," Carly said. "But I'm telling the truth about Ham mooning over Jill. After our wedding reception he kept saying he couldn't believe how pretty you were."

"I'm flattered, Hamilton. I thought you were quite a catch, long before sister Carly there noticed you."

"Oh, I noticed him in college," Carly protested. "I just didn't appreciate him until I met him in London."

"You needed your taste to mature," Hamilton said.

"Your two were fated to meet again." Max glanced at Jill. "I know how that is to rediscover someone. It's fantastic when it works out."

"Like you and Jill," Carly said. "I should have drug her to England with me on that trip, maybe we would have bumped into you."

"I'm not in London much," Max said. "Now if you'd gone to Paris, who knows?"

Jill cleared her throat and looked away. She was feeling nervous suddenly. "Was it hard for you to leave sunny California behind, Carly, for that cool, misty fog of London?"

"It's never foggy," Carly replied. "That's an urban myth. Like the Bobbies not being armed. Or everyone stopping what they're doing to have a lovely tea in the afternoon. The cops have guns now, and unless you spend a fortune and wait an hour to be served in a crowded bakery, 'tea' is a Diet Coke and a packet of crisps."

"Surely you and Julia have a proper tea at home in the afternoon," Hamilton said. "I've seen the leftover scones and raspberry jam. Aren't you being a hard on the Brits, love?"

"Maybe. I think mostly I'm tired." Carly put her hand over his. "Let's go up to our room and let Jill and Max have the rest of the evening to themselves. I'm sure our daughter will be up at some point in the night, her sleeping schedule is out of sync with the time zone."

"Of course." Hamilton waved the waiter over. He and Max jockeyed over the bill for a moment, but Hamilton prevailed and signed it to his room. He stood to help Carly out of the booth. She was unsteady, but it seemed to Jill it was due more to the new high heels than her friend's liquid dinner.

"Max. Jill. We'll see you tomorrow. Cocktails with the old friends, right? Are we all looking forward to that?" Carly asked.

"Like dentistry," Jill cracked, and they all laughed.

Max and Jill parted with Carly and Hamilton in the lobby and headed for the front door. "So will I see you tomorrow before the party?" she asked. "Do you want to pick me up?"

"I thought I might drive you home tonight."

Jill smiled. "My car is here. How would you get back to the hotel?"

"I thought maybe you'd drive me. In the morning."

"In the morning? Are you suggesting you want to stay the night at my place?"

"Oh, I'm not suggesting it. I'm demanding it." His voice was intense with emotion and he pulled her tight against him.

Jill shivered in anticipation of another night in bed with Max. She handed the valet her keys. "I'm a modern woman, Max. Not sure I like you demanding things."

"You can demand right back. I'll try to do whatever you want."

A buttery rush of want warmed the center of her. "Well then, okay. Carly and I have a couple of things scheduled tomorrow afternoon, so I'll drop you here and then we'll rendezvous later for the party."

"Hey, Jill, hold up for a minute!" a female voice behind her called out.

Max and Jill turned around.

Marissa Pierce and Andrew once again stood a few feet behind them, just outside the door of the hotel.

Jill stiffened. The earlier encounter between Max and Andrew had been uncomfortable, but she was hoping that

Max might have defused some of Andrew's suspicions. Across the open space, her gaze locked with her ex-husband's, who was staring at Max with a look that said nothing had changed.

Jill slipped her arm through Max's. "We were just leaving," she said. It was rude, but she did wanted to leave. It was killing her not to confront Andrew over going to see her mother without her permission, but she didn't want to give her ex-husband any opening to escalate things with Max.

"We are, too," Marissa said. "Wouldn't it be fun to stop and have a drink somewhere? We can drop you at your place later. Andrew has a car."

"We don't have time to ferry Jill and her friend around, Marissa. It's late," Andrew said.

"Oh, of course we do. I want to talk to Jill a bit more. I haven't seen her in years." Marissa smiled, obviously tipsy. "God, how gorgeous is Hamilton Stewart? And Carly, has she had work done?"

"No." Jill forced a laugh. "No, Carly's just as god made her."

"Some girls have all the luck, don't they?" Marissa said. She peered closer at Jill's face. "I heard your mother isn't well. What's wrong with her?"

Jill and Andrew locked glances.

"She's in a nursing home. Early onset Alzheimer's," Jill said to Marissa. "Thank you for asking."

"Oh, I'm so sorry. That's the thing where you can't remember anyone, right?"

"Well, that's only part of what it does."

"I went to see your mother, Jill." Andrew said abruptly. "That's a nice place you've moved her into. I'm sure she'll get the care she deserves there."

Jill bit her lip as Max gave her an inquiring look. *Well, so much for heading off a confrontation.*

"I heard." Jill held out her hand. "Would you please give

me one of your business card so I can put a check in the mail to you tomorrow? And for your information, you aren't on the approved visitor list. So please don't go there again. My mother is not up to it."

"You're being a bit melodramatic, don't you think?" Andrew folded his arms. "I just wanted to help you out. Our divorce settlement gave you only a pittance, as I remember. And I have great regard for your mother, who was always very kind to me. Please keep the money, Jill. I'm sure on a teacher's salary, it will come in handy."

"Ah, you sure we shouldn't all just go have a drink?" Marissa said.

"The lady asked for your card." Max's voice was low as he ignored Marissa's question. "Do you have one on you?"

"This is no concern of yours, Kallstrom," Andrew said.

"It is if it involves Jill and her family." Max held out his hand very close to Andrew's chest. "Your card?"

Andrew reached into his coat pocket and took one out, which he handed to Jill with a flourish, the red stone in the St. John's class ring her ex-husband was wearing flashing in the night air.

She took the card. "Thank you. Goodnight."

"See you lovebirds tomorrow at the party." Marissa seemed confused at the tension between everyone. "Should be fun watching everyone get reacquainted."

The valet pulled up with Jill's car. Max held the door for her. Their eyes met. "So you and Andrew reconnected before tonight?"

"Yes." She sounded defensive. "I didn't mention it before because I didn't want to think about it."

Max's jaw tightened. "I'll be right back. Stay put."

She got in the car as Max walked over to Andrew.

"I don't remember you from college, as you know," she heard Max say. "But Jill reminded me that I thought you were a *röv hål*. It's nice to know I was right about that." He nodded. "Marissa, it's been lovely to make your re-acquaintance."

Max walked around the car and got in.

Jill turned away from the pair staring at her. "Feel better now?"

"*Ja.*" Max pulled at his collar. "You should have told me he was giving you trouble."

"Why? I can handle him."

Max pursed his lips.

She put her hand on his thigh. "Let's not go tomorrow," she said as Max clicked his seat belt into place and put the car in gear.

"Because of Andrew?"

"No. Because the past is over. Let's concentrate on the now."

He squared his jaw. "There's nothing for you to be afraid of from Andrew. I'll be there."

She wanted to scoff at Max's words and tell him he had misread why she did not want to go to the reunion party. But he had not.

She did feel anxious about her ex suddenly. He clearly had an agenda, and did not seem to care who knew it. This was a more aggressive side of Andrew than the man she remembered.

"What was all that about a check?" Max asked.

Dave's caution not to discuss anything about Andrew's investigation slammed into her mind. *Hell with it*, she thought. "He went to see my mother at the assisted living home, and left a check to pay some of her expenses."

"I see." He turned and peered at her. "It sounds like you think he was presumptuous."

"More like manipulative. Which is why I'm not keeping the money." She touched Max's arm. "I don't want anything to do with him. I think after tonight he understands that."

"You think so?"

"Yes," she answered firmly. "He's nothing to worry about."

He looked sideways at her. "I'm not worrying," he said quickly. "Why would I?"

"I just meant . . ."

"Sorry. I'm acting too possessive, *ja?*"

"*Ja*. But it's okay." And it was.

They drove on in silence. Jill stared out the window and wished it was a week from now, when the whole reunion ordeal would be over and everyone would leave Santa Barbara and return to the world where they belonged.

Including Max, she thought. With a pang, she realized that wasn't something she wanted at all.

Jill woke with a jerk, a version of the "I'm-falling-off-the-side-of-a-mountain" dream spinning inside her head. For a moment she wasn't sure where she was.

The recognition she was in her own bedroom snapped into place. It was dark and quiet and she squinted at the clock, but could not read it. With a sigh, she rolled over to snuggle next to Max, but the bed was empty. She sat up so quickly her head hurt.

"Max?" she called softly.

The dull buzz of her neighbor's air conditioner going on was the only sound wafting in through her open window. She got up and padded down the hallway. He was not in the bathroom or living room. Rubbing her arms up and down for warmth, she walked into the kitchen, the window lit from a spill of light from the huge moon outside.

She peered out her kitchen window and caught her breath. Max, barefoot and dressed in his suit pants and a white tee shirt, was leaning against a dark car parked in the driveway, talking to a man with bright red hair wearing a black leather jacket. She squinted but could not see who it was.

The kitchen clock read four-fifteen.

What the heck is going on? She glanced down at her nightgown, a sheer blue lace not adequate for her neighbors' eyes.

She hurried back to her bedroom and grabbed her robe and slipped her feet into sandals. When she got to the front door, it opened.

Max stopped and put his right hand against his chest in surprise. "Whoa, what are you doing up?"

She inhaled sharply. "Sorry I startled you. But I woke up and you weren't there, so I started checking and . . ."

"I stepped outside for a smoke," he interrupted. "Couldn't sleep for some reason. I have one every now and then." He pulled a lighter and a pack of cigarettes out of his pants pocket. "See?"

But who were you talking to? She pursued her lips to ask the question, but the realization Max was not going to volunteer the fact he had been talking with the man in the leather jacket stopped her.

Why isn't he telling me about that? And who was that man?

"You smoke? How European," she said instead. "Why didn't you go out onto the back patio?"

"I didn't want to wake you opening the drapes and the slider, but it seems I did. Let's go back to bed." He rested his stubbly chin on the top of her head and put his arm around her. "It's too early to be up."

She walked with him down the shadowy hallway, but stopped at the doorway. Her heart pounded. "I saw you talking to someone outside. Who was it?"

"Oh. You did? You should have said something." He dropped his arm from her shoulders. "It was just a guy. He was walking the neighborhood, looking for his dog."

"In the middle of the night? Whose car was in the driveway?"

"It was his. He parked there and walked the cul de sac, calling the dog. I came outside as he was coming up the sidewalk, and asked him what he was doing in the driveway." Max leaned against the doorframe. "This is an odd conversation. I feel like you think I was hiding this for some reason. I didn't mention it because I didn't want you worrying."

"Worrying? What would I be worrying about?"

"That some random guy is parking in your driveway. Your place got broken into a few days ago, so I didn't want to make a big deal out of it."

"Okay, got it. So let's not make a big deal out it." Jill walked past him into the bedroom.

He followed her. In silence, he pulled off his clothes.

Jill took off her robe and stared at his scarred but powerful body. Their earlier lovemaking had been, if possible, even more satisfying than their first fervent couplings as the newly reacquainted versions of themselves. A few hours ago, she was completely at ease with him.

Safe.

But as she crawled into bed next to Max, earlier doubts she had about certain things burned brighter in her mind.

What do I actually know about this man?

She pulled up the covers as Max embraced her from behind, rubbing his body against her bottom suggestively.

"I want you." He nibbled her shoulder.

"Go back to sleep," she murmured. "I need my beauty rest."

He sighed. "Ah, yes. Tonight we come face to face with the past, and see if we measure up."

"Measure up?"

"Pass the test. Convince everyone I'm not that terrible

guy they thought I was."

"Is that why you're going to the reunion?" She turned to him. "Do you care what those people think, people you don't even remember?"

"I do. It eats at me, what they must have thought of me after I disappeared. How I hurt you. But mostly I care about what you think." He reached out to touch her face, but stopped, his hand falling to the sheet. "I'm sorry if I'm going too fast, but I'm falling hard for you, Jill."

Shock raced through her at his words, his sentiments that so clearly mimicked what she had told Carly about her own growing feelings for him. But instead of elation, Jill shut her emotions down.

She needed to think. About a lot of things.

She touched her fingers to his lips. "Good night." Jill turned over, leaving a space between them, and squeezed her eyes closed, dizzy with conflicting emotions.

This past week, at least six different people from her past had stormed back into her life. The thought of seeing dozens more in the next few days made her feel like she did when she was sick from too many Kirs. Especially as one of them could be a murderer.

But who?

She pressed her hand to her belly and took a deep, steadying breath.

An hour later, as Max snored, Jill knew she was not going to be able to go back to sleep. She crept out of bed, a cold lump of fear coiled in her stomach.

She wasn't sure what she was afraid of exactly, but she was afraid. With that thought, she shut the door of the bedroom and went to sit alone and stare out at the night.

Chapter 15

"Professor Millard, you look lovely, especially your necklace." Jill gave the slight woman a hug, intercepting her at the doorway of the main room at Hill House, where St. John's reunion cocktail party was in full swing.

"It's my very favorite piece," Professor Millard replied, rubbing the heavy coral and turquoise beads with her gnarled fingers. "I feel the sunshine in the stone, no matter how cold it is outside."

"Well, it's spectacular." Jill nodded toward the party. "Shall we go in? There are over eighty of your old students here. It's a huge turnout."

Millard clutched Jill's arm. "Is the handsome Max Kallstrom with you?"

"Yes. He's at the bar with Carly and Hamilton." Things had been strained between them this morning, and again this evening when she picked him up at the hotel.

Jill knew Max was perplexed at her reaction to his statements. She was too, she realized, but her skittishness had more to do with all the things she knew but could not share with him. "Do you want me to go get Max for you?"

"No, I want to talk to you alone about something before we go into that mob. Can you come outside on the porch with me for a moment?"

"Certainly." Jill linked arms with the professor and walked out onto the rustic veranda. They were three thousand feet up in the mountains and the sunset was melting into the ocean thirty miles away.

They sat in chairs at the end of the porch.

"I was visited by two men from the government yesterday," Professor Millard began. "In my office. Very officious pair, grey suits and wing tip shoes. I felt for a moment like I was back at Berkley in the 1960s and about to be arrested."

"You were arrested at Berkley?"

"Of course. Twice. But that's a story for a different day." Millard leaned closer to Jill, peering toward the main entrance of the restaurant as if checking to be sure they were alone. "They asked me about several students in your class. But there were three in particular whose student files they wanted to see. Your ex, Andrew Denton, Eddie Fitzhugh, and Max."

Jill felt as if she could not move. Andrew said he was working for the government. *Why would the FBI be interested in his file? And what did it mean that they wanted Max's records?*

"They specified those three men?"

"Yes, and they were also very interested in my personal correspondence the past few years with Max."

"How did they know about that?"

"I have no idea, but one can assume he's under some sort of surveillance. I told them in no uncertain terms that they would need a warrant to access student information. And then I answered a few innocuous questions and they left." Millard snorted. "I peered out the window and saw them out in the parking lot. They stopped to speak with another man, a red-haired guy on a big motorcycle. He kept waving his arm up at the school, as if he were pointing at something."

"A motorcycle?" The one she had seen more than once this last week flashed in her brain, the red-haired man from last night looming in her memory. "Did it have a blue flame stenciled on the side?"

Millard shrugged. "I don't remember for certain. I

thought I better tell you this as you have been dragged into the orbit of two of those men. Do you know Eddie Fitzhugh?"

"He was the athletic star, right?"

"Yes. Basketball and track. Remarkably handsome. A stud, I think you girls would call him. He's a banker of some kind now I think."

"Really?" Jill's eyes widened. Another man in finance. "I didn't know Eddie that well. He wasn't in the group I ran around with."

"Poor you."

Jill smiled. "He was pretty hunky. Didn't I hear he married someone famous?"

"A model. French, I think."

Another connection to Paris. Could Eddie Fitzhugh be the man Ben Pierce had run into in Paris, Jill wondered nervously. "How predictable for a jock, huh?"

"Yes. At least when he was 20. I was hoping he would mature." Millard leaned toward her. "How are you and Max getting along?"

"It's complicated, if you want to know the truth," Jill said. "I don't know if I trust myself yet to say what I'm feeling is for the man in front of me, or the guy I used to love."

"Go slow with him, Jill. I find Max much changed. Much more melancholy," Millard coughed. "What do you make of the feds' request?"

"I'm shocked, I guess. Who exactly were they? F.B.I.?"

"Their badges identified them as ATF agents. They said they were attached to a task force investigating multinational financial crimes. When I asked why those three students were of interest to them, they told me they couldn't answer my questions, thanked me, and left."

Jill's mouth went dry. Millard had not been told, evidently, that an ex-student of hers had been murdered. "Are you going to tell the guys about this? Max at least?"

"I don't think it's wise. I assumed Max was targeted

because of his work in bonds and investments and such, and because he lives in Europe. But as for Andrew, what exactly is your ex is up to these days?"

"He works as some kind of security consultant." Jill wrung her hands together, wishing she could confide all that Andrew had told her last week about Ben's murder.

"Andrew's a strange one," Millard opined. "I saw him for the first time in years last night, but when I said his name, he peered at me as if he didn't know who I was. He apologized later and said he had a lot on his mind." Millard leaned closer. "Do you think he's still involved with drugs?"

"No, I haven't seen any sign he is."

"He strikes me as someone who is hiding something. I know that look, as I have a lot of experience with that myself."

"She reached into her pocket and handed Jill a thumb drive. "I need your help. I checked through the admission records after the G-men left. Scanned in all the paper file information we had about those three. I want you to look through them and see if there is anything that strikes you as strange."

Jill's hand trembled. "Like what?"

"Did you know Andrew was adopted? The information was included in his health records along with his allergy to certain foods. Or that Max's father was evidently an employee of the Swedish government in some capacity? There was a letter from the Ambassador's office in Max's admission report explaining that personal contact data for his parents was not to be included in any permanent record. There was only a government address in Stockholm."

"No. I didn't know any of that." Max had told her a few days ago about his father traveling a lot for work, but he had not explained it was for their government.

"I don't think either of those things are alarming," Millard continued, "but before I give any one a heads-up about the feds, I'd appreciate your take. Fitzhugh was rumored to be involved in something illicit with a professor, but nothing came of it, according to a letter from the athletic director. If you don't see anything of concern, then I'll tell each of them about my visitors."

"Okay. I'll do it tonight and give you the thumb drive back tomorrow morning." Jill's pulse pounded.

"There you are! I've been looking for you two." Max's voice cut through the dark as he walked up behind them. "What are you up to? Plotting to overthrow the talent show assignments?"

"Hi, Max." Jill stuck the computer stick in the pocket of her silk jacket.

"Women are always plotting something when they sit and discuss men," Professor Millard answered calmly. She stood and took Max's arm, her gold embroidered tunic gleaming in the shadows. "Let's go get fortified, Maximilian. I have the feeling it's going to be a long night."

"Are you coming, Jill? Carly asked me to come and find you." Max's smile was smooth, but his eyes were wary.

"Yes." The thumb drive felt heavy as a lead bar in her pocket.

She followed behind the pair, her mind a tangle of anxiety about Max, secrets from the past, and a red-haired man on a motorcycle who seemed to be circling closer and closer for no good reason she could imagine.

"Well, that went about as well as I thought it would." Carly was sitting with her feet pulled up under her on the sofa.

Hamilton sat beside her, his tie off, holding a glass of Scotch. "I actually had fun," he said. "What about you two?"

Max glanced over at Jill. "I enjoyed myself. Once we got through the cocktail party and settled into dinner, I felt a lot more comfortable."

"You did great fielding all the questions," Carly said. "I would have screamed if I had to tell the same story ten times in two hours."

"I'm getting good at it," Max said.

"Yes, you're very smooth," Jill said. *Too smooth?*

Max frowned as if he read her mind.

The four were ensconced in Carly and Hamilton's luxurious hotel suite. It was nearly midnight. They had gone from the cocktail party to dinner with two other couples, both of whom had been very interested in hearing all the details about the return of Max Kallstrom more than anything else any one had accomplished in the years since college.

"Did you enjoy catching up with old friends, Jill?" Hamilton asked, his eyes intense as he stared at her.

"I did. Everyone looks great. I guess it's because they're all dressed so nicely, and don't have that goofy college hair thing going on." She took off her jacket and folded it over her purse.

She had stuck the thumb drive into her clutch, and was nervously worrying for the hundredth time what she would find on it tonight.

"I enjoyed Eddie Fitzhugh and his wife. He was fun, like in the history class I took with him." Hamilton reached his arms above his head to stretch. "But boy, can he drink. I think he downed four scotches after dinner."

"He didn't drink at all in college." Jill smiled.

"I bet he's worried about Molly," Carly said. "A model's life must be pretty exciting, full of travel and men dying to hit on her."

"I thought Molly seemed very much in love with her husband," Hamilton said. "She listened intently to him while he was regaling all of us with his stockbroker victories. If Eddie's worried, it's about something other than his wife's fidelity."

Eddie had given them a long history of how he went from ex-jock to vice-president at a major American bank.

Another classmate to wonder about, Jill thought. "Susan and Cheryl were certainly interesting. We'll have to go to their art gallery in Los Angeles. Who knew they were gay?"

"I did," Carly said. "Well, I knew Susan was, because she kissed me once, but Cheryl was a surprise." She grinned at Max. "Cheryl couldn't take her eyes off you in college. She was always mooning around after you on campus, if I remember right."

"Susan kissed you?" Jill was surprised. "When?"

"It was nothing." Carly grinned. "Lots of people kissed me."

"Max spurned Cheryl and she became a lesbian," Hamilton deadpanned.

"Hamilton!" Carly shook her head.

"I was kidding. Relax." He patted her leg. "And I agree that you were very compelling, Max, relating your amnesia story. It must be very strange, seeing people who know you, but you don't remember a thing about them."

"It wasn't a story," Carly snapped. "Honestly, sometimes you say things that imply hurtful things, Hamilton"

The other three turned to her in surprise.

"I know what Ham meant." Max raised his eyebrows. "It is strange. As if I'm an imposter in my own life."

Jill blinked, uncomfortable with that image.

"But the best part," Max continued, "was I have found everyone very kind. No one treated me rudely, or pressured me for more details, except for Marissa Pierce. When I offered my condolences again about her brother, she launched into another round of questions as to why I didn't come back to California and reconnect with my friends once I'd recovered."

"What happened to her brother?" Hamilton said.

"Oh, didn't Carly tell you?"

"No," Carly said. "We spent the evening trying to get our cranky baby to sleep. I didn't fill him in on much."

"I remember those days." Max smiled.

"So what happened to Ben?" Hamilton asked again.

"Marissa told us last night that her brother was killed in a hotel fire in France a few months ago," Jill replied.

"Tragic," Max cut in. "She said she's very upset about a lack of accountability as to the circumstances of his death. I asked what she meant, but she didn't elaborate. I'm assuming she meant his family was having trouble with an insurance settlement."

Carly and Jill exchanged looks.

"That's tough. Ben Pierce was a good chap," Hamilton said.

"You knew Ben?" Carly said.

"He was the RA for my dorm during my sophomore year. He was a good guy, gave us idiots a lot of leeway when we broke curfew and got stoned."

Jill was surprised Hamilton had led such a wild life. "Did you keep in touch with Ben after college?"

"No. No, I never saw him after I left for London. Why do you ask?"

"I was just wondering. Max said he thought he met you once, at a meeting in Switzerland. So it's a big world, but a very small one, too."

"What meeting was that?" Hamilton asked Max.

"The World Bank conference three years ago." Max wrinkled his brow. "I thought I met you at a dinner the Brazilian ambassador held at the embassy."

"Nope. Wasn't me. I didn't attend that meeting in Switzerland."

"Didn't you?" Carly said. "When I was pregnant. I thought you went to Geneva that fall?"

"No. I think I can remember where I was, Carly. Which

might be more than you'll be able to say if you keep sucking down wine like it was orange juice."

This exchange changed the dynamic in the room. Jill opened her mouth to say something, but Max cut her off.

"Sorry, I was mistaken." Max turned to Jill. "By the way, Marissa also told me that she cleaned out my dorm room after the car accident, and brought the boxes to the hospital on orders of my mother. I never heard anything about that before, did you?"

"What? No. I never heard that." Jill frowned. She had been hemmed into corners too many times during the evening and had not been able to keep as close to Max as she had wanted to.

"I'm surprised to hear that too." Carly put down her empty wineglass and studiously avoided her husband's eyes. "Why would your parents have asked her to do that? Did they think *she* was your girlfriend?"

"Carly!" Now it was Hamilton who was disapproving.

"I have absolutely no idea." Max loosened his tie and stared at Jill. "But for the record, Miss Pierce is not my type."

"Boobs like that are every man's type," Carly said.

Hamilton laughed. "She has us there, Max. Are you sure you weren't having a fling with the buxom Marissa behind Jill's back?"

"You weren't seeing anyone behind my back unless you were leading a secret life," Jill said.

"If I was, I don't remember," Max shot back. They all laughed uncomfortably.

Jill shook her head. "Gosh, I missed a lot of things tonight. I didn't see Andrew at the cocktail party, either."

"Thank god. He creeps me out," Carly said. "I don't remember him being so serious in college. Every time I saw him tonight, he was staring at someone. Usually Max." She turned to Hamilton. "I saw you talking to him."

"Did you? You should have rescued me. He's a bore." Hamilton pushed his hair off his forehead. "Anyone want more wine? I can order some."

"No, thanks, not for me. I'm glad that party is over," Jill replied. "Maybe we can skip the dinner tomorrow night. Everyone's taken a look at Max, and at me, and knows Andrew and I can co-exist in the same space. And they got to admire you two." She waved at Carly and Ham. "I heard several people comment that you are more gorgeous than you were in school, Carly. Motherhood agrees with you."

"They were lying because I've gained so much weight. I think they felt sorry for me." She nodded at Ham. "They were ogling him though, all of them." Carly said. "Fools for a man in a handmade suit and a British accent."

"I don't have a British accent," Hamilton argued.

"Yes, you do." Jill giggled. "You do, and it's very sexy. No one would think you were an American-born boy."

"Anyone who knows me would," Hamilton said.

"Oh, and those people are few and far between," Carly cracked.

The tension in the room flamed up another notch.

Max got up and sat beside Jill. He draped his arm over her shoulder. "No avoiding the dinner tomorrow. We told Professor Millard we'd come, and she's hell-bent on our doing the talent show. Didn't you agree to sing with me? Even though I don't sing."

Jill leaned into him and pulled her fingers through her hair. "Yes. I did tell her we'd do it. But only a very short version." She started humming "Kiss Me Twice," struck by how appropriate those lyrics were to describe Max and her.

"You're going to have to go on the Internet and look up the words and memorize them, Max," Carly said. "Although I think Millard is planning on running the tape of the original contest in the background, so you can fake-sing along to that."

"I'm good at fake singing," he said. "My daughter says I get the lyrics wrong when we listen to the car radio, even if I don't actually say a word."

Jill met Hamilton's eyes. "Are you going to play piano?"

"No. I don't play anymore."

"Carly said you didn't, which is a shame. I found a cassette tape of the talent show you played in junior year. You were magnificent." She turned to Max. "Hamilton won a state-wide contest. He was incredibly talented."

Hamilton frowned. "I didn't know that performance was taped. Another reason I'm not playing. The comparison from then to now would be shocking."

"You aren't going to play?" Carly frowned at her husband. "Why? Surely you don't forget how to play a piece of music on the piano? Isn't it like riding a bike and swimming? Once you learn, you never forget?"

"I haven't practiced for years. I'm not going to go on stage and make a fool of myself." Hamilton stood up. "I need to get some sleep. If you three don't mind, I'm going to head off to bed before Julia wakes everyone up and wants to play at 3 a.m."

Carly was sullen. "Fine. But I told Millard you would, so don't be surprised if she insists."

"You shouldn't have committed to that for me. You know I don't play anymore."

"Sorry. But you weren't around when Millard asked me," Carly said. "As usual you were flying off somewhere else, leaving the family commitments to me."

Hamilton turned to Max and Jill, the skin pinched around his mouth. "My apologies that you had to listen to this very familiar domestic bitch fest. My wife doesn't keep much to herself about my shortcomings." He left the room, shutting the bedroom door loudly.

The room fell silent.

"What do you say?" Max asked Jill. "I'm ready to call it a night myself."

Jill met Carly's eyes. Her friend was hurt and confused, and most of all, appeared shocked at her husband's behavior. "Why don't you go to your suite, Max? I'll drive myself home tonight."

"Okay. But if you change your mind, stop by. You can stay or I can keep you company on the drive home."

"Thanks." She walked him to the door and they shared a chaste kiss goodnight, but when he hugged her to his chest she felt the banked passion in him. Her body responded to it, though she cut the embrace short. "I'll see you tomorrow," she said firmly.

"Goodnight. Goodnight, Carly." Max pulled the door shut.

Jill sat beside her friend. "Want to talk?"

Carly lay her head on Jill's shoulder. She held up her empty wineglass. "No. I want to drink."

"Are you doing too much of that lately?"

Carly didn't say anything for a moment. Slowly she lowered the glass and set it on the table beside her. "Yes. But it's not a problem. It's a solution."

"To what?"

"To lying in bed staring at the ceiling, trying to figure out what the hell I'm doing with my life."

Jill shook her head. "We're close enough friends that I know you know that's BS."

"It is." She started to cry then, silent tears pouring down her face. "See what I mean about how Hamilton is? He flies off the handle over the oddest things. It used to be so good between us. But now he's gone all the time and when he's home he's preoccupied. He feels like a stranger to me tonight. And if I question him about anything, he gets flinty and defensive. I never know what he's thinking."

Jill hugged her. "Tell him how unhappy you are. It's clear to me he still cares about you."

"Is it?" Carly wiped her hand across her pale face. "It's not to me. I watched you and Max together, last night and tonight. Even with your worries about this whole reunion intrigue, you two are always tuned in to each other. That's how Ham and I used to be. He was there with me, heart and soul. Couldn't wait to be alone with me. That's gone now. And I don't think any amount of counseling can bring it back."

"Nothing good is easy, you know that. You've got to fight for a relationship." Jill sighed. "If Ham's being pulled a hundred different ways because of work, you have to give him a break. I mean, he doesn't even have enough time for his music anymore, right? Think for a moment how he must feel giving up something he loved and was so talented at."

"He gave it up long before we got married. In fact, I don't think I've ever seen him at a piano since we were in college. But you're right about his career." Carly hugged Jill. "I'll think about the counseling. You better get going, but please stop at Max's room. I can tell when he left all he wanted to do was be alone with you."

Jill thought of the flash drive in her purse. And of the conversation with Professor Millard earlier. "He'll be fine. I'll call you in the morning. Get some rest, okay."

"Good night." Carly made no move to get up off the sofa, and was staring at the half-full wine bottle on the counter.

Jill let herself out and walked to the elevator.

After a moment of doubt, she pressed the button for the lobby. She had to get home and look at the information Millard asked her to, though she truly wanted to stay and talk to Carly, help her think things through.

Despite her advice to her friend about counseling, she knew first hand that once some things were lost, like her mother's memory, they were lost forever. Anyone could go to a reunion, but no one could go back in time and be the person they were.

What had Max said? *As if I'm an imposter in my own life.* She pulled her jacket close around her and walked out of the hotel into the night.

Jill drove into her garage at one-forty, a.m. She let herself into the house and threw her purse down on the kitchen counter. After downing two aspirin, she checked the street through the window for strange men walking around. Satisfied the neighborhood was its boring, normal self, she stripped off her new dress, heels, and jewelry as she navigated the hallway.

She dumped all the items on her bed and pulled on her robe, then went into the office and opened her laptop. The paperwork Millard had scanned into documents was standard fare. Names, addresses, past schools. The letter from the Swedish government about Max's parents gave her pause. He had never said a single thing about his father's government service when he was here fifteen years ago, and not much this time around.

Why not?

She blew out a breath in frustration. There was nothing else of note in his file, except that his records had been sent to Oxford University ten years ago, where he had applied to graduate school.

Andrew's were a bit more surprising. His application essay recounted that he was adopted as a child in South America, where his mother was working for the United States government. There was also a letter from his guidance counselor at the ritzy prep school he attended. It was carefully worded, but said Andrew's problems were all in the past.

His health records showed the staff kept epi-pens on hand due to a severe food allergy. Jill frowned as something chewed at the corner of her brain. She sort of remembered that he made a scene once, when they were married, because she bought a jar of peanut butter. But he had never mentioned being adopted.

Jill frowned. Men keep many personal things about themselves secret. She was sure if she was adopted, or if her father worked for the government, that she would have told the men in her life about it.

She started reading through Eddie Fitzhugh's folder when her phone buzzed. The caller ID read 'Marissa Pierce.'

She stared at it as it rang a third time. Then a fourth. She pressed answer. "Hello?"

"Jill. Hi, it's Marissa. I'm sorry I'm calling you so late, but I wanted to see if we could get together tomorrow morning."

"I'll be at the party tomorrow night." Jill hoped the irritation in her voice was not as clear to Marissa as it was to her.

"I need to talk to you before that. Away from everyone," Marissa whispered.

"Are you okay? Why are you whispering?"

"I'm, uh, trying to be quiet. Can you meet me at the Canyon Inn parking lot tomorrow morning about ten? I have some things I want to explain about Ben's death." A sob escaped.

"Oh, I'm so sorry. It must be difficult to talk about Ben with his old friends."

"It is. More than you understand. But more importantly, I also want to talk to you about Andrew."

Jill frowned. "Marissa, I don't want to discuss my ex-husband with you."

"It's not about personal stuff. I can't go into it right now, but he has told me some of the weirdest things, and I think you need to know about them."

"What things?"

"I'll tell you tomorrow, I promise." Her voice echoed, as if she had her hand cupped around her mouth. "Can you ask Max if he'll come, too? I have some of his stuff from college, his class ring and a bunch of papers, and he needs to know that I told . . ."

The phone line went dead, and dial tone sounded in her ear. Jill stared down at the cell.

Marissa has Max's class ring?

With a huge sigh, Jill hit redial. The phone rang and rang but Marissa did not pick up. When it went to voicemail, Jill hit redial again, and the call went straight to Marissa's voicemail again.

Jill set the phone down. She read through the documents for a few more minutes, then closed the computer and got up to make herself some tea. First thing in the morning she would call Dave and fill him in on what Millard had said about the men who came looking for information, and about the strange call from Marissa.

A chill slithered across her neck. She reached her hand to rub it away. No matter what Dave thought, it was time to tell Max, about everything. Everything she knew, including the fact Marissa had his ring. She would freaking ask him what the hell was going on, and pray he would answer truthfully.

Jill put a mug of water in the microwave, and relief flooded through her. A minute later, the microwave beeped, lighting up another thought in her brain.

I could go see Max right now. Crawl in bed with him, and tell him everything that's happened. He needs to know.

And I need to trust him.

Jill hurried back to her room. Fifteen minutes later, she slipped on her jacket, grabbed her purse, and hurried into the garage, pulling the locked door closed behind her. She hit the car unlock button on her key, but then stopped dead in her tracks.

She was not the only one in the garage.

Chapter 16

Jill gasped. The exterior door of her garage was wide-open. A dark sedan was sitting behind hers in the driveway. From the light of the streetlamp, she saw Andrew and a red-haired man in a leather jacket standing ten feet from her. The man had his hand in his right pocket.

"I was about to knock on your door. We need to talk." Andrew took a step.

"Stay right there." She slipped the house key between two fingers to make an impromptu weapon, just as her dad had taught her years ago. "Are you nuts? It's the middle of the night! What are you doing here?"

"Don't be scared." Andrew held up his hand. "I'm only here to bring you up to date on some things."

"Who is your friend?"

"This is Irv, my company's security director. He's here to protect me, not hurt you."

"Protect you from what?"

Andrew sighed and motioned toward the door. "Let's go inside, okay? And you should remember to close your garage door at night. You're inviting someone to break-in again."

Don't go in the house.

Her dad always told her that if someone accosted her, to stay calm, but not to go anywhere with bad guys.

Stand your ground. Yell like hell. But don't leave with them.

Jill made a fist with the hand that held the protruding key. "I'm not inviting you in. In fact, I don't want you on my property. Anything you want to say, say it right where you're standing. And by the way, I'm on my way out to meet several people, and if I'm late, they're going to come looking for me."

"That couldn't sound hokier if you tried. But we can do it your way." Andrew pulled a sheaf of papers out of his jacket pocket and offered them to Jill. "You need to look at these documents."

"What are they?"

"Evidence. I requested copies of Max's car accident report from fifteen years ago. The police say there is no record of an accident involving Max on the night in question. The second item is a reply from the feds regarding my request for the address and background of Ingmar and Kari Kallstrom, Max's parents. There are no records at all on those two. Not birth, death, work, or tax documents. And none I can find for Max."

The news was unsettling, but it fit with what she had learned about Max's father's occupation from Professor Millard's pilfered school records. Besides, she had seen the newspaper clipping Professor Millard had given Max. The accident was real. It was Andrew's story that was suspect. "I'm not interested in any information you've got. I've got some of my own that is a lot more unbiased."

"Oh?" Andrew's arm fell to his side. "Do you have photographs? In particular those taken last week when Max Kallstrom met with a German national in Solvang. A man who is a fugitive, and who has been indicted for bank fraud and embezzlement in England and France?"

Jill's mind churned. *Why is Andrew trying so hard to persuade me Max is a bad guy?* "What's going on with this, Andrew? Are you trying to manipulate me? Maybe I need to do some investigating and find out why you care about my safety, or my mother's nursing home bills. Maybe that Pandora's box on your business card should be pried open so we can discuss a few things about you that you might not want known."

"Like what?"

"I don't know. Like you're adopted? Who knows what other secrets are in your past." She realized immediately that was a stupid thing to say.

"How do you know about that?"

"A little birdie told me."

Andrew clenched both fists and took a step toward her. "Are you investigating me? You're the most ungrateful, thickheaded woman I've ever met. I'm trying to protect you. I know you went through hell ten years ago, and I feel badly about the part I played in that. My interest in you is as innocent as that."

"You don't need to feel anything about me anymore, Andrew. Frankly, I thought you would be keeping yourself busy with Marissa. I hope you've told her about your vested interest in her brother's death. She could get the wrong idea if she finds out you're romancing her for ulterior motives."

"I'm not sleeping with Marissa, if that's what you're insinuating. Some of us smarten up about who we sleep with once we grow up, Jill. You should consider it."

"I want to know why you hate Max so much that you're obsessively trying to get him in trouble."

"I don't hate him. No one hates Max, right?" Andrew inhaled sharply. "It's stupid for you to put yourself in danger because of a past infatuation with a man you now don't know a damn thing about. When this scandal breaks open it could ruin your reputation, and jeopardize your teaching career, if it hits the press."

"What scandal? The one about Ben Pierce being killed by someone who might have been at college when we were? That is a terrible, horrible story, but you don't have any reason to tie Max to it." Jill stepped backward, bumping against the door. "I'm beginning to think everything you've told me is more about a vendetta than an investigation. Maybe you're the one who needs to get over the past."

"You're naïve." Andrew's voice was vicious. "For your information, I've made my final report, and the agency that hired me agrees the evidence I've uncovered is strong enough to arrest Max Kallstrom."

"For what?"

"For questioning in the murder of Ben Pierce, for one thing."

"What?" Jill's mouth was so dry she could hardly get the word out.

"Did you know Max was in France the day Ben Pierce was killed? And his investment company has been implicated in a widening scandal the ATF is investigating. There are other pieces of evidence that I can't share with you. But use your head. The man's past has been expunged, he claims he can't remember things he should, and his present activities are the definition of suspicious. Something sinister is going on with him, and you're being blind to it."

She stuck out her chin. "Just because you can't find an accident report doesn't mean there's a nefarious reason."

"I give up." Andrew held up his hands. "But for your information, the Santa Barbara police have a warrant to hold Kallstrom for federal agents. They've probably already picked him up."

"Wrong again, Andrew." Max's deep voice boomed out from the edge of the driveway. He stepped into the garage from the shadows. "Jill, are you okay?"

Andrew snapped around quickly as the man in the leather jacket pulled a silver gun from his pocket.

Max narrowed his eyes. He was holding a gun, too, and his was quite a bit bigger. "Answer me, babe. You're not hurt, are you?"

"No. No, I'm okay."

"Would you flip on the garage light? I'd like to be able to see more than the whites of everybody's eyes."

Jill flipped the switch and everyone but Max blinked in the harsh fluorescence.

"How's it going?" Max asked the man in the leather jacket. "Did you ever find your dog?" His voice was grim.

The gunman said something under his breath and Andrew scowled.

Max took a step toward him. "Put the safety on the gun, friend, lay it on the ground and kick it under Jill's car. And then put your hands on your head."

The man kept the gun pointed at Max.

Max moved his hand higher and put his thumb on the trigger.

Every nerve in Jill's body twanged as the scene in front of her unfolded like a surreal art movie with villains, guns, and her dark-haired lover. Max, with his past full of secrets, had a look in his eye that said he would shoot if the man did not do what he said.

She inhaled and wondered for a fleeting moment who she should be more afraid of.

"Do what he says, Irv," Andrew said.

The man clicked the safety, put the gun on the ground, and kicked it across the floor. Slowly he folded his hands on top of his red hair.

For a moment no one said anything.

"Why don't you and your buddy take off, Andrew. I think Jill meant it when she said she didn't want you on her property."

"We can't let them leave!" Jill said. "We should call the police."

"Yes, let's do that," Andrew said. "I would like to be here to see your boyfriend arrested."

Jill met Max's eyes. He still held the gun. *What should I do? Can I trust you?*

"Whatever you want to do is fine with me." Max's face hardened. "Innocent men don't fear the cops."

"Here, drink this." Max set a cup of steaming tea in front of Jill.

She was huddled in a kitchen chair, a blanket thrown over her shoulders. She was shaking so hard she sloshed tea out of the mug as she brought it to her lips. She took a gulp and looked at Max.

His expression was calm. "You going to be okay? I locked the garage door. But I'm sure those two aren't coming back."

"You're sure we should have let them go?"

"I'm sure Denton's man has a permit for the gun. And he said he found the garage open. What would the police arrest them for?"

Jill frowned. He's right. Maybe the police would have arrested Max. However, Andrew didn't sound like he was bluffing about a warrant being issued for him.

Where the hell did Max get a gun? And why?

Jill took another sip, her hands gripping the warm stoneware. "How much did you hear of Andrew's story?"

"Enough to know Ben Pierce was murdered. How long have you known that?"

She swallowed and focused on her mug. "For a while."

"Why didn't you tell me?"

"You don't remember Ben. You don't even remember me. Why would I have told you?"

"I thought we were growing closer." Max blinked. "I thought I was getting to know you, but right now I don't feel like I do."

"Join the club." There was more hurt in that comment than she wanted to reveal. And she saw that Max heard it.

"What can I do to make you trust me like you once did?" he asked.

Tears sprang to her eyes. "You seem to forget what happened to me sometimes. How you dumped me without a word of explanation. I was devastated, particularly because I felt like a fool, like I was blindsided."

"Jill, I said the first night I understood that. And how sorry I am . . ."

"Stop." She raised her trembling hand. "I know you didn't hurt me on purpose fifteen years ago. I know that with my brain." She rested her hand on her chest. "But in my heart, the wound is still tender. Raw. What I can't get past is that, once you were well, that you didn't think to reach out to the college, and ask them to help you reconnect with your friends."

"I should have."

"Why didn't you?"

"I don't know."

"If you had, I might never have married Andrew."

Max hung his head and sighed. "I can't undo the past. I would if I could."

So would I, Jill thought. "What made you decide to come over here tonight?"

"I was uneasy after seeing that guy in your driveway the other night. I thought I would drive by, maybe park the car for a while. Make sure you weren't disturbed when you came back from seeing Carly."

"You weren't planning to knock on my door?"

"I have some self-control, but I won't lie. I would have if everything seemed normal."

"So we could have sex?"

His eyes narrowed. "So I could make love to you."

"Nice words." She turned her head.

"I mean those words."

She shook her head as if she didn't believe him.

"You and I have a lot of work to do. I'm sorry I've rushed things," Max said. "I've not considered how big a deal the past still is. But I'm right here. Talk to me."

As usual, when things hurt too much to think about, Jill pushed them away. She pointed at the counter. "Where did you get that gun?" The pistol lay gleaming on the granite, as threatening as a rattlesnake.

"I travel with it."

"What? How do you do that? Are citizens from other countries even allowed to get on planes coming to the US if they are armed?"

"I keep it in my checked luggage. It's legal if you have a permit from your country." Max's eyes darkened. "Which I have."

"Why?"

"I can't discuss that with you."

She set the mug down with a bang. Her shivering stopped, but she felt as if her arms were weighted down. *I'm in shock.* She remembered another time her body's aftermath reaction to the adrenalin rush that came from a near-brush with disaster.

It was the night a decade ago when Andrew Denton had pulled a gun out and waved it around, the night she had shot him.

"Don't you dare tell me you can't discuss something that important. What the hell job do you really have if you've got a permit for a gun? You said you're a financial consultant, and trust fund investor for touchy-feely causes. Are you carrying a gun because you have millions of dollars in cash in your suitcase?"

"Please try and calm down."

"Do not tell me to calm down." Her eyes blazed. "This makes me rethink everything Andrew said about you."

"Does it? Do you think I killed Ben Pierce?" His voice was steely.

She drew back. "No. I don't think that. But were you in France when he was killed?"

"I am in France many days during any given month. Do you know what day Ben Pierce was killed?" He stepped closer to her. "Or why? It didn't sound to me like anything Andrew was saying to you was much of a surprise."

"I don't know what the date was." Her skin flushed. "But what about the other things he said? Why isn't there a record of your car accident? Or your parents? Or your birth? Do you know? Care to share about that?"

"No."

"And what's with that guy you met in Solvang the other day. Did you know he's some kind of international crook?"

"I wouldn't believe everything Andrew told you."

"Why not?"

Max looked away.

Jill cleared her throat. "I need some answers from you, Max. I deserve them."

"I think I deserve a few answers, too." He met her eyes. "When did you find out about Ben? And from who?"

His tone sent a chill skittering down Jill's neck. "You go first."

Max tented his hands together. "There are some things about my family's past that I was not forthcoming about. My father did sensitive work for the government during his career, and made some serious enemies. Certain details about him are still secret. As for me, everything I've told you during the last week about my life and business is true. But I also have professional associations which necessitate my carrying a gun when I travel." He leaned back in the chair. "As for the businessman I met for lunch, *ja*, I'm aware he's wanted by Interpol."

"Holy crap! So what, your dad was a spy and you're some kind of Swedish secret agent?"

His green eyes were weary. "Neither of those statements is accurate."

She waited, but it was clear Max was not going to clarify anything further. "I'm going to tell you some things I've been keeping secret."

Max swiped at an unruly strand of hair that fell across his forehead. "Please, go ahead."

She told him everything. About Andrew's request that she work undercover at the reunion because of Ben Pierce's murder.

She told him what Dave had found out about Ben's career, and about the St. John's ring found at the scene.

And then she told him that Mary Millard had given her a thumb drive full of private student information, and that their professor had been visited by two agents who were seen talking with a redheaded, leather-coat-wearing goon, a twin of the one Max had disarmed in her garage.

Max tensed. He tapped the floor with his left foot, and loosened the shirt button at his neck as she went on.

Jill took a breath. "So what do you have to say about that?"

"Which part?"

"Any of it."

Max sighed. "I'm sorry. This must be stressing you out even more than worrying about your mother."

"What I'm stressed about more than anything is you. Why won't you tell me what it is you do that you need to be armed?"

"Because you do not need to know about that part of my life. It doesn't concern you."

"Jesus! Can't you see when you hedge like that my mind concludes you must be some kind of freaking James Bond or something?"

A shadow of a smile played over his handsome face. "You'd make a great Bond girl."

Jill crossed her arms to keep from smacking him. "This is the night from hell." She pointed to her cell phone. "A few minutes before Andrew showed up, Marissa Pierce called and asked to meet tomorrow so she could tell me something she thought was weird about Andrew, and about your St. John's class ring that she evidently still has."

"I had a St. John's class ring?"

"I never saw one, but that's what Marissa said. Of course, now I can't get her to answer her damn cell." Jill got up and grabbed a box of cookies out of the pantry, crunching one as she paced in a circle.

"What are you planning on doing with all this information?" His words were clipped.

"I'm going to give Millard's thumb drive to Dave Hart as soon as I can call him this morning. And Marissa's phone number. He can call her and maybe he can make some sense of whatever it is that is going on. God knows I can't."

"Professor Millard took a huge risk giving you confidential information."

Jill opened the last sleeve of cookies. "She's worried about her students. She trusts me enough to see if I might see something that was a red flag about the men she was asked about. Which means she wanted me to check and make sure you weren't in trouble."

"Who was she asked about again, aside from me?"

She told him.

"I doubt fifteen-year-old college records would hold any clues to Ben Pierce's death."

"I don't either, and I didn't see anything. But I think the best thing to do is pass them onto Dave. Maybe he'll find something relevant."

"Are you giving him my file, too?"

"Yes. You should be happy. At least it confirms what you said about your father's work." Jill stuck another cookie in her mouth and chewed. It was dry as dust. "Should I not do that?"

Max picked up the box and stared at her for three beats of silence. "If you think it might help him get to the bottom of what's going on, I don't care."

She took a gulp of tea, inordinately relieved that he

hadn't asked her to conceal the truth from Dave. "Would you please go get that gun that was kicked under my car? I'll give that to Dave, too. Let's leave this mess to professionals. Although I guess you're some kind of pro, too. Even if you won't specify what kind."

Max took the two remaining cookies out of the box and stuck a whole one in his mouth.

He crunched for a moment, staring at her.

She could see he was mulling over everything she said. But she didn't have a clue as to what he was thinking.

Max swallowed the second cookie. "These are good. What are they called?"

"Do-si-dos. My neighbor's daughter sells them for her Girl Scout troop." She got up and put the box in the trash, careful not to touch the gun on the counter. "I'm glad they're finally gone."

"I'm not. I like cookies with nuts. These are pecans?"

"Peanuts."

"Oh. They remind me of *Finska pinnar*, *Finnish fingers* you would say in English. Swedes don't eat a lot of sweets, but we like cookies with our coffee."

Am I talking cookies with a secret agent? Jill quashed a laugh that would surely sound hysterical and stared at Max, waiting.

He picked up the revolver from the counter and stuck it in a holster at the base of his spine.

The man has a holster. That confirmed the gun thing was not a rare event. "So what happens now?" she asked.

"I would like to go with you to see Carly's Dad."

"Are you going to explain why you are traveling the world with a gun in your pants?"

A beat of silence passed. "No."

"Or about your special side job?"

"No."

"Then I think it's better if I go by myself. Dave is not going to be happy when I tell him I told you everything. And he'll be even less happy when I tell him what happened tonight. He might call and have you arrested himself."

"Why?"

"He's an ex-detective, Max. Suspicion is second nature to American cops. He's worried about Carly. And me. He's looking into this crazy tragedy of Ben being killed by someone who might be a classmate, so if you're not going to level with him about why you are armed, well, that's not going to lead anywhere good."

"I see." He glanced at the clock. It was nearly four a.m. "You must be exhausted."

"I am. Aren't you?"

"May I stay? I want to make sure you're not paid any more visits tonight. I'll sleep on the couch."

The last thing she wanted was to be alone, but she knew she could not lie comfortably in Max's arms for what remained of the night.

Jill shivered, fatigue, fear, and worry shifting inside her head like sand. "I have to get up early and go see my Mom. Don't worry, I'll be fine. Remember, I've got a gun, too. And bullets."

For the first time since he walked back into her life, Max seemed very much different from the college boy she fell in love with. The lines in his face were deep, and he had a weariness about him, as if he was a man with the weight of the world on his shoulders.

"Everything I told you about my accident fifteen years ago is true," he said. "I hope you are not doubting that. I also pray you are not doubting that when I told you I didn't remember you, I didn't. And I mostly hope you aren't doubting what I said about my feelings for you."

"To be honest, I don't know how I feel about anything

right now." Her voice trembled. "If you would just tell me what's going on."

"We've got the rest of our lives to work this through, Jill. If you'll trust me . . ."

"Trust you? How do you expect me to trust you if you don't trust me? If you have secrets you're not willing to share with me?"

He tilted his head back. The agony she saw in his eyes matched how she felt inside.

"I'll get that gun from the garage so you can take it to Dave." He walked out.

Jill got up and poured a glass of water and drank it down. She picked up the empty cookie box and stared at it, remembering it was the one Andrew had pulled out and helped himself to when he was here.

She frowned.

"We're still on for the reunion dinner tomorrow, *ja?*"

Jill jumped at his voice. "What? Yes, I'll be there. We promised Professor Millard we'd sing that duet."

"Even though I don't sing."

"Just fake it. It seems you're pretty capable of that."

Max drew back as if she had slapped him.

Carefully he set the gun down that he had wrapped in a rag from her garage. He placed six bullets beside it. "Dave may want to find out who this is registered to. I think you should put it in a bag of some kind. Not your purse. You don't want to touch it more than necessary."

"Thanks for the tip."

"You're welcome." A nerve under his eye twitched.

"Don't sit out in your car and watch my house."

"Okay. I'll see you at the reunion dinner." With that, Max walked to the front door. He used more force than necessary to shut it behind him.

Jill stared at the gun, and wiped her eyes.

After a moment, she threw the empty cookie box into the trash and then hurried back to her computer.

He knew now he was going to have to kill her, and the sooner the better.

She knew too much, might guess the rest, and would surely run to the authorities if she did, even if he disappeared.

The man who killed Ben Pierce sat in his car in the hotel parking lot and drank cognac directly from the bottle.

The horizon over the ocean was brightening, the air was warm, the gun in his pocket hard against his back. He took another drink and sighed, wishing he had never come to the reunion.

But it was too late now.

Chapter 17

Jill sat in Dave Hart's tidy office in the back of the house where she and Carly had spent hundreds of hours of their youth. She talked for ten minutes straight to bring him up to date on Professor Millard and the nightmarish confrontation in her garage that ended with Max showing up like the cavalry.

She handed him the thumb drive.

Dave copied the information onto his computer and slid it across the desk back to her. "Have Professor Millard get rid of that."

She nodded and gave him the large baggie with the gun Andrew's man had given up. Dave raised his eyebrows but said nothing.

"Did Andrew specifically threaten you?"

"Well, yes. But, no. I mean, he said he was about to knock on the door when I came out into the garage. And I probably did leave the garage open, I was so upset when I got home."

"Did you feel in physical danger?"

"Yes. But only because they startled me. The man didn't pull out his gun until Max showed up with one. Andrew said he's some kind of bodyguard."

"I don't like this at all." Dave glowered. "And where the hell did Max get a gun?"

"He said he legally carries one for work." She took a deep breath. "He wouldn't tell me anything more. Do you think he's going to get arrested like Andrew claims?"

"I don't know. I don't know what kind of case Denton made to whoever it is he's working for. But I doubt it. My take from talking to my contacts is this is a multi-agency investigation, so unless Max is the mastermind behind the fraud case, or they have proof he met with Ben Pierce in Paris, I doubt they'd move on him on Andrew's say so. They would have to verify everything, and that will take time."

Hearing Dave say that made her angry, and then dizzy. She pawed through her bag and pulled out an envelope and dropped it on Dave's desk.

"I wanted to give you this, too. It's Andrew's business card. If you want to check out those numbers for Pandora Security, there they are. For my money, Andrew has been lying to me the whole time. I am not even sure he's actually got a contract with the government."

"You might be right. But whatever his game is, he's showing a lot of aggression." The ex-detective shook his head. He picked-up the business card. "You got this from Andrew?"

"Yes. I made him give it to me last night."

"Okay."

Jill squeezed her hands together in her lap and watched Dave's face. "Will you confirm the story those men who visited Dr. Millard gave her? Here's their information." She reached into her pocket and took out a folded paper she got from Millard this morning.

He held out his hand. "I will. If these guys are legitimate agents, then they might be interested in some things I've found out about your ex."

"What things? And what do you mean, legitimate agents?"

"Anyone can get a business card printed up. It bothers me that Professor Millard saw them talking to a guy who is the muscle for Denton. They might be thugs posing as feds."

"I didn't think of that," she said. "What did you find out about Andrew?"

Dave spoke carefully. "Don't pass this on to Dr. Millard, or Max, or even Carly."

"Okay."

"As you know, Andrew was an only child, raised by his mother who worked for Immigration. I was told by a retired INS guy who once worked for his mom that the rumor was that Andrew was adopted illegally, and brought back to the States with her."

"I read that he was adopted in the application files." She nodded at the thumb drive. "But why all the intrigue with a criminal? His mother could have adopted a baby here."

"She was single, and spent most of her work life traveling. I don't know, Jill, it was harder for a woman in those circumstances to adopt a child thirty-five years ago."

Jill's head was spinning. "Wow. So his mother used her connections to take a short cut through the laws more than once."

"Yes." Dave leaned forward. "The question I have is, is Andrew Denton even a U.S. citizen? This information, if found out, could complicate his life enormously."

"Why? He was a kid. He didn't sneak into the country."

"Immigration law, as you know, is pretty rigid. Lots of illegal immigrants get kicked out of our country. He could be in a world of trouble if his adoption wasn't on the up and up. He could get deported, even if he isn't at fault. The INS is pretty tough on this issue."

Jill blinked. *Did I hit a nerve when I threw that out at Andrew last night?* "This is all so confusing. Andrew's convinced that Max is a criminal, and that he's hiding things about his life that are making him look guilty, and no one seems to know the real reason poor Ben was killed."

"You're right. I don't know how all those pieces fit together, but for right now, I'm going to tell you what your father would tell you, steer clear of both of those men until we know more."

She had not expected him to say that. "Okay."

"Hang out with Carly and Hamilton tonight. I'll get going on some more calls, and I'll let you know as soon as I find out anything."

Jill nodded slowly. "I'm going over to see my mother and then I've got a couple of errands before I get ready for the tonight. Please call me if you hear anything."

"I will." He stared at her closely. "Carly and Julia are coming to stay at my house next week. You're welcome to stay too. If you don't want to be home until this is all resolved."

"Thanks. But I'll be fine."

"I know you will." He gave her hug. "Keep the faith, honey. This time next week we'll probably know a whole lot more."

Jill hugged him back, and walked out to her car, wondering what shape her life would be in this time next week if they did know how all those puzzle parts fit together.

Jill signed in at Friend's House and was hurrying down the hall when someone called out "Miss Farrell!" behind her. She turned and Karen, the director, was walking toward her.

She stopped, her stomach churning.

"Thank you for waiting, Miss Farrell. I was going to call you but when I saw you signing in, I ran to catch up. I didn't want you to go into see your mother before I spoke to you."

"What's wrong?" Jill turned toward the hallway. "Did something happen?"

"Your mother had an incident. But everything is fine." Karen fell into step beside her as they headed for Dorothy's room.

"What kind of incident?"

"She got out of the building somehow and was missing for an hour or so before we found her. She's unhurt, except for . . ."

"How did she get out? She's in a locked wing!" Jill stopped dead.

"It happens, I'm sorry to say. A visitor or a nurse presses the code numbers onto the number pad and the door opens and they don't notice a resident standing nearby. A lot of them sneak out before the door closes."

"Where did you find her?" Jill started walking toward the door again.

"She was in the grassy area right outside the window of her room, by the bird feeders. She was on the bench there."

Jill pushed her mother's door opened. Dorothy was sitting in the rocking chair by the window, her head back as if she was dosing.

"Hey, Mom, how are you doing?"

Dorothy's eyes fluttered opened and she stared at Jill. "It's Friday."

"Well, it's Saturday, but that's pretty close." Jill was so relieved she felt dizzy. She gently squeezed her mother's shoulder and turned to the nursing home administrator. "She's got scratches on her face."

Barbara walked closer. "Yes. I think she probably picked those up on the bushes by the side of the building. She's got a scrape on her left knee too." She leaned down and raised Dorothy's pant leg to show Jill a small bandage there.

"How long was she gone?"

"The nurse came in at 7:30 a.m. to help her up and walked her to breakfast. When the attendants took the residents back to their rooms, one of them helped your mom down the hallway, but she said she wanted to look out the window, so they left her there. It was about an hour later they found her outside."

"Why didn't you call me?" It was all she could do to not raise her voice. Her hands were clammy and her voice cracked, she was so shocked.

"I was going to. But then I saw you . . ."

"I mean why didn't you call me the minute you knew she was missing?"

"I understand you're upset, Miss Farrell. But our residents aren't confined to their rooms. It's not uncommon for something like this to happen. There are a lot of staff members walking in and out of the buildings. So she wouldn't have gone unnoticed long."

"Buketa, buketa, buketa, Uncle John," Dorothy mumbled. She rubbed her neck and cringed. "Who was that man?"

Jill leaned down to look at Dorothy's skin and saw a red welt where her mother was rubbing. She turned to Karen. "What happened to her neck?"

Karen blinked and walked over to peer at what Jill was talking about. "I don't know. It looks like, what, an abrasion?"

"Where's her necklace?" Jill's voice was getting louder.

"What necklace?"

"Her locket. The gold locket. It has her initials on the back. It's the only piece of jewelry I left with her."

"Let me call the nurse in who found her, Miss Farrell. There was nothing in the report about your mother losing her necklace."

Jill squeezed Dorothy's hand. Her mother was staring at her vacantly. "Mom, did you pull your necklace off? Your locket." She touched her hand to her mother's inflamed skin and Dorothy winced.

"Max," Dorothy whispered, resting her hand on the red line on her neck. "Scat, kitty cat. Don't come back."

Jill hurried into Professor Millard's office at St. John's and closed the door behind her.

"Jill, dear, have a seat." Millard turned her ancient leather swivel chair toward her. It was six-thirty in the evening. Jill had called and offered to drive Millard to the reunion dinner, as well as meet to talk about the files Millard had pilfered. "So what did you think about the records? Anything helpful?"

"Nothing I could see. But like I told you on the phone, Carly's father has a copy of them now, too."

"He's a retired detective?"

"Yes. Not that they ever retire." Jill sat opposite Dr. Millard, the brooding picture of the orchestra conductor behind her looking down on her. "Dave also verified the two men who came to see you are actual ATF agents."

He had not had any luck yet getting a lead on 'Irv', the red-haired guy, who Millard had seen speaking to the agents. The investigator claimed not to know what Millard was talking about, which Dave said concerned him, but Jill wasn't going to share that information with the professor.

"Well, that's good news. Did you find anything that worried you about Max? Did he ever mention the facts about his father working for the government?"

"No. He didn't. But I guess that's not surprising." Jill took the thumb drive out of her pocket and handed it to Millard. "You must erase this, or destroy it. Dave made a copy of it but doesn't want you to have it in your possession. Do the same thing with the scanned documents on your computer, okay? You don't want to be found with personal student information."

"I will. Thanks for keeping my butt out of jail, my dear." Millard slipped the device in her pocket and stood up. "You look absolutely stunning in that color. Pink on blondes always puts me in mind of Mary Cassatt. The female subjects in her paintings are usually in that color, all glowing and soft."

Jill gently touched the dress Carly had brought her from Paris. "It was a gift. I wouldn't have chosen if for myself. Seems too elegant for me."

"Nonsense. It flatters you in every way. Is Max going to meet you at the restaurant, or is he waiting in the car downstairs?"

"I'm not sure." She had called to tell him it was better that they didn't see each other for a few days, but he had not answered. Or called her back.

She had no idea if he was even coming tonight.

The professor linked her arm through Jill's as they walked to the door. "Do I sense trouble in paradise?"

"There are some issues."

"There are always issues in love," Millard said.

"He's a man of secrets, Dr. Millard. It's difficult for me to imagine a future with a man of secrets. And he lives in France. That's a pretty big hurdle all by itself."

"I see." The older woman sighed. "Your heart has a long history with the man, or with two men, the Max of then and now. But to him, you're a brand new love. I doubt he knows you well enough to know how cautious you are."

They walked out to the parking lot.

"I guess I am," Jill agreed. "I like to think everything through. And my mother can't move anywhere now. So it's tough."

"I know it is. But you need to trust your heart. You're a good catholic girl, so don't be afraid to take a leap of faith every now and then."

"That's good advice. But you know, it's hard to leap sometimes. A lot of things have changed about Max since I was with him before. He's secretive, and stubborn, for example. Even bossy." She thought of his insistence he buy her those bullets. "I remember him as much more easy-going."

"We all change," Millard said, stepping into Jill's car. "Haven't you?"

"Yes. I have." She shut the door on Millard's side.

Millard stopped asking questions about Max. As they drove to the restaurant, the professor inquired about Dorothy, and Jill told her about what happened to her mother this morning, and her distress over what seemed like lax standards at the nursing home.

By the time they arrived, Jill's mind was no clearer, and her heart heavier. Millard was greeted at the door by Cheryl and Susan, who whisked the beloved teacher off to another group of alumni.

Jill pulled at the neckline of the dress and searched the crowded room. She spotted Carly standing near the bar, empty glass in hand.

That's not a good sign.

Jill made her way through the sea of beautifully dressed people, stopping once or twice to give or receive a hug from a classmate she had reconnect with at the cocktail party. Millard's comment that Max was "two men" kept replaying in her head.

She agreed. And she doesn't even know that one of them carries a gun.

"God, you look like a princess in that dress. I get an A for buying it." Carly said when Jill walked up. She held the empty glass up to toast her. "And I love the earrings. I told you that you should always wear sapphires. They turn your eyes to that sparkling color the minute you put them on."

"Thank you. You need to move back to the States so you can pick out all of my clothes, and lend me all of your jewelry." Jill touched the dangling earrings Carly had ordered her to wear.

"I may do that."

"Your father and I would throw a party. You look like a goddess, by the way. I love that one-shoulder look." Carly's dark hair was swept up off her face and neck into a Princess Kate type of low chignon, and the sparkly plum sheath hugged every curve of her lush figure.

"Thanks. I like to show the girls off since I stopped nursing. Although I need a bra now with more support. Maybe one with steel under wires."

"I think you are seeing something none of the rest of the world does." She smiled and nodded at the wineglass. "What are we drinking?"

"Whatever this hunk is pouring." Carly motioned to the buff bartender, who moved to their side of the bar.

"Can I get you another one? The same?"

"Yes. I could do this all night long," Carly said.

The young man grinned and handed her a fresh glass of Cabernet.

"Thank you." Carly took a deep sip. "I love California wine. Even the cheap stuff tastes like sunshine."

From the look of her watery eyes, Jill judged that it wasn't her friend's first drink of the evening. "I'll have one, too," she said to the bartender. "So where's Hamilton?"

"I don't know. Possibly at the airport." Carly frowned.

"What? He's not coming tonight?"

"He got a call this afternoon and said he was going to have to leave on the first flight he could get to Brussels." Her voice roughened. "I left at four to get my hair blown out so I didn't have to deal with Julia wanting to help me, and told him he best not duck out on me before dinner, but he didn't commit. He knows I'm pissed. I don't know what the hell he's doing. And right now I can't say that I care."

"I'm sorry. Dr. Millard is going to be disappointed. She was convinced she had talked Ham into being her star attraction at the talent show."

"He had her fooled, then. He kept saying how he didn't want anyone to hear how rusty he is. He was worried Millard would know he wasn't the same musician he once was." Carly shook her head. "Sometimes Ham is so vain. He should be more like Max, who says he can't sing but is a good sport."

"He is a good sport," Jill said. *Among other things.*

Carly squinted at the crowd. "Where is he, anyway?"

Jill glanced around the room. "That's a good question. Max might not show up either." Jill took a step.

"Whoa." Carly grabbed her arm and stayed put. "What happened?"

Jill met Carly's eyes. "I found out last night Max has been hiding significant things from me about his past, and his present. Things that make it hard to imagine how we're going to push this personal reunion of ours into the future."

"Oh my god, it's not because of something my dad discovered about Ben Pierce's murder, is it?"

"Shhh," Jill said softly. The crush of people around them was growing. She spotted Andrew. He was at the doorway, talking to Eddie Fitzhugh. Eddie and his blond supermodel wife were holding court with a big group.

"Come on, let's go sit down, Carly. I need to tell you what happened last night."

"Oh my god, now what?"

"I'll tell you when we sit down."

Carly took a huge gulp of wine and set the glass on the bar. "When does the program start?"

"In a few minutes. At seven o'clock Professor Millard is going to give a short welcome. She's over there with the techs setting up the microphones so it must be close to time." Jill nodded at the dais. She took Carly's hand and they walked to their table. Jill scanned the crowd again looking for Max, but there was still no sign of him.

They were the first to arrive at the table set for eight. Jill leaned close to Carly and quickly filled her in on the visit from Andrew and the armed associate, and about Max showing up at the right moment.

"Where the hell did Max get a gun?"

"He says he travels with one. For work."

"Work? What does he do? I thought he was in investments."

"He does that, but there's something else mysterious going on." She leaned closer. "Andrew told me a few unsettling facts, and your dad is talking to a lot of people to try and find out some answers. Until then . . ."

"Shhh, there he is." Carly put a huge smile on her face, but she squeezed Jill's hand as if she was commiserating. "Max! God, I love a man who knows how to dress. Where did you get that suit? Rome?"

"Good guess. Milan." Max's green eyes flashed. "You look gorgeous."

"Thanks. If my best friend wasn't sleeping with you, I'd ask you to sit beside me."

"Carly!" Jill frowned.

"And if I wasn't enamored with your best friend, I'd be delighted to be your dinner companion," Max said, his voice rough with emotion. "Where's Hamilton?"

"He abandoned me. Nothing new there."

"He had to leave for business?"

"Yes. Something can't wait in Europe. More important than his wife and daughter." Carly reached for her wineglass. "I'll distract my lonely self by staring at you. You look like heaven."

"Thank you." Max inhaled. "What do you think, Jill? I don't want to embarrass you during our duet."

Jill did not stand up to hug him. "Hello, Max. You look fine."

"And you look delicious. Like warm cotton candy." He cupped her chin with his right hand, and leaned down and kissed her hard on the mouth.

The kiss left her breathless. She had been dreading seeing him after their argument last night, as well as Dave's caution to stay clear of him. But her body's reaction to Max's kiss confirmed the one thing she had not admitted to herself until now.

I'm falling in love with him all over again. And despite the questions, I trust him.

"May I sit beside you?" Max asked.

She nodded. "Yes."

He sat and pulled a note card out of his suit pocket. "I brought my music."

"What music?"

"'Kiss Me Twice.' I copied down the lyrics." His eyes crinkled as if he were coaxing her to smile. "You didn't forget?"

"Actually, I did. I should have practiced." She touched her throat. "I'm going to sound like Kermit the frog."

"You'll sound great. But you do remember I can't sing, right? But I will at least know the words."

"It's good of you to do this for Dr. Millard."

"I'm doing this for you. I hope you know that." He leaned forward. "I should have trusted you more. I hope you'll give me another chance to explain some things."

"Max, I . . ." Tears filled her eyes.

He put two fingers on her lips. "Not now. Later. We've got time, Jill. I'm not going to let you get away again."

She blinked and then kissed his cheek as relief flooded through her. Max put his arm around her and squeezed her tight.

The lights dimmed and they all faced the stage where Professor Millard stood at the podium. With a sigh, she relaxed against Max's hard body.

All we have to do is get through this party, she thought. *What did Millard advise me to do? Take a leap of faith?*

Next to her Carly drained her glass and reached for the bottle in the middle of the table. Suddenly Andrew appeared and slipped into the empty seat across from Jill.

"Hello all," he said.

"You're not sitting here." Carly banged the bottle of wine down. "Go." She pointed.

"Since your husband has taken a powder, this seat is empty and I'm filling it. I like the view from here." He turned and stared at Jill.

Jill tensed.

"Let's all be quiet now. The show's about to start," Max said. His stern tone seemed to knock Andrew off-balance.

Her ex-husband turned toward the stage and folded his arms over his chest.

"It's okay," Max whispered to Jill. "Keep your cool."

Jill watched Carly, who picked up her glass and took a long drink.

"Welcome St. John Vianney class of 2001 Reunion Celebration," Professor Millard said into the microphone.

Applause swelled around her, and Jill squeezed her hands into fists.

Chapter 18

In the dark, Jill and a hundred other people watched the flickering images on the screen mounted above them in the hotel ballroom.

Professor Millard narrated as scenes of sporting events and talent shows and graduation speeches filled the air around them. There were spontaneous rounds of applause for Eddie Fitzhugh's winning touchdown, wolf whistles for the cheerleaders, including an almost unrecognizable Marissa Pierce, and catcalls and laughter as the final segment, a ten-minute clip of two of the talent shows the class participated in.

There was a brief few seconds of her and Max, both of them to her eyes remarkably young looking, and then three different thirty-second outtakes of other groups of students singing. Andrew was in one group, which surprised her. Jill had forgotten he liked to sing in college. He was actually somewhat endearing in the clip where he and two other guys did a take-off on the Letterman trio.

The lighthearted acts were followed by a long passage of Hamilton Stewart at the keyboard, masterfully playing the Bach piece he won the California college championship with.

Jill stared at Carly. Her friend's eyes were glassy as she stared rapt at Hamilton's handsome profile on the screen.

She is missing him terribly. Out of the corner of her eye, she saw Andrew turn and she moved involuntarily closer to Max.

Andrew took a handful of nuts from the bowl on the table and turned back to watch.

With a start, Jill contemplated the fact that Andrew was

eating nuts. Peanuts and cashews were mixed together in the bowls of appetizers sitting on the table.

And he had eaten peanut butter cookies at her house.

But he was deathly allergic. Were peanut allergies something people got over?

Jill suddenly found it hard to pay attention as her brain started linking all kinds of snippets of information.

Ben Pierce had said there was something 'off' about his college friend, and he needed to talk to him more before he gave his boss a name.

Was the off thing the fact that the Ben had realized his classmate was not who he said he was? Could the person who killed Ben have been impersonating someone from college?

Someone like Andrew Denton?

Was the man sitting six feet away from her the same man she had once been married to, or was he someone else?

Jill stared at Andrew's left temple. She saw the scar from the bullet, but she would swear there was something different about the man. Andrew's ears seemed more pointed than the college junior she had watched on screen. And his chin weaker. Jill leaned forward, squinting in the shadowy light as the recording of Hamilton's piano piece came to an end.

Jill had the urge to grab Max and tell him what she was thinking, but she was afraid she might tip Andrew off that something was up.

I need to talk to Dave Hart. As bizarre as it would be to say, she was terrified suddenly that the man calling himself Andrew Denton was not really Andrew. And if that was true, she was sitting six feet away from a murderer.

"Excuse me," she whispered to Max. "I need to run to the ladies."

"You okay?" His eyes narrowed.

"Yes. I'll be right back." Jill made her way out of the ballroom and rushed down the hallway to the ladies. She sat on the sofa in the lounge area, which was blessedly empty, and pulled out her phone and dialed Dave.

"Hi, Jill," Carly's father said. "What's up?"

"Dave, I have to tell you something." Quickly Jill rushed through the peanut allergy facts about Andrew, and about her observation that he didn't seem to have an allergy now. "I got to thinking about what Ben Pierce told his supervisor, that there was something off about his friend, and I thought, what if the man Ben met with was an imposter, who was posing as someone else? I mean, what if Andrew isn't Andrew? Maybe Ben was on to him, and Andrew, or whoever he is, knew it and killed Ben. And he's now trying to frame Max." She was horrified at her own words, but knew her reasoning was sound.

"You have the instincts of a detective," Dave replied. "I heard from my FBI contact that ATF is investigating the same angle. They floated the idea that someone had stolen one of your classmates' identity, and that Ben may have stumbled onto that fact when he ran into the guy in Paris."

"Oh my god. You need to tell them about Andrew, and the allergy stuff!"

"Slow down, Jill." Dave took a deep breath. "After our lunch today I had Andrew's fingerprints from the business card run, to see if I got any hits on unsolved crimes."

"And?" Jill felt as if she could not breathe.

"I didn't. But more importantly, the print on his card matches his arrest record from ten years ago. Andrew Denton is the same Andrew Denton you went to school with and married, at least as far as his fingerprints go."

The air seemed to go out of the room.

"Oh crap, do I feel dumb now. I was so sure these were very important discrepancies." Jill slumped in the chair.

"They were. I can't explain about the allergy, but it's a good thing you called. There's some tough developments involving Max."

Before Dave could finish, Jill got a signal in her ear that

a call was waiting. She checked the phone as the number calling flashed. It was Friend's House.

"What's wrong, Dave? Tell me, I have to take another call in a second."

"The feds are going to bring Max in for questioning. Evidently Andrew was on the level about what he had heard. The government wants to interview Max about what he was doing in France when Ben Pierce was killed. And also about his work for the Swedish Intelligence services."

"What?" she gasped. "Max is a spy?"

"I don't know what he is. He works with some kind of special operations unit called the *Nationella Insatsstyrkan*. It's an elite police force. My guys think that's why he came to California, to track down someone they're interested in."

Not to see me. Jill put her hand on her chest and struggled to breathe. Max had told her the first night she saw him that he had come to see her, to find his past, to explain.

If that was all a lie, what else had he lied to her about? "I, I don't know what to say, Dave. But please hold on a minute, I have to take another call." Jill clicked over. "Hello?"

"Miss Farrell?" It was the director at her mother's nursing home.

"Yes. What's going on, Karen?"

"You need to come right away, Miss Farrell. Your mother is missing from her room again, and . . ."

"What? I'll be right there." Jill clicked over to Dave's call. "Dave, I have to go. My mom has wandered off from the nursing home. I need to go right now."

"Okay, go, but call me when you get there. I'll come if you need me."

"Thanks, I will." Jill stuffed her phone in her bag and ran from the ladies room, nearly barreling into Carly.

"Oh my god, Jill. You won't believe what just happened." Her friend was white faced.

"Carly, I have to go. My mother's gone missing again at

the nursing home again. I don't understand this, the place is locked, but somehow she's nowhere to be found."

"What? Oh no." She grabbed Jill's arm. "Do you want me to go get Max?"

"No," Jill's eyes filled with tears. "No, your dad just told me some things that are kind of scary about him. I need to think things through some more."

"What? Tell me!"

"I'm sorry, I don't have time now. We'll talk tonight, okay? I'll just go in a get my wrap and . . ."

"Wait. You can't go back in there right now." Carly pulled Jill into an alcove, checking around them quickly for other people in the area.

"Why not?" Jill stared at her best friend. "What's wrong? What happened?"

"Professor Millard stopped the program, and the police are here." Her friend was white-faced. "Marissa Pierce was found dead a few hours ago. The cops want to talk to everyone. If you go back inside now, you'll never get out of here."

Jill covered her mouth with her hand. "What? How? What happened to her?"

"I don't know. Everyone is so shocked."

"Jesus!" Jill hugged her. "I wish Hamilton was here. Why don't you come with me, okay? I don't want you to stay here either."

"No, I'll stay and try and find out more details. If you need to leave, go now." She hugged Jill.

"Don't tell Max anything," Jill said.

"I won't. Now look, you better take a cab. I'm sure the cops have clamped down on the valet area."

Jill looked past Carly toward the front door. She saw flashing lights and a crowd gathering. "I'll go out the kitchen entrance." She pointed down the hallway. "I can grab a cab to Friend's House from across the street."

The women hugged again and Jill sprinted away. Her

mind was numb with shock about Max, about Marissa, but fear for her mother kept her moving.

The taxi dropped Jill at the entrance of Friend's House, where police cars, two ambulances and an emergency rescue vehicle filled the small front parking lot. Several police officers stood off to the side, staring at a map someone had unfolded on the grass.

"Jill!" Karen called from the front door as Jill sprinted, despite her high heels, down the walkway.

"Have you found her?" Jill asked.

"Not yet. But I'm sure we will any minute." The facility director's face showed the strain of having one of her charges missing. "I'm so sorry."

"I want to help in the search," Jill said.

Karen's eyes widened as she took in Jill's elegant clothes and shoes. "Of course. Come to your mother's room and you can change. I have some tennis shoes I can loan you. And some jeans and a shirt."

"Thanks." Jill was shaking with nerves as the women rushed down the hallway to Dorothy's room. "I can't believe how many police are here. How long has she been missing?"

"About an hour. I'll introduce you to the officer in charge, Sergeant Glass. He's out on the back patio. Once I explained the circumstances, they showed up in force."

"What circumstances?" Jill asked. "An elderly dementia patient wandering around in the dark is urgent, but it looks like a swat event outside." She stopped at the opened door to her mother's room and gasped.

Karen grabbed her arm. "I'm sorry, I didn't have time to explain everything. It appears your mom's room has been ransacked, and the back window screen was slit open. The police think there's a possibility Dorothy was kidnapped."

"What?" Jill's glance moved fearfully around the room.

All the dresser drawers were pulled out onto the floor, and all her mother's things were scattered. There were reddish-brown smears on the window sash. "Is that blood?" she nearly screamed.

"We don't know. Don't touch anything, the police have called for evidence technicians who should be here any minute, but wait here and I'll go get you things to change into." Karen hurried out of the room.

Jill stood immobilized with fear for several moments. Slowly she walked to the window. Outside, floodlights were set up on the grass, and the birdbath threw a grotesque shadow against the wall. "Oh please, where are you?" she murmured.

"Jill, what's happened?"

She whirled around at the sound of Max's voice. "What are you doing here?"

He took a step, his expression wary. "I heard about your mother. Have they found her?"

"No. She glanced at the door. "I need to go help in the search."

"I'll help too."

"No!" She glared at him.

"What's wrong, Jill? Why are you angry at me?"

"Dave Hart told me that you are working for the Swedish government. That you're here in California because of a case you're working on. Not because you wanted to see me."

He drew back, his arms stiffened at his sides. "I have no comment about that, except to say that's not completely true. Seeing you was the reason I came here."

She held up her shaking hand. "Stop. I don't want to hear any more lies, Max. And who told you about my mother?"

He pursed his lips together.

"How did you even get out of the ballroom at the reunion? Carly told me there were police everywhere, because of Marissa Pierce." She took a step toward him, anger building with every breath.

"I went to make a call when you went to the ladies room, and I heard Professor Millard's announcement through the door." He looked at her intently. "And I saw you running across the street to the cab stand, so I caught another one and followed you here." He looked around the room. "I was worried about you, and then when I saw all the police in the parking lot . . . Did your mother do this?"

"No. The director said she might have been kidnapped." Jill's voice broke and she covered her mouth with her trembling hand. "Who would do that, Max? And why?"

He looked like he wanted to come closer, but he stayed where he was. "Don't jump to conclusions. I can't believe she's been kidnapped."

"But look at the window screen. And that smear on the ledge. Is it blood?" Jill clutched her arms to her chest. "My house was broken into. My mother's things in my garage were ransacked. And now this!" Jill pointed at the shambles around her. "What the hell is going on?"

"That's what we're here to find out," a deep voice said.

Jill and Max turned in unison. Three police officers, accompanied by a terrified looking Karen, filled the doorway.

"Are you Max Kallstrom?" one of the officers asked.

"Yes." Max stepped forward, as if to shield Jill from them.

"I have a warrant for your arrest." The burly, balding cop who looked to be in charge, motioned to Jill with his hand. "I'm supervisor Glass. Please step away from Mr. Kallstrom, ma'am."

Jill could not move. "What are you arresting him for?"

"It's okay, Jill. Do as the police officer asked," Max said. "Why don't you go outside and see what progress the officers are making? Call to your mom, like you said. I'll be out to help you soon."

The two cops flanking the burly sergeant walked toward

Max. "I need to pat you down, sir," the olive-skinned woman said.

Max put his arms up. "I'm not armed."

Jill stared at Max. *Where's his gun?*

The cops cuffed him and took all the items out of his pockets.

"Where are you taking him?" Jill asked.

"Santa Barbara precinct. Downtown," Glass said curtly.

The female cop who had gone through Max's pockets handed her supervisor the contents. He shook out an evidence bag and transferred Max's wallet, cell phone, cash, and a few American coins into it.

And a necklace.

"Who does this belong to?" The officer held up the gold chain, with a dangling oval locket. The locket appeared broken, for it gaped open.

"I have no idea who it belongs to," Max said, "or where it came from. I didn't put it in my pocket."

Jill squinted at the shiny piece of gold. She knew who it belonged to. It was her mother's locket. She gasped.

"Miss Farrell, do you know who this necklace belongs to?" The cop asked.

She looked into Max's face, but found no answers there. "Yes," she said. "It's my mother's. It's been missing for a couple of days."

"That's him. That's him," a woman shouted from the doorway. "He's the one I saw leading Mrs. Farrell around the back of the building. I saw him! I remember him! He's a cutie, but he ain't fooling me."

Everyone turned to find the nursing home director with her arm around Mrs. Jeeks, the resident who Max and Jill had almost allowed to escape from Friend's House a few days ago.

"This is the man you saw with Mrs. Farrell?" Policeman

Glass asked.

"Yes. Do you have my dog?" Mrs. Jeeks demanded, pointing directly at Max.

A nurse rushed up behind Karen. "Karen, we found Mrs. Farrell! She's out in front with the paramedics. I think she's okay."

"Did you do this? Did you take my mother, Max?" Jill couldn't believe she was asking this.

Max's face was blank, his eyes unreadable.

"Tell me!" she screamed.

"Jill, you've got to trust me."

"Never. Never again dare to ask me that." She turned and ran out of the room, brushing past the crowd of people, her heart feeling as if would burst.

Chapter 19

"The police aren't sure how Mom ended up in the shed." Jill wearily rested her elbows on the table. The clock showed it was after eight p.m., but bright sunlight still streamed through her kitchen window. "Of course she's no help, and can't remember anything. She may have found the door open and locked herself in by accident. There was a latch inside."

"What I don't understand is why the cops didn't check there sooner last night." Carly picked up the mug of tea and shook her head. The friends sat in the kitchen together, both exhausted. "The building is on the other side of the nursing home parking lot."

"They claim they didn't see her because she was hiding in the corner." Despite the warm temperature, Jill shivered with fatigue. "She does that all the time, hides. It's part of her disease. She doesn't recognize where she is, so she panics. I'm thankful she didn't break her hip. That's what I thought had happened when I saw her."

Carly reached over and covered Jill's hand with her own. "I'm so sorry about all this." She nodded toward the hallway. "Is she asleep?"

Dorothy had spent several hours in the hospital for observation after she was found, but instead of allowing them to discharge her back to the nursing home this afternoon, Jill insisted on bringing her home for a couple of days.

"Yes, she's out cold. I didn't even give her the sedative the doctor sent. I fixed her some soup, which she inhaled, and then she was asleep by six-thirty." Tears welled in Jill's eyes. "I don't know if I can ever think of sending her back to Friend's House. I may have to take a leave from my job and care for her here."

"Oh, Jill, you know she wouldn't want that. And you can't care for her alone. Look how many times she got out the door in the last year when you tried that." Carly squeezed Jill's hand harder. "Its fine for a couple of days while they repair the damage to her room, but you put a lot of effort into researching Friend's House. You said yourself it was a great place for her. You can't blame them for what happened last night."

Jill met Carly's eyes. "What did happen last night? Do you think Max had anything to do with my mother?"

Carly cleared her throat. "Do you?"

"No, I don't believe that." Jill frowned at her untouched tea. "I think poor Mrs. Jeeks remembered seeing Max with Mom when we came to visit a couple of days ago, and that's why she said what she did to the cops."

"That's a possible explanation."

"What other one makes any sense? And anyway, he was with us at the reunion dinner."

"He was, but he showed up late." Carly leaned toward her. "And no one knows exactly when your mother went missing, right?"

"Right. But . . ."

"And what about her locket?" Carly pressed. "The cops found it in Max's suit pocket. You said someone ripped it off your mother's neck a couple of days ago. What was he doing with it?"

"I don't know. He told the cops he didn't put it there." Jill wondered where it was now, again thinking of the locks of hair. "I still think Andrew might be behind this. Max isn't the kind of man who would hurt an ill woman. And while he obviously has a secret life because of his work with the Swedish government, I don't think he lied to me about, well, about everything. Do you?"

"I don't know what to think, Jill. If you had asked me at dinner last night if I thought he was falling in love with you for the second time in your lives, I would have said yes. If he isn't, then he's a pathological liar and a very good actor."

Jill trembled. "And if he's a liar, then everything he told me about wanting to remember the past, about how he feels for me, well, it was all for some other reason. But what?"

"I don't know," Carly said.

Jill's voice cracked. "I'm telling you honestly, he was sincere in wanting to reconnect and find the past. I would know if it was an act."

"Would you?" Carly asked softly. "I mean, it's been fifteen years since you knew him. Memory plays tricks on the best of us. Does Max deserve that kind of faith?"

The women stared at one another.

"I trust my gut that he wasn't lying about wanting to tell me what happened to him," Jill said. "Besides, Carly, no one has made any kind of coherent argument as to why Max would do those things."

"Do you want to hear Andrew's theory?"

"Andrew's theory?" Jill pulled away and stared at Carly. "When did you talk to him?"

"I didn't, but Hamilton did." Carly flushed, her voice roughing with anger. "When I finally got a hold of Ham on the phone this morning, he told me the whole story of what's been going on. Evidently Andrew tracked him down in London a few weeks ago. They even met for drinks! Andrew urged Hamilton to come to the reunion and report back if he noticed anything suspicious about anyone, especially Max, like Andrew did with you. And he got Ham to agree not to tell me about it."

"What? Did Andrew tell Hamilton the same story? That he's working for a government agency?"

"Yes. But unlike with you, Andrew told Ham outright that he had proof Max's company was a target in the fraud case Ben Pierce was investigating, and that Max was implicated in Ben's murder."

"Implicated how?"

"Andrew didn't tell him. I am so pissed that Ham didn't tell me about any of this crap before this morning." Carly crossed her arms and sighed. "He said he couldn't because he didn't want me to tip you off about Andrew's suspicions. He also said the only reason he agreed to come to the reunion was so we could help you because you're my best friend."

"That's pretty great of him," Jill said.

Carly's face softened. "It is. He also said he doesn't trust Andrew. Ham thinks he's got an ax to grind. That he's still in love with you."

"Oh my god, that's ridiculous." Jill rested her head in her hands. "I wish Ham had told you the truth from the beginning. You could have warned me Andrew was doing this, or gone to your dad, even."

"I totally agree. I mean, I didn't tell Hamilton what Dad has found out, because Dad told us to keep quiet, but Ham should have told me that Andrew contacted him, don't you think so?"

"Yes. But we sound hypocritical," Jill said.

"We do, but so be it. I should have trusted my instincts more."

"How?"

"I should have figured out something was going on with my husband when he announced without warning that we were coming to the States for the reunion. Hamilton has been quizzing me for a couple of weeks about you and Max."

"What do you mean?" Jill frowned.

"Ham never wants to talk about college at all, in fact he gets impatient if I refer to friends from those days, other than you. But on the flight home from Rome, he was overly inquisitive. Wanted to know who you and Max hung out with and what you did together in college. I told him a bunch of anecdotes, how you fell crazy in love with him almost at first sight, how you two did everything together, that you even used to cut his hair and wore it in a necklace. And that you taught him to drive my dad's car." Carly frowned. "I realize now he was asking so he could help Andrew."

Jill's heart lurched. "Does Ham think Max is involved in Ben's death?"

"I asked him that and he was noncommittal. He said Andrew called and asked him the same thing this morning. Andrew also told him about Marissa. Hamilton was shocked she was killed. Evidently my husband does remember some people fondly from college."

"God. I haven't even given poor Marissa much thought." Jill realized the police would surely be calling her at some point about the phone call Marissa made the night before she died.

It felt as if she was radiating anxiety out of her pores. Marissa had mentioned Andrew in that call to her the night she died. *Was Andrew going to be implicated in some way, too?*

He was dating her.

All roads led back to Andrew, not Max, in the suspicious connections department, Jill thought. She needed to tell all of this to the police.

"Marissa's poor parents," Carly murmured. "How will they survive losing two of their children under such tragic circumstances?"

"I don't know." Jill sighed. "I saw on the news this morning that the police are looking at images from the security camera in her building."

"I saw that, too." Carly stared at Jill. "Is Max still in police custody?"

"As far as I know. He hasn't been in touch with me." Jill wrung her hands together. "Your dad called a couple of hours ago and said the Santa Barbara PD is holding him for their own investigation about my mother's abduction, and that the feds are pressing them to release Max to them. Evidently they searched Max's hotel room last night and found more evidence tying him to what happened in Paris."

"Oh my god," Carly gasped. "What?"

"Your dad didn't know, but he said things sounded serious. He was also told Max has called his embassy for legal assistance." Jill glanced again at the wall clock. "Your dad said he would call later and give me any update he had."

Carly stood up. "I'm glad Dad's been able to help you with this mess."

"Me, too," Jill said. "It's getting late, Carly. You need to get back to your baby."

"I know. I'm going to head back to the hotel. I told Gloria to pack up everything so we could take Julia to my Dad's tomorrow. I think I'm going to send Gloria back to London. I feel like spending time with my Dad and baby girl without anyone else around right now."

"That sounds like a good idea. But I'm coming over to see you."

"I didn't mean you, silly. And thank god my stepmother is out of town. I couldn't bear that right now." Carly gave Jill a hug and picked up her purse and keys. "Call me later and let me know what Dad said, okay? Or if you want to talk."

"I will." Jill walked Carly to the door and waved goodbye. She locked it and leaned against the smooth wood, closing her eyes for a moment.

What is Max doing right now?

Despite telling Carly she didn't believe he had lied to her about wanting to reconnect when he came to the States, she had a hundred other worries about what he was involved in.

This man of secrets had too many to keep track of.

She prayed he would clear himself of suspicion soon, and get a chance to explain the things he had promised to before last nights' event blew-up in all their faces. Jill cringed when she thought of how harsh her last words had been to him, but more than anything she could not let herself be played for a fool.

The truth would come out. *I just hope I'm strong enough to hear it.*

Dave Hart knocked on Jill's door the next morning at ten. The look on his face told her the news was not good.

"Max is going to be charged in the next forty-eight hours for the murder of Marissa Pierce. Despite that, Santa Barbara PD have been told he will probably be returned to France to face charges in Ben's murder first. There's quite a fight going on over whose jurisdiction trumps whose."

Jill collapsed on her sofa. "What evidence do the police have?"

"Max is on the security camera tape at Marissa's parents' condo at six p.m. the night she was murdered." Dave sat across from her, his hands clasped together, his brow furrowed. "The cops have requested hair, blood, and fingerprint samples from Max to match to evidence recovered at the scene."

"Oh my god. How was Marissa killed?"

"She was shot at close range. In her bedroom. There were signs of a brief struggle, but not of forced entry. The police theory is that she knew and admitted her killer into the house. They have the bullet, so the make of gun used will be identified by the end of the day."

"Did the police find Max's? He didn't have it with him when he was arrested."

"I don't know."

A hollow sound echoed inside Jill's head and for a moment she thought she might faint. She walked out onto her sunny patio, and glanced at her mother dozing on the lounge chair. "What can I do? Can I go see him?"

"Do you want to?" Dave said, following her outside. "I doubt anyone but his embassy people, or an attorney, will be able to until he's formally charged."

Jill winced as the words 'formally charged' knifed through her brain. "Yes, of course I want to see him. I'm sure there is an innocent explanation for why Max went to see Marissa. Remember the phone call she made to me about having his college ring? Maybe he went to get it."

"They also found Ben Pierce's cell phone in Max's hotel room."

Jill opened her mouth and then shut it without uttering a word.

Dave handed her a business card. "No telling what else they found. Detective Steve Martin is handling the investigation. Call him. I spoke with him this morning and told him you had pertinent information." Dave glanced at Dorothy and sighed. "Anything he asks, you just tell the truth. I know you want to help Max, and that you believe in him, but the only way you can is to stick to the facts."

"Okay." Jill squeezed her cold hands together. "When you found out Max was working with that security group in the Swedish government, the . . ." Her mind blanked. "What is it called?"

"The *Nationella Insatsstyrkan*. It's a paramilitary unit within the Swedish police force. According to my FBI source, their officers carry Sig Sauers, by the way. Is that the kind of gun Max had with him?"

"I have no idea." She leaned forward. "What is it that group does?"

"They respond to everything from terror threats to financial fraud."

"If Max was working in some capacity with that organization, that could be why he was meeting with that guy on the Interpol wanted list that Andrew told me about, right?"

Jill saw pity in Dave's eyes.

"Don't try and work this out yourself. Call the detective and tell the truth. Don't hold anything back because you're worried it might hurt Max in some way." Dave patted her shoulder. "Carly and the baby are at my place. You're welcome to come by anytime. She wanted to come with me this morning, but I told her to chill for a while. But call her and let her know how you and Dorothy are doing, okay?"

"I will." She pressed her fingers so hard against the thin paper card that they trembled. "I'll call Detective Martin right now."

He nodded at her slumbering mother. "Is she staying here for good?"

"No. Even if I hired three shifts of home health care aids she wouldn't get the kind of therapy and care she was getting at Friend's House, and we'll run out of money fast. I will probably take her back there. But I need a few days to figure it out."

Dave hugged her. "I know you'll do what's best for your mom, honey. But be sure you do what's best for you, too. Okay?"

"Thanks, Dave. Tell Carly I'll call her tonight."

"Will do."

Chapter 20

Jill glanced at her watch. She was sitting on a hard chair at an empty desk in the Santa Barbara police station, waiting for Detective Martin to return. Uniformed officers milled around, talking, joking, and more than one had glanced in to look at her with speculation.

Detective Martin had taken her statement, asking all the questions she had expected about the incidents at the nursing home, Max's return, and her phone conversations with Marissa Pierce. He also asked her one question she had not been prepared for.

"Has anyone suggested to you that Marissa Pierce was having an affair with Hamilton Stewart?"

"What?" she had blurted out. "Since when?"

"No one told you those two were involved?" Detective Martin had replied. "Do you know if Mr. Stewart's wife, Carly, thought her husband was seeing Miss Pierce?"

Jill had told him the truth, that Carly had expressed a worry that Hamilton was seeing someone, but she didn't know who. She was going to have to admit this to Carly, and hoped that her friend would forgive her for sharing her confidential thoughts.

Jill rubbed the center of her forehead. *I thought Marissa was involved with Andrew, despite his declaration that he wasn't sleeping with the ex-cheerleader. But Hamilton? Detective Martin has to be wrong about that.*

Doesn't he?

A commotion outside the door made Jill look up.

Two policeman were leading a man through the outer office. The man was dressed in prisoner denim, handcuffed, and his ankles were shackled. He stared straightforward, his face calm.

Max.

Jill gasped and covered her mouth with her hand. The policemen stopped outside the office. "Detective Martin wants a few words with you before the transfer. Sit down, Kallstrom. The bus isn't going to be here for an hour or so."

Max sat in a chair ten feet away from her. One of the cops left, and the other sat next to his prisoner. Both men stared at her.

"How's your mother?" Max asked softly.

"She's fine." Jill walked to the doorway, leaning against it for support.

"I didn't take her out of her room. And I didn't take her necklace."

"How did it get in your jacket?" Her voice was brittle.

Max clenched his jaw.

Jill sighed. If Max was being set up for a series of crimes, he was not doing very much to help himself. She saw the cop listening carefully, his body tense.

She crossed her arms over her chest. She had a million questions, but suddenly her mind felt empty.

"I don't suppose you could leave me and the lady alone for a few moments," Max said to the guard.

"No can do," the cop replied.

Max stared back at Jill. "I'm sorry. I'm sorry I didn't get a chance to tell you everything I need to before all hell broke loose."

She was sorry, too, but mostly she was angry again. He should have trusted her, she thought. "Where are they taking you?" she asked, her voice tight.

"Los Angeles."

"Why?"

Max glanced at the cop. "Evidently the feds are trumping the local boys for wanting to accuse me of things I didn't do."

The cop smirked and shook his finger at Jill. "Don't believe this guy and his 'I didn't do it' line of bull. I've seen a lot of fine women like you waiting around for men who didn't deserve them."

"Thanks," Max said drily. He stared at Jill, taking in her face and body. "I'll call you as soon as I can."

"I don't think we have anything to talk about, Max."

"Don't give up on me. You didn't before. Don't do it now."

She didn't answer, but turned and walked back into Detective Martin's office, her skin hot and cold at the same time. Her face flushed when she heard the other policeman return and tell Max it was time to go.

The sound of his leg shackles clanking together was the only sound Max made as they herded him down the hallway.

Tears filled her eyes. Her brain felt frozen with suspicion, and fear. *I let him make a fool of me again.*

She sat heavily in the chair at the detective's desk, unable to think of a single thing she could do to make any of the fifty things wrong in her life one bit better.

At home that night Jill stared at her cell phone. It was after nine and she owed Carly a call. Her best friend had left two messages, but she could not seem to screw up the courage to call her back.

She had to tell her what the Detective said about Ham and Marissa, and that she'd told the cops Carly had worried Ham was having an affair.

I shouldn't have told them that, she thought.

When Dave Hart called, she had not been able to bring herself to tell him about the detective asking about Hamilton. But sitting alone now, she had the sudden thought that maybe he already knew, and maybe so did Carly, and that was why she and the baby were now staying with Dave.

The only new information Dave had passed on was that Andrew was also seen on the security tape from Marissa's condo the day she was killed.

What that meant is anyone's guess, she thought.

Exhaling loudly, Jill got up and rummaged in the refrigerator. The home health care aide who had watched her mother for a few hours today had offered to share her homemade tamales with her, but Jill had declined.

She wished she had one now. She took out bread and popped two pieces in the toaster, and opened the peanut butter, her go-to dinner when she was on her own. Her mind kept returning to Max.

She was furious with him, but her heart ached as she imagined what he was enduring. *What will he tell his daughter?* It was going to take time to clear all this up, especially to explain why he was seen going into Marissa's.

As far as explaining away how he was found with her mother's locket, the more she thought of it, the more she was convinced that someone had stolen it from her mother and had put it in his pocket to frame him.

Andrew's been there. Could he have done such a thing? It had a lock of Max's hair in it, and if it was found on Marissa's body, it could have been taken out of the locket. *Could the crime lab people tell how old a strand of hair was?*

As for the cops finding Ben Pierce's phone, well, Max might be a lot of things, a lot of things she didn't have any idea about, but he wasn't stupid. Only someone stupid would carry around a cell phone belonging to a man he had murdered. That evidence had surely been planted, too.

Her front doorbell chimed and Jill jumped. She licked a trace of peanut butter off her finger and squinted out the front window. There was a car in the drive, a silver compact she didn't recognize. She hurried to the door and looked out the peephole.

Andrew stared directly at her through the tiny lens. "I need to talk to you," he said at the top of his voice.

Shit.

"Now, Jilly."

"Go away," she yelled. "I'm not interested in talking to you."

Anxiety pumped through her. Even though Carly's dad had validated Andrew's credentials as an investigator, she didn't trust him at all.

"I'm not the bad guy," he shouted. "Come outside for five minutes. I need to tell you a couple of things."

The check, she thought. *I can give him the damn money and make it clear I don't ever want to talk to him again.* She hurried down the hall to her bedroom, grabbed the check from under the mattress, and a few moments later pulled open the front door.

"Here." She held it out, eerily mimicking Andrew's movements when he pushed a vase of roses at her a few days ago.

"Your mother could use that," he said.

"My mother is no concern of yours."

Andrew pursed his lips and grabbed the check. He stuck it in his coat pocket and then glared at her.

Jill stepped outside, pulling the front door closed behind her. "You want to talk? Talk."

"I told you Max was trouble," he said. "You should have listened to me."

She crossed her arms. "Why didn't you tell me you enlisted Hamilton Stewart to spy for you?"

He blinked. "Who told you that I did?"

"Did you tell the police Marissa was sleeping with

Ham?"

"You said I was sleeping with the lovely Marissa the other night. Changed your mind?" He laughed sarcastically.

"Don't make jokes, Andrew. The poor woman is dead."

He sobered. "I know that. No, I didn't tell the police that Hamilton was sleeping with her. Why would I? Marissa never confided anything like that to me. Who said they were having an affair anyway?"

"I have no idea. But the cops think they were."

Andrew frowned. "That's interesting. I know Marissa was attracted to Hamilton. She chattered on and on the other night about how he dressed, and how polished he was. But she did the same thing about Carly. And Max. She was star struck to see all her old idols close up after all those years." He stuck out his chin. "But you know, if the cops think she was screwing Hamilton, maybe she was. Our class isn't known for marital fidelity."

"Stop acting like a jealous thirteen year old boy," she shot back. "Now look, the cops also think Max killed Ben and Marissa, and that's not true, and you know that it isn't. Someone is giving them bad information and trying to frame Max. You need to keep investigating. You've overlooked something."

Andrew threw his head back and laughed. "Oh my god, Jill, are you that naïve? You continue to think the best about everyone, despite proof to the contrary."

"There's no real proof Max did anything wrong."

Andrew shook his head. "He met with a known felon involved with a worldwide financial fraud scheme. He pulled a gun on me. Ben Pierce's cell phone was in his hotel room! And, according to a cop who told me off the record, his hair was found at the murder scene." Andrew pulled on his necktie, the red stone in his college ring sparkling. "I think you've taken leave of your senses."

"Why, because I think someone could be framing Max?"

"Because you aren't facing the facts."

She blinked. "Marissa told me on the phone that she had Max's class ring. If she did, then whose ring was found at the scene of Ben's murder?"

"When did she tell you that?" Andrew's voice was shocked.

"She called me the night before she was killed. So if Marissa had it, then the cops will find it when they go through her room. But they might not know about Ben's murder details. I think you need to tell them if they find a ring it's important. That could prove that Max is innocent."

Andrew's eyes narrowed. "You realize that you're a weak witness for his defense, don't you?"

"I'm an honest witness," Jill said. "And if you are interested in solving Ben's murder, like you say you are, then explain to me why Max would have killed him."

"If Max is guilty of bank fraud, which the facts say he clearly is, perhaps he went to see Ben and tried to bribe him, or intimidate him."

"And when Ben wouldn't cooperate, what, Max killed him? Why would Max think that would stop an investigation? Ben wasn't working alone, for god's sake."

Andrew frowned. "It's clear you've given this a lot of thought. But you're forgetting a couple of things. One, criminals often don't act in a logical way. And two, Max Kallstrom has gone to some lengths to hide his identity. If you ask me, I think he killed Ben because he was trying to buy time so he could disappear with the monetary fruits of his crime, before the investigation was complete."

"Then why show up at the reunion? Why would he risk it?"

Andrew opened his mouth, then closed it with a click of his teeth. "To see you, I imagine. Test the level of gossip about Ben. Look, I don't have all the answers as to how or why Max Kallstrom has acted as he has, but it is clear he has secrets. And he's a man. And men, even if they are a thief and murderer, feel love. And lust. Maybe you were his Achilles heel."

"So you don't believe he has amnesia about the year he was here for college?"

"No." Andrew stuck his left hand in his pocket. "No. I don't believe that for a minute. I think it's a smokescreen to distract people. Give them something to talk about other than us."

"Us?" Jill's voice rose. "Jeez, Andrew, I didn't get asked a single question about our break-up. Let it go." She stared at the scar on his forehead. "No one even asked me about shooting you."

"A couple of people asked me about it," Andrew said defensively. "It was humiliating," he added.

Jill blinked. "Why aren't you allergic to peanuts anymore?"

"Now that is a true non sequitur." Andrew narrowed his eyes. "I once thought I was allergic to peanuts, but it was actually all the illegal chemically-enhanced weed I was ingesting. One I got clean, the allergic reactions went away."

She considered that for a moment. "Look, cash the check and consider all issues between us now complete." Jill half-turned away and grasped the doorknob. "For the record, I am glad you beat the drugs. Goodbye, Andrew."

"Wait."

She turned. "What?"

"Will you please go to dinner with me?" Andrew put his hand on her arm. "Let's go back a week. I want to see you. We once had things to talk about. Let's give it another try."

Talk about an Achilles heel, Jill thought. Andrew's the one who can't let go of the past. Somehow she kept from rolling her eyes. "No. Thank you, but no."

He squeezed her arm harder. "You gave Max a chance. I

deserve at least that much."

Jill pulled away and held up her hand in warning. "That hurt. Jeez, just when I thought you weren't a total shit, you act like one."

"Fine." Andrew ran his eyes down her body. "I'm staying around for Marissa's funeral, and I'll be at the hotel for another week before I head back to San Francisco. You know how to reach me."

She slammed the door behind her, locking both locks as loudly as she could. *Some men did change, and some didn't.* Andrew was definitely category two.

Her cellphone was ringing on the table in the kitchen and she picked it up. It was Carly.

Jill swallowed hard. She was going to have to toughen up and deliver a piece of gossip that might ruin her best friend's life.

Chapter 21

Jill checked on Dorothy in the guest room. Her mother was mumbling in her sleep, but showed no signs of waking up. She closed the door and the chimes hanging from the knob tinkled softly in the night.

She had placed a string of bells on the handle to alert her if her mother tried to leave the room, but so far the last couple of nights Dorothy had shown no ability to get out of the house on her own.

With a sigh, she headed for her bedroom, her mind full of thoughts about Max. She had not heard from him since she saw him at the police station two days ago.

It seems like a month. She slipped on a nightgown and opened both of the windows to let in some air. She kept her AC turned off because her mother seemed always to be cold, but the house was stifling.

She took out the bottle of sedatives and considered taking one, but decided against it and crawled into bed. Her sleep was fitful, filled with nightmare scenarios of crowded rooms and loud music, starring Max, Carly, and poor Marissa Pierce as partygoers she could not get though the dream room crowd to talk to.

Three hours later, Jill woke with a start, drenched with sweat. She lay still for a moment, controlling her breathing, quieting her nerves. Outside, a night bird called to its mate as a breeze rustled through the lemon trees on the patio.

She thought of her recent barbecue with Max and missed him so badly she ached. *If I call the jail, would they let me speak to him?*

But what jail? She didn't even know where he was being held.

Rubbing her welling eyes, she dragged herself out of bed and checked her mother. Dorothy slept soundly, the sheet pulled up around her shoulders.

Jill headed for the kitchen. She grabbed a bottle of water from the fridge and peered out into the night. No unfamiliar cars were in her driveway or on the street. She leaned against the counter and sighed. She was not one bit sleepy, though she had averaged only about four hours a night the last few days.

Next week school would be back in session, and she had not done any work to deal with that. Her students had two more weeks of lectures, which she had planned out and had given many times before, but she needed to re-design her final exam.

Deciding to try and refocus her attention on something normal, Jill tiptoed back into the guestroom and pulled her laptop and some folders off the desk, and then shut the door behind her. She was walking back to the kitchen when she stopped.

Was that a noise in the garage?

The sound of muted rustling did not fit the normal night sounds. She took a step closer to the garage exit opposite the front door. Slowly she leaned forward to listen, but all was quiet.

Tell me I didn't forget to close the garage again. She visualized coming in from errands earlier, but could not remember if she had hit the button before she stepped inside.

Jeez, maybe I'm getting Alzheimer's.

This was a constant worry now, especially during times of stress, even if she knew it was surely not true. "This is ridiculous," she murmured.

She set her laptop and paperwork on the kitchen table, turned on the teakettle, and headed resolutely back to the foyer. *I'll open it a crack, confirm everything is closed properly, and then sit down and get to work.*

She turned the knob and pushed the door open, and flipped the light switch. Her car was parked, and the garage was closed. But there was a cardboard box sitting on car's passenger side trunk.

The top was open and several books were piled next to it.

"What the devil?" She stepped down onto the concrete and headed for the box.

"Hello, Jill," Ben Pierce's killer said.

She yelped and grabbed her throat.

A man rose from the crouch he was in beside the washing machine. He grabbed Jill with one hand, and aimed a gun at her head with his other. "Stand still and be quiet. I won't hurt you unless you scream."

Shock and bitter anger nearly brought her to her knees as she registered who he was, and what a massive betrayal he had pulled off. Furious, she slapped at the gun and twisted out of the man's grasp, and turned to run.

Before she completely filled her lungs with air to scream, his pistol cracked against her skull and knocked her to her knees.

There was black, and then nothing.

From the depths of her consciousness, Jill imagined she heard her mother calling her.

Jill, Jill, come inside for dinner. It's time to eat!

She opened her eyes slowly, as the dream images receded, but she couldn't focus. Blinking, Jill turned her head and the room around her settled into view. She was in her own bed and the lamp next to her was turned on low.

The man who had bashed her senseless was standing across from where she lay, leaning against her dresser.

He was holding her jewelry box.

Their eyes met. "I tried to find the locket in here last week," he said. "When I couldn't, I realized I better check the nursing home to see if your mother had it. I'm surprised you let her keep something so nice with her. Don't those old bats misplace everything?"

Jill squeezed her hands into fists and only then realized they were tied together in front of her. Her feet were also bound.

I'm trussed up like an animal about to be slaughtered.

Her body jerked as blinding pain, radiating from the side of her head, rolled through her, followed by a wave of nausea. She moaned and closed her eyes, for a moment blotting out the man's traitorous face.

"Breath deep a couple of times and you'll feel better. Well, at least a little better."

She exhaled and opened her eyes. "Why?"

The intruder put the jewelry box down. "Oh, it's a long story, Jill." He slid a lighter out of his pocket, and picked up the lavender candle that had scented her recent joyous nights of love.

He stared at her hard for a moment, and then flicked on the flame and lit the candle. He sniffed it and set it gently on the dresser. "We don't have time for the whole sordid tale, but I'll fill you in on the highlights. I guess I owe you that."

"You owe me a hell of a lot more than that, you son of a bitch."

"No, I don't." He seemed weary. "But I can understand your anger."

"I doubt that." She strained against her ties. "How could you be such a filthy liar? How could you do this?"

"Surely you understand I have feelings, too?"

"You? You're sick. And twisted. And hateful. Whoever the hell you really are."

The target of her rage raised his silky eyebrows. "Well, so you finally understand you can't believe everything you see. Okay, well, I'll start with my name, my real name. It's

Peter. Peter Cullen. I'm just a poor bloke from a poor family." He grinned. "Hey, that's almost a song lyric, isn't it?"

"Untie me! And get out of my house"

"Come on now, really? You know I can't do that." He folded his arms, raking his eyes over her body. "Now, I've digressed. Back to my youth. I was poor. Dirt poor, as you Americans say. Only hope I ever had of being not poor was one blood relation, a Mr. Henry Stewart. You see, Henry fucked my mom for a couple of years pretty regular. He left me inside her during one of his visits, and to show his support he gave her a fiver now and then when he came to call, but when I was a young lad he decided he had enough of us.

"Poor mum died without a quid to her name, and I wanted to go to University, which was a joke, as I didn't have much of an education to that point, nor any money. But I thought, when I was about sixteen, and my poor mum died, that I'd go up to visit old Henry, see if maybe he'd help out, considering he was my father." Peter smiled sadly. "Sent me packing, saying I had no proof who my dad was, although he a good laugh out of the fact that I was a dead ringer for his only legitimate family, his orphaned nephew. He was so tickled by the fact he showed me a photo of the kid, and Henry was right. Hamilton Stewart, recent arrival at the Oxford I dreamed of going to, looked exactly like me."

Oh my god, Jill thought. *Can this be true?*

Peter Cullen narrowed his eyes at Jill. "You following this okay, girl? That's a bad bump you got on your noggin."

She felt paralyzed, and wondered for a moment if she was dreaming. But the ties chaffing her hands and feet reminded her she was very much awake.

He's a madman. A madman she knew as Hamilton Stewart, her best friend's husband. But this man was not Hamilton, not the Hamilton she had known at St. John's College. Not Hamilton at all.

"What did you do to Hamilton?" she asked.

"Oh, the poor lad drowned sixteen, seventeen years ago now, I'm sorry to say." He looked off into space, a rueful look on his face. "One lazy afternoon while on summer break. After old Henry died and left Ham all that money, I visited my dear cousin, told him my story. He was a sweetheart, actually. Said he would try to help if he could, that we would visit his solicitor and see if he could help with my university fees. He couldn't get over how much we resembled each other, too. Only real difference was that I'm a leftie. No one remembered that Hamilton wasn't I guess."

A movement outside the window beside the dresser caught Jill's attention. There was a shadow, a faint silhouette. *Who is outside?* Her body quivered with fear.

"Anyway, Cousin Hamilton invited me to stay with him during his holiday at the shore," Peter continued. "He was working on his music, had started writing it as well as performing. Sat on his bum by the piano day and night. Except for when we'd go off for a swim. Quite boring."

"You're despicable."

Peter narrowed his eyes at Jill. "Now, now, let's not be so judgmental. We can't all be the kind, forgiving girl you are. Anyway, my plan came to me all of sudden. One day after lunch, dear Hamilton got a cramp while he was swimming, quite a bad one. His lips were blue and his eyes wild. He was thrashing around, calling for my help, and I realized, well now, here's an opportunity." He blinked. "So I stood by as he went under. I let him stay there long enough to get the job done, and then I hauled him out. I buried his body where, as far as I can tell, no one has found it yet, and went back to school in Oxford. And became him." His eyes widened as if he was hearing the story for the first time. "Pretty amazing. A real life changing-places story, staring me."

"And no one noticed?" Jill was mesmerized by his evilness. "No one realized you weren't Ham?"

"No. And I was as surprised as you, Jilly girl. But then, Hamilton lived alone. Just him and the piano. Only one man seemed to have a doubt that I was him. I think the guy had been buggering dear old Hamilton, if you don't mind hearing such a thing. The good professor showed up a bit tipsy one night, looking for a slap and tickle. Well, I might be a lot of things, but queer isn't one of them. So it was sad when the unlucky bloke turned up the victim of a hit-and-run accident. Sad for him, anyway."

Jill swallowed the sob filling her throat, distracted again by the movement of the curtain across from her. She kept herself from staring at it, but she was now sure someone was outside, watching.

Whoever you are, please call the police, she prayed.

"So, how's that for a dramatic twist? You didn't notice anything different either, did you?"

"No. But your accent is totally British tonight," Jill replied loudly, returning Peter's unwavering stare. His hardened face did not look like Hamilton at all now.

"Yeah, well, no need to pretend now, is there?"

"You pulled off quite a scam."

"I have, haven't I? It's amazing how most people take you at your word, face value, if you'll forgive the pun. You say you're someone with confidence, and no one doubts you. Must be how Max feels, huh? Showing back up in your life, not remembering you, but counting on you to trust what you remembered about him. Maybe he's a killer, too."

"That's a terrible thing to say."

"It is, isn't it? But I'll have to live with that. And I will." He glanced at his watch. "I'm going to fly home in the morning and wait for the return of my dear wife and child."

"Carly . . ." Tears flooded down Jill's face as her rage turned to pain as she realized that her dearest friend was married to this monster, and there was nothing she could do to change that horrible reality. "You won't hurt her . . ."

"Oh, no, don't worry about that. Carly's a love. She doesn't suspect, because thankfully she really didn't know Hamilton all that well. Hadn't ever slept with him, or anything, score one point for the homo, thank you very much. And I am very grateful for that, you know, because I fancy her, I do. She and the wee one are a bonus. I got the education I dreamed of, and a great job and life, along with a perfect family. Great for a bloke's confidence, too. Too great, actually. Because I thought if I'd fooled her, I could fool anyone Hamilton had ever known."

"Did you?" Jill asked. From the corner of her eye, she caught another shift of light against the screen. *A hand? Was someone about to burst into the room?*

She raised her voice. "You seemed to have fooled everyone at the reunion."

"Here? Yes, I did. But I messed up somehow, a few months ago when I was in Paris."

"Ben Pierce." She shuddered. "He guessed you were an imposter?"

"Ben. Yeah. I guess Andrew told you all about that, eh? He did, poor bugger." Peter stood up straight. "Ben said he heard something in my voice. I did research later and found out our Ben studied linguistics in graduate school. I guess he pegged me pretty easy as not being a natural born Yank. So that was the end of him."

"But why did you come to the reunion?" Jill's mind turned to her mother's safety. She had to keep Peter talking in the hopes whoever was outside would come to their rescue.

Delaying Peter's plans, whatever they were, was her only chance to stop him.

"The biggest reason was that I needed a class ring, as old Ben had put up a bit of a fight and I accidently left mine behind in Paris. I knew that mistake might get people sniffing around our St. John's alums, excuse me, your alums. See how well I've adapted to being Hamilton?" Peter grinned.

"I knew people would show up here with their rings, and I needed to have one to be safe. I figured I could snag one from a hotel room. I'm good at getting in and out of places."

She stared at Peter's hand, the blood-red stone sparkling like a demon's eye. "Whose ring are you wearing?"

He held up his fist and admired it. "This, strangely enough, is Kallstrom's. Which brings me to my second reason for coming to town. First thing I did was call Marissa, which of course I had to do to see what her brother Ben had called and told her about meeting me in Paris. I knew he had spoken to her because her number was the last he'd called on his cell. Anyway, lo and behold, the chit was thrilled to see me. Said Ben had mentioned running into me, but she didn't tie it to his dying shortly after."

"She didn't know Ben was murdered."

"Right. The poor lass was saved that sad news. Which was good for me, you see, because evidently she had a yen for Cousin Ham since her school days. When I expressed some interest in those enormous tits of hers, she had me undressed and plowing her good in record time." Peter snickered. "She wasn't very subtle about our hooking up some more when I ran into her at the events this week, but thank god Andrew, your ex-better half, was fortuitously squiring her around, too."

Jill flinched at the mention of Andrew. He was going to feel humiliated to find out he had been so wrong about Max.

"You don't like Denton much, I can see." Peter studied her face. "Did you know he's still got it bad for you? He called me up a couple of months ago to enlist my help in investigating old Ben's death, which gave me quite a fright, if you want to know the truth. But it became clear right away Andrew had his mind set that Ben's killer was Max. He let jealousy get the best of him, but as his mistake benefited me, I played along. And I reinforced them when I left Ben's cellphone in Max's hotel room."

She felt no triumph hearing him admit he had framed Max. "The cops are going to find out Max is innocent. They'll look for other answers. They'll find out about you."

"You think so? I don't. Especially with you out of the way." His voice was harsh suddenly, no longer relaxed. "So sorry, Jill, but once I decided to pin Ben Pierce's murder on Max, it became clear that I was going to have to involve you in my mop-up activity." He shook his head as if he was actually sorry. "I know Andrew's already convinced, and has the cops looking at Max hard, but when you turn up dead, well, they'll throw away the key. Justice will be a little blind as far as any loose ends about Max Kallstrom's innocence."

She strained again against the bindings. "You're not going to get away with this. Someone will find a fingerprint, or check your travel, or find Hamilton's body someday. You'll be caught. If you are smart, you'll run now. You created a new identity for yourself once, if you leave now you might be able to get away with it again."

Peter shocked Jill by laughing as if he was delighted. "Some people never do change, do they? Carly always said you were a Pollyanna, believing in truth, justice, and smart American girls getting themselves out of trouble. Sorry, love. This is the perfect crime. The cops will think Max killed Peter, and Marissa."

He slipped the gun he had smacked her with in the garage out of his pocket. "What's Max doing with this, by the way? I found it in his hotel last night when I left the cellphone."

Jill glared at him.

"You don't have to tell me if you don't want to. But it came in handy with Marissa."

"Why did you kill her? You said she didn't realize you weren't Hamilton." Jill inadvertently glanced at the curtains, but quickly turned back to stare at Peter. "How could you do that?"

"I had to. When I heard Marissa on the phone with you, I realized she could gum things up if she gave Max his ring. I needed it, you see, to help in the frame, and if I asked her for it, or just stole it from her place, she might have been trouble down the line."

"You're disgusting."

Peter moved closer to the bed. "I'm an opportunist, more's the truth. I'm fast on my feet. When Carly told me weeks ago about you keeping some of Max's hair in your locket, I filed it away. Because of that, I was able to leave some nice evidence under Marissa's fingernails your Max will have a time explaining, thanks to Andrew pointing the coppers at him. Poor Andrew. Sucks to be a two-time loser I imagine." Peter moved toward the door. "I've enjoyed our chat, but I need to get going now."

Her brain felt as if it were on fire. Jill shook her head, risking a sideways glance at the window. There was nothing to see now except black night.

She wet her lips. "What were you looking for in the box in the garage?" *Keep him talking . . . ...*

Peter stopped, his hand on the light switch. "Your cassette tapes from the school recital Hamilton performed so well in. Aside from being a leftie, I also have no musical ability at all, you see. When Millard pressed me to play, she seemed suspicious to me. I saw something in her eyes the other night, she was squinting at me. So I nicked a couple more out of the old crone's office. And came to get yours. Tiny loose end. But a loose end nonetheless."

"What are you going to do with me?" Jill moved her arms out from under the covers and struggled to scoot up to a sitting position. "I'm tied up. I can't get to my mother if she needs help."

"Oh, your Mum's fine. She woke up a while ago so I gave her a drink of juice and a sedative. She's dozing out on the patio now, happy as a clam." Peter walked to the window and pulled the drapery completely open. "See her out there?"

Jill inhaled, praying there was nothing outside that would escalate the surreal into the deadly. She saw only the dimly lit figure of her mother on the lounger, not moving. "So now what?"

"I'll be back in a second with a nice cuppa. You're looking a peaked yourself, dear girl. I need to give you something to sleep. This candle will help relax you, too."

Peter grinned, a cold gleam in his bright blue eyes. "You'll dream sweet dreams and this will all be over soon."

As soon as he left the room, Jill rolled over and managed to sit up. Her feet were bound tightly so she reached down and tugged at the satin binding from her robe that Peter had used, but it didn't budge. She bit at the ties on her hand, making zero progress as her brain screamed for her to get to a phone and call for help.

She struggled wildly, but had no idea where her purse was. For a moment she considered going to the window and yelling her lungs out, but knew Peter would silence her, and then her mother would be at his mercy. Just then her neighbor's air-conditioning unit kicked on, drowning out her thoughts.

I can't risk it. She searched the window for a sign of another person, but saw nothing. The shadow she had seen outside could have been a cloud over the moon, she realized with a sinking heart. She began to panic, realizing that if Peter Cullen had told her as much as he had, that he must have plans to kill her.

"Jill." Her whispered name floated through the air like a wasp. She sat bolt upright and squinted at the window.

Max pressed his face against the screen, his finger to his lips, signaling for her to be quiet. He ran a blade down the middle of the screen, slicing it open with a glint of silver.

A moment later, he was in the room, his arms around her.

Jill trembled so violently she thought she might shake apart. "Cut me loose. I can't move."

"Shhh. Where's your cellphone?"

She shook her head. She couldn't remember where her purse was.

"Mine died." Max cut the silk binding her legs with one stroke. She fell against him as he carefully slit the heavier cord wrapped around her wrists.

She rubbed her hands together and they crept toward the door. "Patio." He whispered. "Get outside and call for help."

Jill clung to Max for a second, not wanting to leave. She had no idea why he was no longer in police custody, but she felt no fear.

She heard Peter in the kitchen, slamming cupboards while he looked for god knows what. "He has a gun."

"I saw it." Her lover's eyes darkened and his lips pursed into a grim line. He still had the penknife in his hand and pushed her gently into the hallway. "Go now, get out through the living room."

She would have to carry her mother off the patio if she couldn't wake her, and drag her to one of the neighbors and call the police. "I don't know how you made your way here tonight, or why, but thank you."

Max touched her face, his mouth softening for an instant. "You've trusted me, forgiven me, and did everything you could to help me. I'm amazed at your kindness. It's I who need to say thank you." He pulled her closer. "And I will when this is over. But now you need to get out of here and take care of your mother. Go. We need more help."

She kissed him hard and hurried out of the room. Her aching legs faltered and she almost fell hurrying down the hallway. She glanced back fearfully and saw Max, standing still as a pillar, watching her. She slid the screen door carefully, and ducked out onto the shadowy deck.

Get Mother. Go next door. Call 9-1-1.

Her eyes adjusted to the darkness and Jill stopped in shock. Dorothy was not on the lounger.

The patio was empty.

Chapter 22

Jill whirled around and hurried to the side alley that led to the street. The gate was wide open. She ran out to the front yard but there was no sign of her mother anywhere.

She glanced at her neighbors. *Should I go to the door and bang on it, scream for them to call the police?*

No, I have to find Mother first.

Jill made a 360-degree check of the area and saw a flash of light through her kitchen window. Her mother was inside the kitchen at the counter, looking out at her!

"Mom!" Jill gasped and started toward the house just as the kitchen light went off.

Jill darted back into her yard and ran across the patio and into the living room, right into the grasp of Peter. He pushed her roughly against the wall, his gun pressed against her chest.

"Hold still," he ordered. "Where's your mother?"

"I, I don't know. She's outside somewhere," she lied, waving toward the patio. *Mom must be hiding. In the powder room or out in the garage,* Jill thought, knowing how doors confused her. "I need to go out and find her."

Peter pulled her hair, so close to her she could smell his stale breath. "If the cops show up, you're both dead."

"I didn't call them." Her eyes darted toward the kitchen. *Where is Max?*

She gasped then, seeing Max laying in the hallway at the edge of the living room, face down.

"Oh my god, what have you done?" At that moment Jill saw Peter's shirt was covered with blood.

"Max stabbed me. So I shot him." He pulled her past Max's unmoving body and pushed her down onto her bed, yanking off his necktie. "Tie your feet together." He picked up her robe and pulled off the belt. "I'll do your arms."

"I'm not moving until you let me help Max."

"God damn it, Jill, tie your feet together now or I'll shoot you right now. Then what will your mother do?" He pointed the gun at her and pulled the trigger back.

With shaking hands, she bound her ankles together, praying her mother stayed in whatever hidey-hole she had found. She held out her hands, her voice shaking. "Why don't you leave? Get out while you can."

"Thanks for the advice," Peter said sarcastically. Savagely he wrapped the belt tighter and fastened it securely to the wrought iron headboard. "I've got my own plan."

He was pale and his hands shook. She saw a wound trailing blood on the side of his neck.

Her arms screamed with pain from the tightness of her bindings. "What are you going to do now?"

Peter grabbed a tee from her drawer and stuck it inside his shirt against a second wound on his shoulder. "What I should have done a half an hour ago. I'm taking your car. Where are the keys?"

"In my purse," she said, remembering in a moment of clarity where she had left it. "It's inside the closet, on the floor. But what about Max? If I'm tied up, I can't help him."

"He's dead. Or will be in a minute." Peter shoved her head against the headboard. "Sorry, lass. You're done rescuing people for the night. This is goodbye." He pushed a silk scarf into her mouth. As she watched in horror, he then picked up the lit candle from the night table and tossed it into her open bureau drawer. The smell of burning silk filled the air immediately.

"They'll blame that on your mum playing with matches,

no doubt." He dropped Max's gun on the floor out of her reach. "And they'll think Mad Max tried to kill you because you knew too much about his plan. But you fought back, brave girl, and shot with his own gun. It will be very easy for Andrew and the cops to explain the whole thing."

Peter pulled Max's motionless body into the bedroom by his feet and left him on the floor next to her bed. With a final look around his well-staged mayhem, he disappeared from sight.

Her entire body shook from fright. *What am I going to do?* She tried to roll, but couldn't because of how tightly Peter had tied her to the headboard.

Max groaned. Jill looked down and saw his hand jerk, as if he was trying to push himself upright. His dark hair was matted with blood.

Tears welled in her eyes and her throat felt like it was closing. She ordered herself to calm and worked to push the handkerchief out of her mouth.

The smoke was becoming thicker and more acrid as items inside the dresser drawer began to smolder. She prayed someone had seen or heard something, and had called the police.

Without warning, a gunshot rang out, and a man screamed.

Jill froze. *What happened? Were the police here?*

Pale as a ghost, her nightgown spattered with blood, her mother walked through the door. Jill's father's service revolver was clutched in her right hand.

Her mother waved the gun around and then pointed it at Max. "Fire," Dorothy said, her eyes wild.

Jill finally managed to spit the gag out of her mouth. "Mom, put the gun down on the floor. Go outside and scream fire. Please! Go now!"

Dorothy stared at her blankly.

"Mom! Listen. Go outside. You have to help us both now," Jill screamed, straining against the binding, trying to free herself from the headboard.

"Who is that man?" Her mother dropped the gun and stumbled out of the bedroom doorway, swallowed by the smoky darkness.

"Jill," Max moaned and rolled on side. His face was covered with blood. "Jill."

She yearned to touch him but couldn't move. She began to cough as her eyes watered and panic built in her chest. The smoke was thickening, and the heat and flames intensified across the room.

"Max, can you move? Max, crawl out of here if you can. Max!"

He grabbed the side of the bed and pulled himself up. His eyes were agonized. He tried to stand. "Jill . . ."

Their eyes met. "Max, mother is out there somewhere. Please go help her if you can." She was finding it hard to breathe and convulsed with coughing.

Max managed to stand and he reached for her, his hands fumbling with her bindings. His forehead was a red gash, and his right arm was drenched with blood.

Across the room, the dresser flashed into blue flame. Max fell across the bed.

"Turn your head into the mattress," he said. "Cover your mouth and don't breathe the smoke."

Her eyes met his, and then Max's closed and he went limp.

Jill screamed and pushed him off of her, breaking free from the ties on her arms, and both of them tumbled to the floor. Jill's ankles were numb and she knew she didn't have the time or strength to get the bindings off.

I'm going to die here tonight, she thought. Before Max knew she loved him, before they had another chance.

Suddenly there were sirens, so loud they seemed inside the house. There was pounding on the front door, and then she heard voices. She buried her head into Max, her consciousness fading.

"Jilly! Jilly, where are you?" Andrew rushed through the hellacious smoke, calling her name. He grabbed her. "Oh my god. We have your mother outside. Is Max . . .?"

"I told you that you were wrong about Max," she whispered. The room filled with jostling and shouting emergency personnel. Jill closed her eyes and prayed she would wake up, not at all sure that prayer would be answered.

Dave Hart was sitting beside Jill's hospital bed.

She had been in intensive care for one night, and was now on day three of rehab due to smoke inhalation and shock.

"Hi, Dave." Her voice was scratchy and hoarse.

"Hey, kiddo." Dave patted her hand. "How you feeling?"

"Pretty good, I guess," she said. "How's Carly?"

Dave's face darkened. "She's shattered. It's going to take quite a while before she's able to accept everything that's happened."

Jill's swollen eyes teared up. "I honestly cannot imagine how she will get through this, but please send her my love. And tell her I'll be here for her."

"She's coming to see you later today. She wants to be sure you're alive." Dave's voice roughened. "And that you forgive her."

Tears ran down her raw cheeks. "Oh, Dave, she didn't do anything that needs to be forgiven."

Dave hung his head. "She blames herself for being fooled, for bringing that man into all of our lives."

"Oh, god, no, don't let her do that. She met a man and fell in love. Who could have imagined what he really was?"

"Not me." He cleared his throat, his face grimmer still. "And I should have. Anyway, we'll help her get through this. She has that sweet baby. That will help."

Jill nodded, overwhelmed at the thought of how Carly would have to one day explain the imposter to her daughter. "The police say my mother shot Peter Cullen."

"That's what it looks like." Dave nodded. "She must have been in the hall closet, where you kept your dad's gun. It's a miracle she knew what to do with it."

"It's more a miracle that there was a bullet in it. I never loaded it after Max had it cleaned."

"Max told the cops he checked it then and there wasn't a bullet in the chamber. But there were three in the belt holding the holster. Your mom must have loaded one." Dave shook his head. "How she remembered how to do that is beyond any of us."

"Instinct."

"That. Or maybe your dad was watching out for all of you."

Jill sighed, not ready to believe in that theory, however lovely to contemplate. "The doctor asked her what happened, but she seems to not understand the question. But physically, at least, she's doing well. She wasn't exposed too much to the smoke."

"I know." Dave patted her hand. "I wanted to tell you that Detective Martin called. He said Max has been completely cleared of all the crimes he was charged with."

"I heard. I spoke with Max briefly on the phone last night." She looked away, remembering the awkward conversation. "He sounds terrible, like a two-pack-a-day smoker."

"He's going to be okay, too. Thanks to you and your mom."

Jill turned to Dave. "He's the one who saved us. Instead of leaving, flying back to Paris when he was released, he came to me. He nearly died defending us against Peter Cullen."

"He's quite a man."

"He doesn't see it that way." She thought briefly of his words on the phone last night. "He blames himself for not telling me about what he was investigating, or about his suspicions about Hamilton."

"Do you blame him?" Dave asked quietly.

"He should have trusted me. If he had, things may have turned out differently." Jill shivered when she thought of how close they had both come to being killed.

Max was recuperating in a room on another floor, recovering from being nicked by a ricochet piece of the bullets Peter fired, as well as being stabbed twice by the knife he had first wielded against the madman.

"Max would have died from loss of blood if the bullet had hit him full force, Detective Martin said," Dave offered. "It was a miracle he got away from Cullen."

"Two miracles that night." Jill sighed.

"Is your mom still in the hospital?" Dave asked.

"No. They took her back to Friend's House today," Jill said. "I think that's the best place for her. My house is going to have to be repaired from the fire. No place for either of us for a while."

"What are you going to do?"

"I think I'll rent an apartment for a bit, stay close and supervise the work. I'm supposed to be released tomorrow. I need to go back to school this week, too." Jill's voice broke.

Dave sighed, looking older than his sixty years. "The police in London are searching for Hamilton Stewart's body. I don't know when Carly will be able to go back home."

"Tell her I said she needs to take it one day at a time," Jill murmured.

"You, too, Jill."

She nodded.

Dave got up and kissed her cheek. "I'll be in touch."

"Thank you for everything, Dave."

"Stay strong. And remember how much you're loved. By many."

Jill watched her best friend's father leave with tears in her sore eyes. She didn't feel loved today, she felt alone. She missed her mother.

And Carly.

And Max.

A knock sounded at the door and Max stuck his head in. His dark hair had been completely shaved off in the emergency room, and he was dressed in baggy hospital patient clothes. "Hey. I was hoping I would find you sleeping." He had an envelope in his hand, and the wariness she had seen too many times before was in his eyes.

She blinked. He was the dearest sight she could imagine. "Sorry to disappoint you that I'm awake." She nodded at the envelope. "You want to read it to me."

"No." Max walked to her bedside and put his hand gently on Jill's shoulder. "You're going home tomorrow, I hear."

"Yes." She ached to touch him, but sat completely still. She wondered what was in the envelope.

A farewell note. A goodbye.

She had not had one from him the last time they parted, fifteen years ago. Tears welled in her eyes and she touched her fingers to her eyelids to hide them. "When are they kicking you out?"

"Today, I think."

"When are you flying back to France?"

"Tomorrow."

She looked away. "I'm sure you can't wait to see Olivia. Does she know what happened?"

"Her mother told her I had an accident. I'm going to talk to her about it when I see her. Tell her a little, but not too much of the details. Not yet, anyway."

"That sounds like a good plan."

His green eyes stared at her. "How are you holding up? Really?"

She rolled her shoulder and he dropped his hand. She took a breath. "My throat hurts, but I'm going to be fine. I need to go to physical therapy for a few weeks. Evidently one of my lungs is a bit damaged."

"We're blessed," he said simply.

"Yes, we are. Thank god Andrew got it in his head to come to my house to warn me you had been released." She smiled grimly. "I've had to adjust my feelings a bit about my ex-husband."

"He was obsessed. He had his facts completely wrong, but I'll be forever grateful to him." Max smiled faintly. "I spoke to him this morning. He came by to apologize about his suspicions. He's really not a bad sort. Have you seen him?"

"No."

"He's still in love with you," Max said tightly.

Jill let out a rattling breath. "He's not in love with me, Max. Andrew came back into my life to try and make it up to me. His behavior when we were married still embarrassed him. I told him yesterday when he called that he has more than settled the score now, and that I forgave him. I hope he forgives me, too." She stared at Max. "I did marry him for the wrong reasons. But I'm not going to dwell on that. I'm done with the past now. I'm letting go of those old wounds. For good."

"What are you going to do if Andrew asks you to reconsider him in the future?"

"He won't." She smiled faintly, remembering Andrew's last words to her. *"You're in love with Max again, aren't you? Still in love with him, I guess."*

Max blinked, a look of anguish in his eyes. He sat on the

bed next to her. "Are you done with me, too?"

The tears came harder and Jill could no longer control them. "Max, our being together is impossible. We have separate lives, on separate continents."

He kissed her gently, then not so gently. He held her face in his hands. "Nothing is impossible. We can make this work, this new love, if you'll try."

"I don't know if I can, Max. You should have told me the truth, the whole truth, about why you came back to California."

"I know. But don't let my mistake ruin what we have now, Jill." He handed her the envelope. "Open this."

She wiped her eyes. "What is it?"

"There's an airline ticket, open ended, for you to come to stay with me in Paris. Meet Olivia. See if you like the house, and the neighborhood. If not, we'll get something else. There's also a copy of my resignation from the *Nationella Insatsstyrkan*. I am going to concentrate on my business now, and work half-time from the States and half-time from Paris. I am done with the *Nationella*. I'm exclusively a family man now. Hopefully with a new wife. And more children."

Jill rocked back in shock. "A new wife?" She tried to keep from smiling, but couldn't. "That's quite a lot of changes in your life."

"I don't want to rush you, Jill, but I do want you to know that I will never leave you again. Unless you throw me out. And even then, we'll I'm pretty tenacious."

"Are you giving up your work with the government for me?"

"For you. And for Olivia." He looked grim. "When I was laying on the floor in your room, all I could think of was that I was about to lose both of you. It was worse than dying, the thought of that. It's one I won't forget."

She squeezed his hand. "I was thinking the same thing. What is it you did, actually, for the intelligence people?"

Max took a breath and briefly outlined his relationship with the organization. He worked occasionally in the fraud division for them if they needed someone with a 'real life' who could allow his company to be used as bait. He had agreed to help in an international fraud scheme that Ben Pierce's division was investigating without realizing the implications to his own life and safety.

"Small world," Jill said. "Neither you or Ben had any idea the other was involved."

"No, we didn't. And even if I had been told his name, I wouldn't have realized there was a connection to my lost past."

"But Ben would have recognized you, had you met on the street like he met Peter Cullen."

Max shrugged. "Who knows? It was tragic that Ben ran into Peter Cullen and realized the man was an imposter. But there was nothing Ben could do about it. Just like there was nothing Carly could have done but accept him as Hamilton Stewart, because she didn't remember well enough."

"It's so unfair."

"But it's how life is, *ja*? You've learned that with your mother's illness. And with the accident that separated us for so long."

"*Ja*." Jill touched his face. It was a different face than she first loved all those years ago. But every smile line and crease, every plane, every mark on it was newly beloved.

Max was a lot like her father, she realized. Always put his family first. Protective. Loyal. Loving.

Gently she touched the bandage over his stiches. "You look good bald."

Max rubbed his head and chuckled. "Better me than you, *ja?*"

They both laughed and he hugged her hard to him. "So will you marry me, Jill, and be my wife?"

Despite the odds, it looked like Max Kallstrom, the great love of her past, would now also be the great love of her future.

Jill exhaled and rested her head against his chest, hearing his heart beat strong and calm. "Yes, Yes, I will."

Also from **Soul Mate Publishing** and **Emelle Gamble**:

SECRET SISTER

"Secret Sister is compulsively readable. I defy anyone not to race through the pages to find out what happens to Cathy and Nick — and Nick and Roxanne!" Patricia Gaffney, New York Times Best-selling author of *The Saving Graces*

"Lovers of women's fiction have a new must-read! Secret Sister by Emelle Gamble has it all . . . romance, drama, and suspense . . . I could not put it down." Beth Harbison, New York Time's best-selling author of *Chose The Wrong Guy, Gave Him The Wrong Finger* and *Shoe Addicts Anonymous*

To their friends, Nick and Cathy Chance have the perfect marriage. High school sweethearts who've been together for ten years, they've weathered challenges and are as committed as they were when they first fell in love. Cathy trusts Nick, Nick's world revolves around his wife, and the future looks golden.

To everyone who knows them, Cathy Chance and Roxanne Ruiz have a perfect friendship. They connected in grade school and since then have been each other's confidant and trusted advisor. Cathy loves the gorgeous Roxanne like a sister, Roxanne has fun-loving Cathy's back in every situation, though lately there's been tension between these two best friends . . .

And then, on a sunny summer morning, the unthinkable occurs, throwing into doubt the truth of what each of these people really know about themselves and one another.

Will Roxanne's sacrifice be too little, and too late? Should Nick's love for his wife be strong enough to risk trusting his heart more than logic? Can Cathy's devotion to Nick give her enough strength to convince him to see her for who she really is?

SECRET SISTER proves how strong, how stubborn, and how trustworthy love can be as Nick and Cathy and Roxanne are challenged to overcome the secrets, the lies . . . and one extraordinary twist of fate that turns their lives upside down.

Available now on Amazon: http://tinyurl.com/h3kquyz

DATING CARY GRANT

A modern Manhattan fairy tale starring . . .

Tracy Connor, a New York City career woman who loves her job and classic movies.

Mike Connor, her estranged husband, a small-town Mayor who loves his wife but doesn't seem to have enough time to see her.

The handsome stranger, Philip Adams, who lives downstairs from the small sublet Tracy has temporarily moved into. He's charming, funny, and looks a lot like her very favorite screen icon, Cary Grant.

Dating Cary Grant is a romance all about New York city career woman Tracy Connor struggling with real issues with her real guy, her husband of six years, Mayor Mike Connor of Cukor, Connecticut. Tracy is a smart woman, but some of her problems with relationships are partially caused by her unrealistic expectations that real guys should—and can—behave like matinee idols. Mike's problems are also caused by the fact that he's such a great guy and overextends his heart, and his appointment calendar, to every constituent, friend, or stray animal who crosses his path.

Tracy is also being stressed by a TV reality show intent on showcasing Tracy and Mike's personal life, as well as the imminent takeover of her employer, a small, private television station, by a billionaire with unlimited funds and no taste.

Dating Cary Grant considers just how selfless a man needs to be to meet his wife's expectations, and just how honest a woman must be with herself about what she's willing to give, and give-up. And Cary Grant is along to help prove that any woman's search for 'Mr. Perfect' might take her to a surprising place to find him.

Available now on Amazon: http://tinyurl.com/jxj7xu8

CPSIA information can be obtained
at www.ICGtesting.com
Printed in the USA
BVOW06s1742061116
467079BV00010B/79/P